ABOUT THE AUTHOR

M. L. Tompsett is an emerging author of action paranormal fantasy romance. This is her first book published.

A bit about the Author

M. L. Tompsett has been creating worlds to escape to since she was a little girl. Years later, she is still enjoying her writing in her imaginative make-believe worlds with interesting characters. Finally, moving forward to the big wide scary world of digital and print publishing.

M. L. Tompsett is married to her childhood sweetheart. They live in Victoria, Australia, and have two fully grown, extremely talented sons.

Her books are now out in print soft, cover books, ebooks, and now venturing into audible. She is excited to see something she has been working on for far too long finally become a reality.

When M. L. Tompsett is not busy tapping away on her keyboard, creating her next page-turning book with a cup of tea and a bag of licorice, you will find her either creating digital book files for one of her talented clients or taking random photos around Australia.

facebook.com/M.L.TompsettAuthor

instagram.com/mltompsett.author

bookbub.com/profile/m-l-tompsett

THE GUY NEXT DOOR

SEX, LIES AND FAMILY SECRETS
BOOK ONE

M. L. TOMPSETT

TOMPSETT PUBLISHING™

Book One: **The Guy Next Door.**
Sex, Lies And Family Secrets. **By M. L. Tompsett**
Copyright © 2016 by M. L. Tompsett
Print: ISBN 978-0-9953858-1-8
Large Print ISBN 978-0-9953858-6-3
eBook 978-0-9953858-0-1

Cover art designed by **Tompsett Publishing**™ Cover
images licensed via Adobe Stock and DepositPhotos.

This book in the series edition published by **Tompsett
Publishing**™ & **M. L. Tompsett Author**™ in Victoria,
Australia

* **Disclaimer:** This publication is a work of fiction. All names, characters, businesses,
places, events, and incidents are either products of the author's imagination or are used

New Revised Printed Edition 2026 Font Times New Roman 12.5 pt

* **This book** contains coarse language, adult sexual themes, blood, vampires, young love, soulmates, violence, nudity, and handsome-muscled men. *If you are offended by any of these themes, this book is not for you.*

This book is written and edited in Australian/UK English. Which means spelling will be different to that of the USA English spelling.

For my Family

To my boys, thank you for allowing me to type and create, including driving you all mad with the world of Alexia and Drake, all things in the world of romance – love you guys. P.S - Heads up. Sorry, there will be more.

This journey has been a long one, but one I am glad to have travelled.

Just think, thanks to a fantastic song by Shakespears Sister, a haunting ballad - named - STAY. My imagination soon created the characters Alexia and Drake and their battle to remain together and a far away kingdom named Darshia. All this drama materialised in my head and here we are, with my first book - THE GUY NEXT DOOR.

Friends, family and loved ones, you all know who you are, without the generous words of wisdom, encouragement and sounding boards, I would still be typing away and not be publish today. Thank you, for your ears and your reading abilities.

And for you the reader - For anyone contemplating, writing for enjoyment, I would encourage you to try it. Grab that pen and paper or computer and have a go. Once you start, you never know where your imagination might take you. You can do anything you put your mind to. Travel to places only you can see, until you introduce them to everyone in your fantastic and creative words. Never allow someone to dictate, 'you can never do something you enjoy.'

Your little typist with a wicked imagination of fiction paranormal fantasy romance

- - M. L. Tompsett.

ALSO BY M. L. TOMPSETT

In the Series

Sex, Lies And Family Secrets

The Guy Next Door - *Book one*

Dark Surprises - *Book two*

You Never Know - *Book three*

It's You - *Book four*

What You Know - *Book five*

OTHER VAMPIRE BOOKS

Her Vampire Fated Mate

Paranormal Fantasy, *including Vampires and Witches*

Plus many more…

All books are available at all good eBook outlets and Audible stores.

ALSO BY M. L. TOMPSETT

OTHER BOOKS

Contemporary Romance

SECOND CHANCE AT LOVE- SERIES

Insta Bride

The bodyguard's convenient marriage

Ghost of a chance in love

Secret Heiress

Urban Fantasy

Shifter Romance

Kept in the Dark of Love and Lust

Kept in the Dark of Lies and Deceit - Book Two

Paranormal Urban Fantasy *including Dragons, Shifters, and Elves*

Plus many more…

All books are available at all good eBook outlets and Audible stores.

Dark Ones, assassins and fighting to survive, become Alexia's new way of life. In this new series of Sex, Lies And Family Secrets: The Guy Next Door.

Alexia Steele is about to face the hardest challenge in her young life. The love of her life - Drake, is gone and Alexia's mother just revealed a massive family secret, changing her life forever.

Arriving with her mother in a mysterious new world where Dark Ones roam, Alexia is on a mission to protect the people she loves at the same time fighting to stay alive and discover who is trying to kill her.

Alexia starts her search for her next-door neighbour, the absent love of her life - Drake. Will their love be strong enough to reunite them, or is Alexia already too late?

It soon becomes clear not all family can be trusted and will the person who wants Alexia dead succeed in their evil plans for power.

You're never too old to create the world to escape in,
The world to fight for what you want,
Learn to love and be loved
And succeed in what you do.
The world only you can conquer and rule.

— M. L. TOMPSETT

CHAPTER ONE

"REMEMBER, BABY. I WILL ALWAYS LOVE YOU."

Romantic declaration number one, straight out of my soap opera of a life.

Does he mean it?

For now, I'll go with the flow and stare up at Drake's annoyingly perfect face — chiselled jaw, soulful eyes that I love, and that smug little smile that says, *Yes, I know I'm irresistible.*

My body trembles like it's auditioning for a dramatic action scene, ready to explode into glittery confetti of ecstasy. And yet, somewhere in the back of my lust-fogged brain, I'm irritated. I'm certain I'm mad at him. I just can't remember why. Something about betrayal? Blood? Abandonment? Ugh. Whatever. Right now, he's hot, I'm melting, and my subconscious clearly has no boundaries.

"I love you, Drake," I whisper, breathless, like I'm starring in my own steamy novella.

He moves — masterfully, of course. Because why wouldn't he be a master of everything? His heated flesh glides between my thighs like a sensual ballet, and I'm seconds away from shattering into a thousand sparkly pieces or exploding like my own NYE fireworks display.

I shift my hips, desperate for more. So close. Just a little more. Come on, universe, don't be stingy.

His lips graze my shoulder — warm, possessive, and just the right amount of sinful. I tilt my head like a willing sacrifice, and bam — teeth. Sharp teeth pierce my flesh. Goosebumps erupt like popcorn along my body.

Yes. Bite me. Love me. Worship me. Take what you need.

The pull at my neck heightens my sensations; I'm on the edge of utopia — a blissful, mind-blowing state where two lovers understand each other's every need.

Time slows, part of me wants to explode and shatter, soak in my impeding life changing orgasm, the other... Bugger... I can't wait any longer and have to bite back. Because apparently, I'm not just a snack — I'm a connoisseur.

My teeth pierce his succulent neck, like a hot knife slicing through butter. His blood tastes like heat, passion, love, and danger and something I shouldn't crave, but do. Oh, I do. And I like it. A lot more than any sane person should.

His hips thrust forward, hitting all the right places. Ahhhh — oh, yes. "More. More," I chant.

Yes. This is it. This is the moment. The stars align, the heavens sing, my toes tingle, and—

SCREEEEEECH.

Wait. What the actual hell?

A screeching banshee noise invades my ears, murdering the mood with all the grace of a chainsaw. The soft moans and pants? Gone. Replaced by the spawn of Satan: my alarm clock.

My eyelids crack open enough for me to realise darkness surrounds me. My heart gallops like it's trying to escape my chest. I squeeze my eyes shut, desperately clawing at the dream like a toddler reaching for a stolen cookie.

Noooo. Stay. Please stay. My hand flails through the air like a sleep-deprived lunatic, grasping nothing but cold, cruel reality.

And just like that, the fantasy evaporates. Drake's perfect face? Gone. His panty-melting smile? Gone. His very lickable lips? Also gone. I'm left with drool on my chin and a pillow that's seen better days.

I slap the alarm clock like it insulted my ancestors. Sweet silence. Finally.

My hand slides across my mouth. Moist. Ew. Drool. Because apparently, I'm a romantic mess and a slob.

I inhale the crisp morning air like I'm preparing for battle. Exhale. And boom — reality hits me like a truck full of emotional baggage.

I'm single. Alone. Devastated. Confused. Sad. And now — angry. Because of course I am.

He said he loved me. Said he'd always be there. Cue the dramatic chest ache. I rub the spot like it'll fix the gaping hole where my heart used to be.

We were peas in a pod. Childhood besties. Fourteen years of friendship, and now? Poof. Gone.

Yesterday, Mum saw my tear-stained zombie face and

didn't even flinch. She wrapped me up in a warm, maternal burrito and let me ugly cry all over her.

I cringe and shudder with embarrassment when I think about my gross, runny nose, and her clothing turning into my human-sized hanky.

Drake left, and I am caught in the emotional rollercoaster of a love so intense it vanishes right before my eyes, breaking my soul.

Instead of yelling at me like any sane parent might, Mum goes full Mother Teresa. She hugs me, listens to my sob story, and doesn't even call me an idiot. Bless her.

I relive the breakup. How Drake packs his bags, drops the *"I'm out"* bomb, and vanishes like a magician with commitment issues.

And yes, I'm angry. Emotional. Possibly overdramatic. But let me explain.

Drake Smithlyn. Six foot three. Muscles for days. Jawline sharp enough to cut glass. Scruffy golden brown hair. Smile that melts panties. Lips that deserve their own fan club.

He's been whispering sweet nothings in my ear since we were five. Always protecting me. Always by my side. Basically my emotional support beefcake.

We finally level up from the friend zone. Two virgins, one bed, and a whole lot of awkward fumbling. Romantic, right? Until we practice, and practice some more. Each time better than the last.

Then comes yesterday morning. The horror. The trauma. The moment that will haunt me forever.

Drake's guardians — Lucile and Michael — walk in on us mid-passion. And not just any passion. Oh no. They catch him drinking my blood. Like a vampire. Because apparently, that's a thing now.

With his bags packed by his feet — Cue banishment. Drama. Tears. And me threatening to kick his arse if I end up pregnant. Because he didn't think to wear a condom.

Drake's response? "Sorry, baby, I come from a special family." Oh, how convenient. Special family. No babies allowed. Thanks for the heads-up, Dracula.

Turns out, he wasn't using protection every time we made love. Surprise! And I'm left wondering if there's even the slightest chance I could be carrying his child.

I tell Mum everything. She mutters something about "Dark Ones." I blink. She walks out. I panic. She returns — with a dusty, ancient book like she's Gandalf revealing my destiny.

"It's time, Alexia," she says. Dramatic much?

Clearly not buying this epic fantasy talk, which even comes with its own book... Apparently, I'm part of a secret vampire lineage. Can you believe that? Because I don't. Did I mention, this vampire family is from a long line of royalty? Yeah, just what I need to hear on top of everything else. Dark Ones. Born, not turned. No sunburns. Me — No fangs — yet. Just blood cravings and existential dread.

Mum chose not to become one. Turns out that is also a thing. I, on the other hand, have apparently kick-started my transformation by letting Drake treat me like a blood smoothie — and yeah, I drank from him too. And liked it. A lot more than any sane person should. So now I'm apparently halfway to vampire royalty with a taste for drama and plasma.

So instead of planning my epic eighteenth birthday bash, I'm packing for a road trip to a hidden kingdom called

Darshia. Because why not throw in a secret vampire realm while my life implodes?

This will be no family road trip. No. Dad stays behind. *"For his own safety."* While Mum and I drive off into the unknown, I feel like I'm starring in my own supernatural soap opera, and I didn't even get a script.

I place my hand on my belly. It's puffy. Tender. As for my bladder it's full — I squeeze my pelvic floor and shake and wiggle my hips. Yep — Time to pee before I wet myself. Next, on what could be my last day alive — Brush teeth. Shower. Dress into comfortable clothing. While pretending I'm normal.

I run my tongue over my teeth. No fangs. Still human-ish. I'll play along until I see actual proof. Because right now, Mum's story sounds like a rejected Twilight fanfic.

Oh no. Something is not right. My throat's doing weird things. Saliva overload. I swallow. It doesn't help.

I slap a hand over my mouth. Pressure builds. Yep. I'm going to hurl.

Because nothing says "welcome to your new vampire life" like morning nausea and emotional trauma.

CHAPTER TWO

ARE WE THERE YET?

No, seriously. Are we? Because if I have to spend one more minute in this car, I'm going to throw myself out the window and let the forest deal with me. I'm sleep-deprived, nauseated, and possibly dying of some roadside plague. Meanwhile, Mum's over there looking fresh as a daisy, like she's on a scenic drive to a spa retreat. Thanks for the solidarity, Mother.

She finally pulls the car onto a dirt driveway that looks like it was designed specifically for horror movie jump scares. I squint through the windshield and — oh, you have got to be kidding me.

This place? This is where we're going? It's the perfect setup for a murder scene. Thick forest. Creepy bushland. A decrepit building that screams serial killer hideout. And an open car park that's basically begging for a chalk outline.

I turn to Mum, eyebrows raised to full sarcasm mode. "So… this is the place, huh?"

She nods, hesitates, bites her lip like she's trying not to say, I was expecting Hogwarts. "Well, according to the directions, we've arrived," she says, sounding about as convinced as I am that this isn't a setup for a vampire-themed prank show.

I glance back at the building. It's dark, weird, and looks like it was built by someone with a grudge against architecture. Creepy doesn't even begin to cover it. If this isn't our destination, I'm staging a mutiny.

Mum checks the dashboard again, rereading the directions from her ancient family journal. Yes, the infamous journal — currently lying open like it's waiting for a dramatic gust of wind to flip its pages. Apparently, this sacred relic has been passed down through generations of vampire queens. Because of course it has.

Turns out, the Royal Blue Dark Ones mostly birth girls. Royal vampire girls. Because patriarchy? Not in this bloodline.

Mum's been apologising nonstop for hiding this whole vampire soap opera from me. She keeps reminding me I was supposed to get the journal on my eighteenth birthday, like it's some kind of cursed tiara. Surprise! You're royalty. Also, you might crave blood. Happy birthday.

She lifts her chin like she's about to deliver a speech to the United Nations. Her gaze sweeps across the car park, then back to the building. The car hums like it's trying to fill the awkward silence. We roll forward, slowly, like we're approaching a crime scene.

The building — if you can call it that — looks like a timber hunting lodge that gave up on life. I'm filled with a delightful cocktail of dread, nausea, and "please let this be a prank."

Mum kills the engine. I sit there, unsure if I'm relieved or just too tired to care. My legs are cramped, my back is screaming, and I'm pretty sure my soul is trying to escape through my eyeballs.

I scan the area. No signs of life. But my skin prickles like someone's watching us. Fantastic.

I glance at Mum. She's already out of the car, looking around like she's arrived at Disneyland. Her face lights up with excitement. This is real to her. Dark Ones. Vampire family reunion. She's practically vibrating.

She whips out her phone and starts texting with a grin that screams "update time." I bet it's Dad. Probably sending him a play-by-play of our descent into vampire territory. Her way of keeping him safe and far, far away from the bloodsucking drama.

On the road here, she even sent him a pic of me mid-puke. Classy. I'm convinced they've got a bet going — how many times will Alexia hurl before reaching the gates of doom? Honestly, I wouldn't put it past them.

Dry biscuits and ginger ale have become my lifeline. I'm basically surviving on grandma snacks and spite.

I shake my head at their twisted little conspiracy and glance back at the building. Then I notice the gate. Oh, the gate. Twenty feet high, double cast-iron monstrosity, held up by columns that look like they were designed by someone with a flair for intimidation.

A cyclone fence stretches out from the columns, disappearing into the trees like it's guarding the secrets of Area 51. And yes, I bet it's electric. Because why not?

I listen. Yep. There's a hum. The fence is definitely electric. And the razor barbs on top? Just in case the message wasn't clear: "Go away or get impaled."

The hair on the back of my neck stands up. A buzz starts in my head. Pressure builds. Someone's coming.

I casually turn my head toward Mum, pretending I'm not ready to throw hands. Footsteps crunch on gravel. We both freeze, then turn toward the sound.

I plant my feet on the same little stones, body tense, ready for action. Dad's voice echoes in my head: "Look after your mother, Alexia. You know how to fight. Protect. And don't play by the rules if you're ever in trouble."

Gotta love Dad. He raised me on street fighting, kickboxing, and martial arts. Plus a few extra moves he swore I should never use unless absolutely necessary. Secret weapons. I'm basically a walking combat manual.

So yeah. Let them come. I'm ready.

I SHAKE MY HEAD AT MUM AND DAD'S LITTLE PUKE-TRACKING conspiracy, then glance back at the gate — because apparently, we're starring in a supernatural prison break. The thing is massive. Double cast-iron, held up by columns that look like they were designed by someone with a flair for intimidation and zero chill. A cyclone fence stretches out from either side, disappearing into the trees like it's guarding the secrets of Area 51.

And yeah, I bet it's electric. Because why not?

I listen. Yep. There's a hum. The fence is definitely electric. And the razor barbs on top? Just in case the message wasn't clear: "Go away or get impaled."

The hair on the back of my neck stands up. A buzz starts in my head. Pressure builds. Someone's coming.

I casually turn my head toward Mum, pretending I'm not ready to throw hands. We lock eyes, then turn toward the sound of approaching footsteps.

Feet shoulder-width apart. Body tense. Ready. Dad's voice echoes in my head: Look after your mother, Alexia. You know how to fight. Protect. And don't play by the rules if you're ever in trouble.

Classic Dad. He trained me in street fighting, kickboxing, martial arts — and a few moves that probably aren't legal in most countries. I'm basically a walking combat manual with a side of teenage angst.

So yeah. Let them come. I'm ready.

The footsteps get louder. Two men appear, dressed like they just stepped out of a luxury catalog for supernatural bodyguards. Dark suits. Sunglasses. Polished shoes that probably double as weapons. I bet they're steel-capped. Because of course they are.

I eye them casually. Okay, fine — a little less casually. Their suits are tailored within an inch of their lives, hugging hard-muscled bodies like they were born in Armani. On any other day, I'd be drooling. Today? I'm too nauseated to care. Sad, really.

Mentally slapping myself, I force my brain to stop ogling and start assessing. Focus, Alexia. These guys could be friendly — or they could be the type who shoot first and monologue later. The guy on the left has a suspicious bulge under his jacket. Spoiler alert: not the fun kind. Definitely packing heat.

Hand-to-hand combat? I'm your girl. Guns? Not so much. A bead of sweat slides down my spine. Cute. Time to channel my inner ninja and not die.

Mum's patience runs out before mine. She taps her foot like she's waiting for a waiter to bring her the bill. Our eyes meet. Her brow arches. I bite my lip to keep from laughing. Now is not the time for sarcasm-induced giggles.

She squares her shoulders and unleashes her full *"I'm-a-lawyer-and-you-will-listen"* voice. "Gentlemen, I take it you work for the Queen — Queen Alexettia? We require a meeting with her as soon as possible. Can you arrange that?"

The men blink. Literally just stand there, dumbfounded. I almost applaud. "Well?" Mum presses. "Can you assist us?"

Their expressions shift — just slightly. Like they're listening to someone we can't hear. Mind interference, Mum called it. Apparently, some Dark Ones can communicate telepathically. Because of course they can. I'm still trying to wrap my head around the fact that I might be one of them. Yay me.

They stare into space for a few beats, then snap back to reality. The guy on the left gives us a smirk that makes my skin crawl. He's totally undressing us with his eyes. Gross. I glare at him like I'm about to kick him in the shin. He doesn't flinch. Typical.

The one on the right finally speaks, voice deep enough to rattle the car windows. "We have confirmation from our Queen. You may enter Darshia and drive straight to the royal castle. Someone will be there to greet you and escort you both to where you need to go."

Cool. Vague instructions and zero enthusiasm. Do we follow the yellow brick road or what? I glance at Mum and give her the universal "let's bounce" look. She nods. We're done here.

"Thank you, gentlemen," Mum says, all polite and professional, before turning back to the car. I monitor the Men in Black through the window reflections like I'm in a spy movie until we're safely inside.

The gate creaks open behind us like it's been waiting for this moment all century. Security cameras swivel toward us like robotic vultures. So that's how they saw us coming. Creepy surveillance level: expert.

Mum starts the car. "Here goes nothing," she murmurs, pressing down on the accelerator.

I nod as the car drives through the open gates, and the atmosphere instantly shifts as I watch silently in the side mirror while they close behind us. We continue forward onto what I now call the "*not-so-yellow brick road.*" It's dark blue, narrow, winding, and flanked by trees that look like they're plotting something.

Then it happens.

The car jolts. The air shifts. Something changes.

Without looking at Mum, I mutter, "Did you feel that? I think something just happened." My hand flies to my stomach. Please, ginger ale, don't fail me now.

Mum's voice is quiet, but loaded. "I don't think we're in Kansas anymore."

Oh, great. We've officially crossed into metaphor territory. I nod, not sure if I want to laugh or cry. Probably both.

Whatever just happened, we're not in the creepy carpark anymore.

We're in Darshia.

And I'm not ready.

THE DEEPER WE DRIVE, THE DARKER IT GETS. THE TREES overhead knit together like they're trying to block out reality, creating a tunnel that feels less enchanted forest and more *"you're about to get eaten."* I glance at Mum. The dashboard light casts dramatic shadows across her face, and I give her the classic "how much longer?" look.

She responds with her patented "we'll be there soon" expression. No words needed. We're fluent in silent sarcasm.

The engine hum shifts — yep, she's speeding up. Apparently, Mum's decided that if we're going to get murdered by supernatural royalty, we might as well arrive early.

Minutes pass. The trees thin. Civilisation — or something like it — emerges. Elegant townhouses pop up like they've been waiting for us. No slums. No graffiti. Just pristine buildings that look like they were built by immortal architects with a flair for drama.

These houses are sturdy, flawless, and suspiciously timeless. Like they were plucked from a historical drama and dropped here for aesthetic purposes. No expense spared. No people visible. Just vibes.

And then Mum breaks the silence. "Alexia, before we reach the castle, I need to explain a few things."

Oh, great. Serious Mum voice. I turn in my seat. Her face shifts from excited to grim. This is not a drill.

"Since we pulled up at the front gate... has your head felt funny?"

Uh-oh. We're officially in mind invasion territory. I remember her saying something about vampires — sorry, Dark Ones — being able to read minds. And apparently, I'm a natural blocker. Yay me. Let's hope that superpower hasn't expired.

Note to self: Read the damn family journal. Preferably before someone tries to mentally hack me again.

I think back. Yeah, I felt pressure. Buzzing. Like someone trying to pick the lock on my brain. But then I did... something. Instinct, maybe. And it stopped. Mostly. It keeps trying, though. Like a nosy neighbour peeking through the curtains.

"Mum, just say it. Yes, I've felt pressure in my head. Since the gate. It comes and goes. Is this that vampire mind invasion thing you mentioned?"

She peeks at me, smiles faintly, then focuses on the road. Her brows do a little dance of concern.

"Yes, Alexia. That's exactly what I meant. Someone's trying to get into our heads. I hope you're blocking them. We can't let anyone know who we are. It might not be safe. And remember — Dark Ones. Not vampires."

Oops. Right. Dark Ones. Eye roll activated.

I take a deep breath. Slowly exhale. This is officially the weirdest day of my life. And that includes the time I accidentally dyed my hair green.

I nod. "Yeah, I figured we were keeping our identities on the down-low. Those two guards didn't know who we were. Didn't use our names. So I've been blocking. A lot."

I rub my temple. "Whoever it is, they're persistent. And when those two guys kept zoning out? I swear they were talking to someone. In their heads."

Mum's eyes widen. Her mouth opens slightly. Bingo. I've hit a nerve.

So yeah. Trust level with the Dark Ones? Currently at '*nope.*' If they want to know something, they can ask me to my face. Preferably without the creepy mental peeping.

Mum's voice cuts through my internal rant. "Whoever it is, we need to stay alert. Always."

Agreed. Because if this is the welcome wagon, I can't wait to see what the royal family's like.

"Anyway, enough of that. How are you feeling?" Her tone softens. "Still nauseated? Want more dry crackers?"

She glances down at the empty box I've been munching like it's gourmet cuisine. Her smile is sympathetic as my stomach lets out a dramatic growl that echoes through the car like a demon trying to escape.

"Don't worry, Alexia. We're almost there. I think that's the castle up ahead."

I shift my gaze to match hers. Something looms behind the trees and buildings. The closer we get, the clearer it becomes.

And yep — there it is. A massive, old, dark stone castle

with high outer walls and tall, narrow windows that scream "we don't do sunlight here."

I lean forward, forehead nearly smacking the windshield, just to get a better look. Multi-level towers rise inside the walls like they're auditioning for a historical drama. It's the kind of place you expect to see knights brooding on balconies and ghosts pacing the halls.

Wow. Just... wow. At least it doesn't look like Dracula's vacation home, but it's still giving major "I drink blood and judge peasants" energy.

And weirdly? It doesn't look out of place. Towering over the surrounding buildings like it owns the block. Darshia isn't just a town — it's a full-blown supernatural city. From what I can see, it's bigger than my hometown, which is saying something. I can't wait to explore, meet people my age, and maybe find someone who doesn't want to bite me. Fingers crossed.

I stare up at the castle in awe and immediately pity the poor souls who have to clean it. That thing would take a team of twenty and a week just to dust the chandeliers. It must be worth a fortune. Are Dark Ones rich? Is there a vampire stock market I should know about?

Goosebumps crawl up my arms. Reality check: I'm about to walk into a castle full of blood-drinking royalty. This is fine. Everything's fine.

Okay, Alexia. Suck it up. You're smart. You're strong. You've survived worse. Probably. I take a slow, deep breath and glance at Mum, trying to read her face.

"Yep," I say, voice miraculously calm. "Pretty sure that qualifies as a castle."

MUM TURNS HER HEAD, CATCHES MY EYE, AND FLASHES A smile that's way too excited for someone about to walk into a vampire — sorry, Dark One — castle. She's practically glowing. Great. She's in full "I'm about to meet my long-lost supernatural family" mode.

"Alexia," she says, voice low and serious, "don't be surprised if the Queen already knows who we are. But remember — do not tell anyone. We hide our identities until we know who to trust. Even with Grandma Ma. Keep your shields up. Be prepared for anything."

Oh, fantastic. So now we're in a royal soap opera with secret identities and telepathic espionage. Who needs TV when my life is basically Game of Thrones: Vampire Edition?

And then — oh... ow. What the hell was that?

A weird tapping sensation hits from inside my belly, followed by a jab that makes me wince. I rub the spot, eyes wide, and glance at Mum. Her gaze drops to my hand, then back to the road, then back to my belly. She's officially concerned.

"What's wrong, Alexia? Are you okay?"

I look from my belly to her face, trying to decide if I'm about to cry, laugh, or throw up. Probably all three.

Her eyes flick between me and the road like she's calculating how fast she can get me to a supernatural ER. "Ah, Alexia... when we reach the castle — assuming Grandma Ma lets us stay — I think it's time you see a doctor."

Butterflies. Not the cute kind. The kind that feel like they're trying to claw their way out of my stomach. I stare down, waiting for the next sensation. Please don't let this be another puke moment.

Thank the gods I packed stretchy pants. They're the only thing standing between me and a full-blown wardrobe malfunction. My belly's swollen, bloated, and officially rebelling. I need a shower. I need food. And — oh no. No, no, no.

I'm craving Drake's blood.

What. The. Hell.

Seriously, brain? That's your idea of a snack? Blood? From the guy who ghosted me after turning my life into a supernatural circus?

I cover my mouth and yawn, trying to shake the exhaustion. This trip has drained me. I want a bed. A hot shower. A meal that doesn't come in cracker form. I want to not feel like I'm turning into something I don't understand.

I'm trying to go with the flow here, but my brain is still stuck on the whole "Dark One" thing. At least now I know Darshia is real. I've seen the name on shop fronts, signposts, and enough signage to confirm this isn't some elaborate prank.

Oh gods. My heart races, thumping against my ribs like it's trying to escape. We're really in Darshia. Mum's little bedtime story? Not so fictional after all.

This is happening.

And I'm not ready.

CHAPTER THREE

Mᴜᴍ ꜰʟᴀsʜᴇs ᴍᴇ ᴀ ǫᴜɪᴄᴋ sᴍɪʟᴇ, ᴇʏᴇs sᴘᴀʀᴋʟɪɴɢ ʟɪᴋᴇ sʜᴇ's about to meet her long-lost vampire — sorry, Dark One — family and not walk into a supernatural identity crisis. She looks like she belongs in this castle, perched in a royal wingback chair like she's auditioning for Queen of the Realm.

Meanwhile, my stomach decides to make its presence known. Loudly.

Not again.

It groans like a dying whale, echoing through the fancy gold-accented room like a hunger anthem. Mum gives me a sympathetic look. "Soon, Alexia. We'll grab something to eat soon."

Soon? I need food now. Or blood. Or both. Honestly, I'm not even sure anymore. My cravings are multiplying like rabbits, and my stomach is staging a full-blown rebellion. Great. First impressions: starving, possibly feral girl with a growling belly and questionable bloodlust.

I shift in my seat, trying to look composed while my insides scream for sustenance. The room is grand — high ceilings, gold trim, expensive everything. And here I am, bloated, nauseated, and seconds away from either vomiting or biting someone.

Then the pressure starts again. That lovely Dark One mind trick buzz. Fantastic. Just as I'm about to mentally scream, the door creaks open.

And my jaw drops.

Standing there is a young woman who looks like she could be my sister. Or my clone. Or my evil twin. She's a little older, but the resemblance is freaky. I glance at Mum, whose face is doing mental gymnastics trying to figure out who this mystery woman is.

I keep my expression neutral — barely — until Mum stands. I scramble up too, because apparently we're doing the formal thing now. But seriously, this woman cannot be Grandma Ma. She's way too young. Where's the ancient, wrinkled matriarch I was expecting? Did she get a supernatural facelift? Or is this her daughter? Granddaughter? Clone?

The woman walks toward us, and the hairs on my arms stand up like they've just sensed a power surge. Yep. That's Dark One energy. And it's strong. Stronger than anyone we've met today. Okay, maybe this chick really is Alexettia. And if so — damn, she looks good for her age.

"Hello, ladies. Thank you for waiting." Her voice is smooth, posh, and very I-own-this-room. She gestures to the chairs. "Please, sit. There's no need to stand. After all, we're family, are we not?"

Family? Oh, we're diving straight into the drama, huh?

I glance at Mum, shrug, and sit. My stomach immediately betrays me again with a loud, angry growl.

"Great. Just great. Not now," I mutter under my breath.

I look up — and she's staring at me. Fabulous. Can the floor just swallow me whole?

She steps closer, graceful and intense, eyes scanning me like she's trying to read my soul. Good luck with that, love. I activate my mental firewall and smile sweetly.

"You're good. Actually, you're both impressive," she murmurs, eyes flicking between Mum and me. "I'm having trouble reading either of you."

Wait — did she just say that out loud? Or did I hear it in my head? Either way, she's confused. And I'm thrilled. Because if she can't read us, we might actually survive this visit.

Mum catches my eye and smiles. Yep, we're thinking the same thing. Our thoughts are locked down. Score one for Team Steele.

But I'm done playing polite. I want answers. And food. Preferably both.

I stand, extend my hand. "Hi, I'm Alexia. This is my mother, Amelia. Amelia Steele. Pleasure to meet you. And you are…?"

She takes my hand. Her grip tightens. I match it. Oops. Maybe too much. I do have manners. Somewhere.

She doesn't let go. Okay, weird. A buzz starts in our joined hands, then vanishes. I stare at her face, trying to decode her eerily familiar features. Same big dark brown eyes with a blue ring. Same bone structure. Same everything, minus a slightly broader nose and longer hair.

She could be my twin. And I do not like it.

Finally, she releases my hand and glides behind the massive desk like she owns the planet. She settles into the throne-like chair and smiles at Mum.

Pressure hits my head again. I shut it down. Fast.

She tilts her head, watching me like I'm a puzzle she's dying to solve. I'm officially unnerved. Darshia is starting to feel less like a magical kingdom and more like a trap.

"Alexia, you are strong. Stronger than your mother, Amelia. But you both excel at blocking." She turns to Mum. "Amelia, I know you're not a Dark One, though you carry the traits."

Then she looks at me. And I brace myself.

"As for you, Alexia... you are no longer human."

Excuse me, what?

No longer human? Did I mishear that? Is this some kind of initiation speech?

"And are you here because of your pregnancy?"

Okay, what the actual hell.

I whip my head toward Mum, eyes wide. My hand instinctively covers my belly. Pregnancy? No. Just no.

This is BS.

I shoot up from my seat. "Hang on a bloody minute. I think you're wrong." My voice is shaking, but I don't care. "How can I be pregnant?"

Drake's words slam into me. Special family. No condoms. Oh my God. Pregnant. No. No way.

"And what do you mean I'm no longer human?" My legs

go numb. Thank the gods I'm still sitting, or I'd be a puddle on the floor.

She cuts me off with a smile that makes me want to scream. "Alexia, I can sense, smell, and detect your children's heartbeats."

Children. Plural.

My mouth drops open so wide I'm surprised it doesn't hit the floor. Heartbeats. As in more than one. Twins.

Oh my Gods. No. Just no. Oh, fuck.

This has to be a dream. A nightmare. A hallucination brought on by crackers and trauma.

But it's not. I know it's not.

Mum rushes to my side, wraps me in her arms, rubs my back like she's trying to keep me from combusting. I cling to her warmth, trying not to lose it completely.

I force myself to focus. To breathe. To not scream.

"Look," I say, voice louder than intended, "you already know who and what we are. Now, will you be polite, explain exactly who you are, and answer our questions?"

She smiles. Of course she does. Like she's enjoying watching my life implode.

"Yes, Alexia, I will answer your questions," she says, turning to Mum. "Just as soon as you, Amelia, inform me who your mother is."

Mum's jaw tightens. She stands, calm but clearly done with the cryptic nonsense.

"I take it you're Alexettia. Thanks, by the way, for your introductions. Your manners astound me. No wonder my great-great-grandmother Allasett left here to start a new life with her husband."

And there it is.

I watch Alexettia's face. For a split second, she's shocked. Then she smiles.

And I know — we've just dropped a bomb.

"What do you know of my daughter, Allasett? Is she alive? Where is she? Tell me. Now."

Well, that escalated quickly.

Alexettia's voice jumps a pitch, laced with just enough aggression to make the air feel heavier. Interesting. So the Queen of Darshia has feelings. Who knew?

She hasn't officially introduced herself, but let's be real — I've connected the dots. This woman, who looks like she could be a Vogue model with a side hustle in ruling empires, is not young. She's my Grandma Ma. Queen Alexettia. And damn, she looks good for her age. Like, suspiciously good. Botox? Blood magic? Probably both.

Focus, Alexia. Now is not the time to be wowed by supernatural skincare.

I glance at Mum. Her eyes narrow. Uh-oh. That's her "I'm about to verbally decapitate someone" look. Not good.

"Look, Alexettia," Mum says, voice sharp enough to slice through royal protocol. "We came here today to find some very much required answers."

Oh, she went there. First-name basis with a queen. My shoulders flinch. So much for manners. But when Mum's annoyed, etiquette dies a swift and brutal death.

"If you act like a grown-up," she continues, "we can sort everything out and hopefully get some answers. You can behave like a good host and provide us with refreshments, or we'll see you tomorrow."

Okay, now Alexettia's face is doing the "what the actual hell" expression. It's kind of hilarious. Mum just told the Queen of living vampires what to do. And we're still breathing. Miraculous.

Way to go, Mum.

But then the hairs on the back of my neck rise. Crap. I thought too soon. The air shifts. I feel it — her power. It wraps around me like an itchy electric blanket. Unpleasant. Unwelcome. And very much a warning.

Her face morphs from regal to sour. No, scratch that — she's pissed. Like, *"I could snap your spine with a thought"* pissed.

Okay, time to intervene before we end up as royal snacks.

"Alexettia. Grandma Ma," I say, voice calm but firm. "For everyone's benefit, maybe afternoon tea would be useful right about now. A little break. A little civility. Also, it's kind of rude not to introduce yourself. We're family, and in our family, we don't treat each other like second-class citizens."

Her face changes colour. It's a little funny. Also terrifying. I sit tall, lift my chin, and brace myself. She's trying to get into my head again — I can feel it. Time to deploy mental defence mode.

Which nursery rhyme should I think of to block her out?

Ah, yes. The classic.

Mary had a little lamb, little lamb, little lamb...

Over and over. On repeat. Loud and obnoxious. If she wants to dig around in my brain, she's getting preschool chaos.

I keep my expression neutral, my posture defiant, and my

internal soundtrack ridiculous. Because if I'm going down, I'm going down singing about livestock.

CHAPTER FOUR

GRANDMA MA FINALLY DECIDES TO PLAY THE GRACIOUS HOST. About time. She introduces herself — officially, thank the gods — and summons a spread of food and drinks that could feed a royal court. Which, I guess, is fitting. There are pastries, delicate little sandwiches, and tea that smells like it was brewed by angels with a side hustle in herbal alchemy.

I inhale everything like a starving gremlin. With my stomach no longer threatening to eat itself, I gently place my teacup back on the desk and try to look calm, collected, and not like someone who just devoured three croissants in under two minutes. I keep my mind clear, shields up, because who knows what kind of mental eavesdropping is happening in this castle.

Mum's been quiet for a few minutes, which is never a good sign. I watch her out of the corner of my eye. Her temple vein is pulsing. Uh-oh. That's the warning light. She's about to go full verbal nuke. And considering she's sitting across from a Dark One Queen, I'm not exactly thrilled about it.

She sets her teacup down with the kind of precision that says I'm about to ruin someone's day, then shifts in her seat like she's settling in for a courtroom takedown.

Here we go.

"See, now that wasn't so hard, was it?" she says, smiling sweetly. Too sweetly. "If you'd introduced yourself from the start, we could've already sorted a few things out."

I gulp. Mum, what are you doing? Do you have a death wish?

The hairs on my arms rise like they're trying to escape. I glance at Grandma Ma — Alexettia — who's watching Mum with a twitch at the corner of her mouth. Is that… a smile? No way. Does she actually enjoy being challenged?

That can't be common. I mean, who tells a vampire queen off and lives to tell the tale?

Still, I'm not taking chances. I'm keeping my sass on a leash. I want answers, not a one-way ticket to the dungeon.

Then — knock knock.

We all turn toward the sound. The opulent double doors creak open like they're auditioning for a gothic drama, and in walks a man who looks like he just stepped off the cover of Supernatural Surgeons Monthly. Early twenties, tall, dark hair, long white medical coat, and a black bag that screams I'm here to poke you with something sharp.

Great. What now?

I HESITATE. BECAUSE OBVIOUSLY, LETTING A STRANGER WHO claims to be a doctor poke and prod me in a vampire castle isn't exactly on my bucket list. But here he is — white coat, black bag, polite smile — and apparently older than he looks. Which, in this world, probably means he's pushing two hundred and moisturises with unicorn tears.

"Ms Alexia," he says, voice calm and annoyingly soothing. "Yes, I am a Dark One. And yes, I am older than you think."

Great. Another immortal with a skincare routine that defies logic.

"This world might be new to you," he continues, "but there is much to learn. My qualifications in the medical field are long and up-to-date."

I give him a nod that says I'm listening, but also mildly suspicious. Because let's be honest — I'm still trying to wrap my head around the fact that I'm pregnant. Pregnant. With twins. In a castle. Surrounded by vampires. Sorry — Dark Ones.

"So… about my pregnancy," I ask, trying to sound casual while internally screaming. "Have you dealt with this variety before? Is it common?"

He pauses, meets my eyes, and drops the bomb. "Yes, Alexia. The last similar pregnancy was thirty years ago."

Thirty years. Cool. So I'm a medical anomaly. Fantastic.

He starts the exam. Blood pressure cuff goes on. He pumps it. Waits. And then his smile vanishes.

"What is it?" I ask, already bracing for bad news.

He shakes his head. "Alexia, I'm going to take your blood pressure again."

"Why? What does it say?"

No answer. Just more pumping. More frowning. More ominous silence.

"Alexia, when was the last time you had your blood pressure taken?"

I frown. "I don't know. A while ago?" Where is this going?

"It's high," he says. "Too high. And as a Dark One, that shouldn't be possible."

Right. Because apparently, vampires have perfect vitals. Of course they do.

"Well," I say, trying not to roll my eyes, "that's just it. I'm not a full Dark One."

He nods, finally remembering I'm a half-baked supernatural hybrid. "Yes. I need to remember that. As a human transforming into a Dark One, we must monitor your blood pressure closely. My advice: avoid stress. Rest."

Avoid stress? I'm pregnant with twins. In a vampire kingdom. My ex-boyfriend might be my soulmate. And I'm apparently halfway to undead. Sure, I'll just relax.

Then comes the handheld machine. He presses it against my bloated, naked belly, and suddenly — sound. Tiny galloping heartbeats. My babies. I hear them. And I cry. Because of course I do.

Two babies. Twice the chaos. Twice the love. I wipe my tears and glance at Mum, who's also crying. Great. We're a mess. A sentimental, hormonal mess.

Then the doctor drops another bomb. "Alexia, you've found your soulmate."

Excuse me?

He looks me dead in the eye. "Do you know what a soulmate is and what it entails?"

I shake my head. Because no, I do not. I'm still trying to process the twins.

He explains. Slowly. Carefully. And I sit there, stunned. Apparently, this type of pregnancy only happens between specific soulmates. And Drake and I? We're that type.

Of course we are.

I stare at him, mouth slightly open. Unbelievable. Drake's blood fetish? Confirmed. His lack of condoms? Also confirmed. And now this? Soulmates. Rare pregnancy. Twins. Transformation. I'm one dramatic plot twist away from a CW series.

Then the final blow.

"I'm sorry, Alexia," he says, voice gentle but firm. "In the next day or so, if you do not consume Drake's blood, you will slip into a coma. And your twins will die."

Silence.

How did my life turn into this?

Once upon a time, I was a normal teenager. I went to parties. Taught martial arts. Saved money. Had plans. Had Drake.

Now? I'm sitting in a vampire castle, pregnant with twins, and apparently one sip away from a coma.

Where the hell did that girl go?

GRANDMA MA'S EXPRESSION CONFIRMS IT — DRAKE COMES from a family of Dark Ones. Of course he does. Because why wouldn't my ex-boyfriend-turned-blood-drinking-soul-mate be part of the supernatural elite?

But then she drops the real bomb: his family lives here. In Darshia. Right under our noses. And I'm flabbergasted. Because for years, I was told his parents were in a tragic car accident when he was three. That's why he lived with guardians. That's why he was always so... guarded.

And now? They're just casually part of the local Dark One aristocracy. Cool. Love that for me.

It hits me — Drake's family is here. So what are we waiting for? Let's go find them. Let's fix this. Let's get the blood I apparently need to not die.

I start to rise, but Grandma Ma places a hand on my arm. Her grip is gentle but firm. "Alexia, my sources have discovered Drake's parents are not home."

Great. Just great. So now what? I stare at her face, which morphs into a smirk. A look I'm not sure I like. It's the kind of smirk that says I know something you don't, and you're not going to like it.

"I have a plan, Alexia," she says. "But first, I need to explain more of our history before showing you to your room."

History? Seriously? I don't have time for a supernatural TED Talk. I need blood. I need Drake. I need a miracle.

"Come," she says. "It will not take long."

Spoiler alert: it always takes long.

She launches into the Dark One curriculum. Apparently, when their kids start school, they're taught all the rules, the consequences, and the whole how-not-to-die-by-soul-mate-separation thing. By eighteen, most of them have found their soulmate and completed the protocol to become full Dark Ones.

Fun fact: Dark Ones can still eat food and drink liquids. But if they're soulmates? They can only digest each other's blood. Romantic, right?

Those who haven't found their soulmate can either stay human and age like one, or go through the turning process and become a full Dark One anyway. But they live lonely lives, hoping to find their match. They can still consume any blood, but it's not the same. It's not... bonded.

And the turning ceremony? Top secret. Only a handful of ceremonial priests know how it works. Not even the Queen gets the full details. Which is comforting. Not.

So here's the short version: I've found my soulmate. I'm slowly turning into a Dark One. And the babies and I need Drake's blood. Like, yesterday.

And we're running out of time.

I'm officially shite scared. What the hell am I supposed to do? Drake's off doing who-knows-what in who-knows-where, and I have zero way of contacting him. No phone. No magic mirror. No carrier bat.

And if I don't find him soon? I die. The babies die. We all die.

No pressure.

I'd prefer to meet my babies. Hold them. Name them something ridiculous. But let's be real — I'm far too young to be a mother. I still haven't figured out how to fold fitted sheets. But what choice do I have?

If I don't find Drake, I don't have to worry about becoming a mother.

Because we'll all be dead.

Morbid Alexia.

Yep. That's totally morbid.

Great. I'm now officially freaking out.

CHAPTER FIVE

MY BRAIN IS STILL SHORT-CIRCUITING FROM GRANDMA MA'S cryptic "I have a plan" declaration. What kind of plan? A rescue mission? A blood transfusion? A dramatic soap opera twist? No clue. After her brief history lesson on Dark Ones — complete with soulmate lore and blood digestion rules — she whisks Mum and me off to our rooms like we're VIP guests at a supernatural spa.

And then the door opens to my room.

My eyes practically bug out of my head. Oh. My. Gods.

This isn't a room. It's a five-star luxury suite disguised as a bedroom. Light floods in from massive windows. Plush carpet stretches wall to wall like it's trying to seduce my feet. And the bed — oh, the bed. A canopy king-size masterpiece piled high with pillows and cushions. I'm already planning my future naps, dramatic flops, and late-night sobbing sessions.

Mum and I do a quick room comparison like we're judging a reality show. Then I dive into my private bathroom.

White marble. Everywhere.

The bath? Basically a swimming pool. The shower? Big enough to host a party. A marble bench inside, multi-spray massage heads, and enough space to reenact a steamy romance — if I weren't bloated, hormonal, and emotionally wrecked.

Double-sink vanity. Heated towel racks. Mood lighting. A flat-screen TV embedded in the wall. I can literally soak in the tub and binge-watch vampire dramas while becoming one. Irony, anyone?

The castle staff have unpacked my bags, washed and dried everything, and organised my walk-in robe like I'm royalty. Only problem? Most of my clothes don't fit anymore. Thanks, pregnancy.

Overwhelmed doesn't even begin to cover it. My hormones are staging a coup. I decide a long shower might help me decompress before I spiral into a full meltdown.

Spoiler: I cry. Hard.

Warm water and tears mix as I sit on the marble bench, letting the jets massage my aching body while my brain tries to accept the fact that I'm turning into a Dark One. Drake's family lives here in Darshia. I'm pregnant — with twins.

Just over a week ago, I had abs. Now? I have a belly that kicks back. I'm still in denial, but at least I finally understand the nausea, the vomiting, the bloating. Yay for answers. Boo for existential dread.

I finish my shower, wrap myself in a fluffy towel, and chug a bottle of water like it's wine. And then I see her.

Grandma Ma, sitting quietly on my bed like she's waiting to deliver another bombshell.

My instincts go full alert. Something's off. She's watching

me. Studying me. And I'm standing there in nothing but a bath sheet. Fabulous.

I smile awkwardly, because what else do you do when your vampire grandmother is eyeing you like a science experiment?

She doesn't make me wait long.

"My men have been busy checking security footage," she says, voice all regal and commanding. "We've discovered Drake is here in Darshia."

My heart skips. My eyes widen. My belly does a happy little flip. Drake is here.

I look down, hand instinctively rubbing my belly. "Yes, little ones," I whisper. "We're close to finding your father."

Trying to sound normal and not like a squeaky fangirl, I ask, "Where did you find him?"

She smiles — again — and walks toward the walk-in robe like she's about to reveal a secret passage. My patience is hanging by a thread. I bite my lip and start counting in my head.

She tilts her head, glancing over her shoulder. "Child, your Drake has been here in Darshia for three days."

"What?" I gasp. "How? Mum and I took nearly three days to drive here."

She turns slowly, still smiling. I'm starting to hate that smile.

"Alexia, Drake and his guardians travel here by portal. It's located close to your home. Instead of taking days, it takes moments."

My mouth drops open. Portals. Freaking portals.

All the blood drains from my face. I need to sit down. I rub my belly again, and one of the babies kicks. Great. My child already knows when I'm stressed. Sensitive little bean. I whisper an apology and try to calm down.

The doctor said I'm nineteen weeks. Nineteen. Weeks. I collapse onto the bed, knees giving out. I look at Grandma Ma, who's still wearing that smug expression.

"Why didn't we know about the portal?" I ask. "There's no mention of it in the family journal. It would've made life so much easier."

If portals exist, we could've travelled safely. I could've avoided three days of nausea and roadside vomiting. And maybe — just maybe — I could finish school without anyone knowing I had babies.

Because if the doctor's right, they'll be born before the semester starts. I could graduate. Pretend none of this happened. Live a double life. Easy, right?

"Damn Drake and his 'I can't make you pregnant' crap," I mutter. "Just wait until I catch up with him."

Grandma Ma chuckles. She's clearly enjoying this. She wants front-row seats to the showdown. And yep — I just said that last part out loud.

"Come, Child," she says. "It's time you dressed. I have clothes for you that will be perfect for tonight."

Tonight? What now?

"You and I will go out to a little dance club. I've been informed your Drake will be there."

She smirks again. I officially hate that smirk. Plus, she knows more than she's willing to share.

"Come now. Move it. I want to witness your Drake's

reaction when he sees you here in Darshia — especially when he notices your expanding belly."

I instinctively cover my stomach. Protective mode: activated. We might have newly met, but I still don't trust the woman.

"While getting ready," she adds, "I'll help with your hair and makeup. You can tell me all about Drake and your history together."

We step into the walk-in wardrobe.

And I freeze.

Where did all this clothing come from? Stylish outfits fill every shelf and hanger. It's like a boutique exploded in here.

Okay. Time to focus. Get dressed. Shield my thoughts. Block my mind. Because something about Grandma Ma doesn't sit right. There's a vibe. A bad one.

And tonight? Tonight might be the beginning of something I'm not ready for.

A FEW MINUTES AGO, I WAS IN A CASTLE. NOW I'M BEING ushered through a sketchy side door into a nightclub that sounds like it's hosting a rave for the undead. The bass thumps like it's trying to crack the foundation, and the air smells like sweat, alcohol, and questionable decisions.

Grandma Ma — sorry, Alexettia — told me to call her by name while we're inside. Apparently, her subjects won't recognise her without her royal drag. No crown, no throne, no problem. Just a queen slumming it in stilettos and silk.

What am I getting myself into?

Her guards flank us like we're VIPs at a concert. They're dressed in civilian clothes, but the way they move? Yeah, definitely bodyguards. The kind who could snap necks while sipping cocktails. They keep a respectful distance, but I can feel their eyes scanning every shadow, every twitch, every potential threat. Comforting. Sort of.

The club is dancing chaos. Lights strobe like they're trying to induce seizures. The crowd pulses like a living organism — sweaty, loud, and half-feral. I'm pretty sure someone just howled. Not metaphorically. Like, actual howling.

I clutch my belly, which is currently doing somersaults. Whether it's the music, the nerves, or the twins reacting to the sensory overload, I don't know. But I swear one of them just kicked in Morse code: *Get us out of here.*

Alexettia leans in, voice smooth and smug. "If you and Drake had been raised here in Darshia, you would've known you were soulmates from the start."

Oh, well, thanks for that. Just sprinkle a little salt on my emotional wound, why don't you?

I nod, trying not to scream. Soulmates. Right. The guy who vanished after drinking my blood and leaving me pregnant with twins. That soulmate.

My mind drifts to Lucile and Michael — Drake's guardians. Did they know? Did they suspect? Because let's be real: Drake and I have been sharing a bed since we were kids. Not in a creepy way. Just… comfort. Safety. I slept better with him nearby. Always did.

So why did they treat us like we were innocent little besties one minute, then yank him out of town like I was a threat the moment they caught him drinking my blood?

Did they know what we were? Did they know what we'd become?

And if they did... why didn't they tell me?

I glance around the club, scanning faces, searching for him. My heart thuds louder than the bass. My palms are sweaty. My stomach is a mess. And my emotions? A full-blown hurricane.

I'm about to come face-to-face with the boy who broke me, bonded me, and possibly saved — or doomed — my life.

And I'm doing it in a nightclub.

Wearing stretchy pants. A top to die for.

Pregnant -With twins.

This is fine. Everything's fine.

Wait until I find Drake!

THE MUSIC IS LOUD ENOUGH TO LIQUEFY MY BRAIN. EVERY beat feels like a punch to the skull, and I'm pretty sure my eardrums are filing a noise complaint. I weave through the semi-dark chaos of the club, dodging dancers like I'm in a supernatural obstacle course. Since when are my ears this sensitive? I used to love club music. Now it feels like sonic warfare.

My nostrils flare. I gag. The air is thick with sweat, alcohol, and the unmistakable stench of sex. It's like someone bottled every bad decision and sprayed it across the room. My stomach rolls. The twins are not impressed.

I shake my head, muttering internally, *Oh, this will be fun. Not*. What fresh hell has Alexettia dragged me into? And

THE GUY NEXT DOOR

Drake — he's supposed to be here. He better not be grinding on some random chick, or I swear I'll turn his balls into earrings. Mood jewellery. Very exclusive.

We settle into an elevated VIP area that overlooks the dance floor like a throne room for the queen of disco chaos. A waiter materialises like a ghost and hands us icy drinks. Mine's a mocktail — thank the gods. Sweet, fruity, and cold enough to soothe my throat and nerves. I sip slowly, trying to look casual while scanning the crowd for the man who ruined my life and possibly saved it.

My foot taps to the beat of a new song, something catchy and annoyingly good. The dancers below are a blur of limbs, sweat, and questionable morals. Everyone looks human. Mostly. I could've enjoyed this place — if I'd known it existed. If I'd known Darshia was real. If I wasn't pregnant and emotionally unstable.

I push the sadness aside. Focus, Alexia. You're here for Drake. Not regrets.

I set my glass down and lean forward, eyes scanning the crowd. The view from up here is disturbingly clear. Some dancers are practically reenacting adult films. Others are drinking blood mid-grind like it's a casual cocktail. Dark Ones. Out in the open. No shame. No secrecy. Just full-on vampire rave mode.

Then I see him.

Across the dance floor. Familiar build. Familiar smile. Familiar ugh.

Drake.

He's dancing with a woman. She's all curves and confidence, rubbing against him like she's auditioning for a role in his bed. My body goes rigid. Jealousy? Rage? Hormonal fury? All of the above.

I watch as Drake's expression shifts. He pulls away. She moves closer. He steps back again. Okay, interesting. Maybe he's not a total man whore. Still, he's down there dancing with someone who isn't me. And that's a problem.

I rub my belly, instinctively protective. These babies are his. He has a lot to answer for. And he will.

I glance at Alexettia. Her eyebrow arches. That smirk again. She saw everything. Of course she did.

"Come, Alexia," she says, standing with regal flair. "Time to show these people how to dance. And time to see your beloved."

Oh, fabulous. Confrontation time.

I finish my drink, and before I can set it down, a server snatches the glass like I'm royalty. Which, technically, I kind of am. I scan our secluded perch and spot one of Alexettia's guards lurking in the shadows. Stealthy. Impressive. Note to self: learn their names. Preferably before I need one of them to save my life.

I follow Alexettia down the spiral staircase. The music shifts — deeper, slower, more sensual. My body responds before my brain catches up. The beat is hypnotic, and I move with it, hands above my head, hips swaying. I'm not just walking — I'm dancing. And I'm heading straight for Drake. *He who cannot make me pregnant.* Ha. Joke's on him.

The closer I get, the stranger it feels. A pressure builds in my head — not the usual Dark One intrusion. This is different. Sharper. Focused.

I keep four dancers between us, watching him through the

crowd. My hand goes to my temple. The pressure intensifies. I concentrate. And then — I hear him.

Drake's voice. In my head.

He's complaining about the song. About the woman annoying him. His lips aren't moving, but I hear every word.

'This female stinks. What did she spray herself with? Shit, here comes another one.'

I freeze. What the actual hell?

I'm hearing Drake's thoughts. Loud. Clear. Unfiltered.

Is this normal? Should this be happening? I need answers. I need that damn family journal. I need a manual for How to Be a Pregnant Psychic Vampire in Ten Easy Steps.

I turn to Alexettia, signalling that I need to talk. We slip off the dance floor and into a quieter nook. She gives me the hurry up look.

I lean close and yell over the music, "Alexettia, I need to ask you something. I don't know how to explain it, but the closer I got to Drake, the more I could hear him. In my head."

Her expression shifts. Not surprised. Just mildly amused. Like I've finally caught up.

"Alexettia, is this normal? What does it mean?"

Her smile grows. "Oh, my Child. If what you've said is true, your Dark One powers — and your bond with your beloved — are increasing."

Well, that's… cool. Terrifying. But cool.

Who needs a phone when you've got telepathic power?

My mind spins. I turn back toward the dance floor,

searching for Drake again. And I feel Alexettia behind me, her breath warm near my ear.

She's not done talking.

And I'm not done unravelling.

I KEEP MY KNEES LOCKED, SPINE STRAIGHT, PRETENDING I'M not seconds away from collapsing under the weight of Alexettia's power. It's crawling along my skin like static, tingling, prickling, almost suffocating. She's not even trying to be subtle. Her energy is everywhere — like royalty and thunder had a baby.

"Alexia," she says, voice smooth and smug, "this is one benefit of mating with your soulmate. You can speak privately. No one else can hear."

Well, that's convenient. Who needs texting when you've got telepathic pillow talk?

"As Queen," she continues, "I can hear conversations. But your Drake? He doesn't have your strength. If he did, I wouldn't be able to hear a single word he's muttering. I think your Drake is missing you."

I focus. Hard. And there it is — Drake's thoughts, raw and unfiltered. *He wants to be home. With me. Wrapped around me like a blanket of safety and love. Not here. Not with strangers. Not with women who smell like desperation and cheap perfume.*

'I am not marrying one of these desperados.'

"What?" I whip my head toward Alexettia. "Grandma Ma, did you just hear Drake? Is it true? Are his parents here tonight to introduce him to his future wife?"

Her face says it all. That smug little twitch of her lips confirms it.

Shite. No. No, no, no. This cannot be happening. Drake. Engaged? To someone else? When we've mated? When I'm carrying his children?

I am his soulmate — dammit.

"Come, Child," she says, already moving. "It's time we confront Drake and his parents once and for all."

You bet your sweet queenie arse we will.

She strides ahead, poised and lethal, reaching for my hand like we're about to storm a battlefield. We plunge back into the crowd, weaving through hot, sweaty, gyrating bodies. A few men try to intercept me, flashing smiles and flexing muscles. One look from Alexettia and they scatter like scared puppies. Ha. Men.

I still can't wrap my head around it. Drake's parents — alive, well, and apparently not in a hospital bed. Everything I was told? Lies. Fabricated fairy tales to keep me in the dark.

Three dancers block my view, but I catch glimpses of Drake. He's moving to the music, dancing with another woman. His back is to me. Good. He doesn't see me coming.

I match his rhythm, slipping between bodies until I'm right behind him. My body moves with his, like we're synced. Like we've never been apart.

I reach for his mind.

'Drake, can you hear me? If you can, keep dancing. Don't let anyone know you know who I am.'

He tenses. Just for a second. Then resumes dancing.

'What? ...Alexia, is that you? But how?' His voice is stunned, searching.

I keep swaying, keeping the beat, keeping the secret.

'Drake,' I said, *'don't let anyone know you know who I am. Keep dancing.'*

His emotions hit me like a wave — confusion, disbelief, longing. He's unravelling. I feel it.

'Okay, Alexia, I don't understand how you're speaking to me or if you're really behind me. But I'm turning around. I need to see your beautiful face.'

Oh gods. His words. He knows exactly how to twist my heart into knots.

He turns slowly, in sync with the music. Our eyes meet. His gaze softens, confusion melting into love. That smile — his panty-dropping, heart-melting, soul-crushing smile — spreads across his face. And I melt. Just a little.

I've missed him. So much.

'Baby, how are you here? Am I dreaming? You shouldn't be here. I must be dreaming.'

I wink. He moves closer, wraps his arms around me. I loop mine around his neck, breathing him in. His nose brushes my neck, lips trailing soft kisses along my skin. Oh yeah. This. I missed this.

I tighten my grip, grounding myself in his touch.

'Drake, I have something to tell you. It's important.' I tilt my head, meet his eyes. *'Drake, listen, I really need to tell you something.'*

He pulls back slightly, eyes searching mine. Does he even realise we're speaking mind-to-mind?

We keep dancing, bodies moving like they remember each other.

'Alexia, how are you here? You shouldn't be here. If my parents see you, they'll cause trouble. Humans aren't allowed here.'

Oh boy. We have a lot to unpack. We both have luggage.

I press my fingers to his lips, silencing him. Then I guide his hand to my belly.

'Drake, remember the last thing I said to you? "If I'm pregnant, I'll hunt you down and kick your arse." Well, guess what? I'm here. And I'm kicking your arse. So before you freak out and panic your parents, stay calm. Walk with me off the dance floor. We need to talk.'

His hand moves across my belly. His eyes drop, then rise again. Confusion. Awe. Panic. It's all there.

He pulls me close, arms tight around me.

'Um... Baby, how are you pregnant? You shouldn't be pregnant. Especially this pregnant.'

I wrap my arms around him, inhale his scent — warm, familiar, intoxicating.

'No shite, Sherlock. Now shut up and kiss me.'

And he does.

Our mouths collide, lips burning, tongues battling. It's not just a kiss — it's a storm. A release. A reunion. A promise. Our bodies respond instantly, heat rising, passion igniting. If we don't stop, we'll be joining the other dancers doing more than just dancing.

His taste is addictive. My body is on fire. My hormones are screaming. I want him. All of him. Now.

His essence wraps around me, pulling me under. I'm drowning in him. And I don't want to come up for air.

I OPEN MY EYES WIDE, BREATH CATCHING AS COOL WALL STONE presses against my overheated back. Wait — when did we move? How did we end up tucked into this shadowy niche of the club? And... why is my arse bare and feeling the breeze?

How in the world did my legs become wrapped around

Drake's waist? Since when did my stretchy pants vanish? Gone. As well as my underwear? MIA.

Fabulous. One minute we're kissing, the next we're halfway to nakedville in a public club. How does he do this to me so fast? My brain's short-circuiting, and I don't even care.

His hands roam, his touch electric. My body responds like it's been waiting for this moment since the day he left. The music pulses around us, but it's just background noise now — our rhythm is our own. Drake's hand sweeps against my heated, damp core. His fingers slide through my warm, slick folds. Oh, God, yes, that feels so good. My eyes close shut when he increases his touch. His magical fingers find their target and play with my clit to the beat of the music.

I'm not thinking. I'm feeling. Every inch of me is alive, burning, aching, wanting. Oh boy, I need him to fill me now. My weeping core seeks more of his touch, and I'm wide open, ready for him to fill me, making us one.

My hand doesn't wait as I slip it between us, undoing his button and sliding down his zipper, releasing his hot, engorged length into my waiting hand. Eager for more, I move my hips forward. It doesn't take long for Drake's heated, solid, silky length to find its target. He doesn't hesitate with a firm thrust of his hips.

Air rushes out of my lungs with the force of his engorged length filling me. My eyes roll back with each one of his thrusts. Each thrust is better than the last. My weeping, heated flesh holds on, unwilling to release him as my hips move in time with his. While the heels of my feet dig into his arse, pushing him in deeper, touching all those places only he can reach.

We move together like we never stopped, like we were made for this. His mouth finds mine again, and the kiss is molten, messy, and maddening. I'm drowning in him, and I don't want to come up for air.

Then he whispers, voice rough and desperate: "Baby, I need you to bite me. I want to feel you. I need you now, Alexia."

The pull of his blood is irresistible. My gums tingle, my instincts flare. I break the kiss, trail my tongue along his neck, and feel the shift — the drop of my incisors, the hunger rising. I sink my teeth into his skin, and his blood floods my mouth like fire and honey. It's everything. It's him.

He groans, body tightening around me, pulling me closer, deeper. I drink, and the world narrows to this moment — his blood, his body, his soul. I seal the wound, kiss his neck, and feel him tremble beneath my lips.

We kiss again, blood still on our tongues, mixing, binding. His thrusts grow stronger, more urgent, and I'm lost in the storm. My body arches, tightens, explodes. He follows, holding me like he'll never let go.

We stay like that for a moment, maybe longer, much longer — breathless, tangled, undone. Our hearts slow. Our minds return. And I remember why I came here.

'Drake,' I whisper into his thoughts, *'we need to talk. I have a car outside. Ten minutes. You can come back after.'*

His mind brushes mine, thoughts jumbled and dazed. *'Okay, baby. We better be quick. My parents can't see us leave. But first — we clean up. Gods, I missed you.'*

We pull apart, smiling, breathless. He slips from my body as I slide down his, legs shaky, heart still racing. A nearby bathroom catches my eye. Drake hands me my clothes — where he found them, I have no idea. I use the nearby single bathroom and clean up fast, dress, and meet him back in the shadows.

The heat of the club, the sweat of strangers — it's nothing compared to the warmth of Drake's touch. I turn toward the exit, reach for him. His hand finds mine, fingers intertwining like they never stopped.

Together, we move as one, slipping through the crowd, heading for the door.

And whatever comes next — we face it together.

CHAPTER SIX

As soon as I make it through the exit, the noise level drops like someone hit mute on the chaos. Cool night air rushes over my flushed skin, clearing my head just enough to register the sight waiting for me.

Grandma Ma — Alexettia — is standing beside the open car door, arms crossed, wearing her patented don't-mess-with-me expression. Lovely. Just what I need after a psychic makeout session and a near-murderous dance floor reunion.

Then it hits me.

Buzzing. Pressure. Like a swarm of bees trying to drill into my skull.

Grandma Ma is knocking. No — she's barging into my head.

Not without my permission, lady!

I grit my teeth, but something shifts. A prickling unease crawls up my spine. Something's coming. I glance around, scanning shadows, then flick my gaze to the guard behind her. He's tense. Alert.

Fine. I sigh and lower my shields, letting the grumpy queen into my head.

Before I can say a word, she's already barking orders: "Alexia. Child, we do not have much time. Walk faster."

What's the rush? I glance at Drake, wondering if he recognises the woman glaring at us like we're late for a royal execution. Judging by his blank expression, nope. So much for being raised by Dark Ones and knowing your own damn queen.

I shoot back, "Okay, Grandma Ma, we're coming." Hopefully, I don't sound like a sulky toddler in her head.

I'm about to introduce them when the hairs on my neck spike. Danger. Real, tangible, creeping danger.

I freeze. Turn.

Three figures emerge from the alley, shadows peeling back to reveal men in dark clothing. At first, they look like your average thugs — until they step into the streetlight.

Red eyes.

Glowing. Freaking. Red. Eyes.

You've got to be kidding me.

Whatever they're selling, I'm not buying. And I definitely don't have time for this. I'm seconds away from telling Drake about the twins, and now I've got to deal with demon-eyed creeps?

Drake moves in front of me, all protective instinct and testosterone. Great. Now he's playing bodyguard. Cute. But unnecessary.

Because I'm not some helpless damsel. I'm a pregnant,

pissed-off, half-turned Dark One with a black belt, street-fighting reflexes, and zero patience for glowing-eyed creeps.

Then all hell breaks loose.

The three figures lunge.

I mentally number them. Bad Guy One, Two, and Three. Middle guy — Number Two — comes straight for me. He's built like a fridge, bald, boots like anvils, and eyes that scream murderous intent. His stance is wide, heavy, predictable. Amateur.

I wait. Time slows. My breath steadies. My weight shifts to the balls of my feet.

Then I move.

I pivot hard, my right leg snapping out in a low arc — heel-first into his ribs. Crack. He grunts, stumbles sideways. I don't wait. I spin again, this time higher, faster, my left leg slicing through the air and connecting with his jaw. His head whips back. Blood sprays.

I follow through. Elbow strike to the temple. Palm heel to the nose. My fists blur — jab, cross, hook. Each hit lands with precision, vibrating through my bones. Pain flares in my knuckles. My ankle screams. Worth it.

He's still standing. Barely.

Time to end this.

I shift my weight, chamber my leg, and launch a roadhouse kick straight to his temple. My heel slams into the side of his head with a satisfying thud. His eyes roll back. He drops like a sack of bricks.

I bounce on my toes, adrenaline surging. My body's in full fight mode — hyper-aware, hyper-fast. I slam a follow-up kick into the back of his knee. Pop. The joint dislocates with a sickening crunch.

I wince. My foot throbs. Bugger, that hurts. I shake it out, hoping I didn't just sprain something. No time to check.

I drop to one knee, press my fingers into the nerve cluster between his neck and shoulder — pressure point. He's out cold. Good.

I scan the scene. Drake's still fighting Number Three. Grandma Ma is squaring off with Number One. Her guard's down. Not good.

I move.

I dart behind Number Three, silent and fast. He's focused on Drake, which is his mistake. I leap, twist mid-air, and drive my heel into the back of his skull. His body jerks, then crumples. Unconscious before he hits the ground.

No time to celebrate.

I spin — just in time to see Number One raise a weapon at Grandma Ma.

I lunge.

But before I reach her, her security finally shows up. About freaking time. A shot rings out. Loud. Final.

I whip around.

Number One stumbles, a dark hole in his forehead. He collapses. And then — he disintegrates. Poof. Dust. Gone.

What. The. Hell.

I'M STILL PROCESSING WHEN DRAKE WRAPS HIS ARMS AROUND me, pulling me into his chest. His face buries in my hair, breath ragged. His hands move protectively over my rounding belly, grounding me in the chaos.

And for the first time in forever, I feel safe.

Which is weird. Because I've always been the one doing the protecting.

But tonight? I held my own. Took down two of the three creeps. Protected myself. Protected my babies. Helped Drake. All in under two minutes.

Not bad for a pregnant teenager with a supernatural identity crisis.

I allow myself a small, smug smile.

Then I feel it.

Something hard. Pressed against my lower back.

Oh, for the love of—

I wiggle. Yep. Definitely hard. Definitely long. Definitely Drake.

Seriously?

It's been twenty-five minutes since he last… used his hard length. Apparently, fighting turns him on. Typical teenage male.

I reach out with my mind. *'Um, Drake, what do you think you're doing? This is not the time or place.'*

I grind my butt against him just to make a point. His body tightens around mine. His lips brush my neck. Shivers. Damn him.

'Baby, I was scared for you. For our baby. I never want to

see you in danger again. I love you too much to lose you now that I have you back.'

His kisses trail along my neck, slow and reverent. My eyes flutter shut. Hormones, you traitorous little monsters.

"Drake, we really need to talk. Let's sit in the car while Alexettia deals with the creeps," I manage out loud.

His lips pause. His thoughts scatter. And that's when I realise — he doesn't know we've been mind-talking this whole time. He doesn't know I can hear everything.

Yeah. Not telling him that just yet.

"Alexia, who is this woman with you? Who are those men? And why does she look like you?"

I glance at Grandma Ma and send her a message. *'I'm taking Drake to the car. Can your guards handle the rest? I don't want those guys anywhere near me again.'*

She stops mid-conversation, eyes locking with mine. Then her voice slides into my head.

'Wow, Alexia, my child, your powers are improving. Technically, you shouldn't be able to speak to me like this. I didn't allow it. Impressive. Yes — take Drake to the car. Talk. I'll join you shortly. My men will handle the criminals. They'll be questioned thoroughly. But that's not your concern now.'

I nod, take Drake's hand, and lead him toward the car. Because it's time for answers.

And this time, I'm not leaving without them.

CHAPTER SEVEN

THE SECOND I SINK INTO THE COOL, BUTTERY LEATHER OF THE palace car seat, my body sighs in relief. But my neck? Oh no. It's doing that creepy hair-raising thing again. Fantastic. I'm officially Spiderman. Or Spiderwoman. Or just a hormonal Dark One with a sixth sense and zero chill.

I turn my head toward the club. And there they are. A group of men slinking out of the alley like they're auditioning for a villain montage. Oh, this does not look good. Cue ominous music.

I reach out with my mind, fast and hard. *'Excuse me, Grandma Ma?'*

Her reply is instant and annoyed. *'What is it, Alexia?'*

Welcome to my world, lady. I mentally roll my eyes.

'I've got a bad feeling about that group of men who just exited the alley.'

I keep my eyes locked on them. Their body language screams we're here to ruin your night. And I'm not in the mood.

Grandma Ma's voice shifts into full royal command mode. *'My Child, the driver will take you and your Drake back to the castle.'*

She moves away from the men, melting into the shadows with her guards like some supernatural ninja queen. And I'm left wondering — is she going to be okay?

'I can hear your thoughts, Alexia.' Oops. Forgot to shield. Again.

'I will be safe. Do not worry. We'll meet back at the castle shortly.'

Right. Mental note: tighten the mind-shield. Grandma Ma doesn't need a front-row seat to my internal chaos.

The car pulls away, leaving her behind. I lean back, trying to relax, but my heart's doing a full cardio workout. There's no reason to panic. We're safe. Grandma Ma's safe. Everything's fine.

Except it's not.

Drake's warm hand lands on my knee, and suddenly I'm

bombarded. His thoughts. His emotions. All of it. Because I forgot to shield again. Brilliant.

"Baby, what's going on? And what about the woman with you? We just left her behind. I need to get back before my parents notice I'm gone."

I turn toward him as the car's interior lights fade on, casting soft shadows across his face. Concern is etched into every line. Cute. But not helpful.

"It's okay, Drake. She'll meet us later. Right now, we need to talk. Your parents can wait."

I manage a small smile, even though my insides are twisting. Someone out there wants to hurt us. And I still don't know who or why. I'm not in Kansas anymore. And where the hell is my fairy godmother?

I look into his eyes, trying to find the right words. Nothing. Blank. Great.

"Drake, you have to let me finish talking before you interrupt me. Okay?"

He smiles, moves closer, wraps one arm around my back, and places the other on my belly. His version of go ahead. So here goes.

Deep breath. Slow exhale.

"Drake, remember how you said you come from a special family and couldn't get me pregnant?"

He jumps in. Of course he does. "But baby, as far as I knew, I shouldn't have been able to get you pregnant."

I give him the look. The one that says shut up or die. He gets it.

"As you can see," I continue, gesturing to my belly, "you did. Very much so."

I glance down, then back at his face. Why am I nervous? I've fought monsters tonight. I can do this.

"Turns out, my mother's side of the family is like yours. Found that out the night after you ghosted me."

His eyes widen. His thoughts spike. He still hasn't figured out we've been mind-talking. Silly male.

"And don't forget, Drake — you're not the only one who consumed blood in bed."

I inhale sharply, then dive in.

"Since arriving in Darshia, I've been informed I'm pregnant. Why? Because we shouldn't have consumed each other's blood. Or had unprotected sex. Multiple times. Before turning eighteen. Apparently, that's a major taboo. And — surprise — we're soulmates."

I pause. Let it sink in. Then drop the final bomb.

"Oh yeah, by the way — we're having twins. The doctor confirmed it this afternoon. And this pregnancy? It's on fast-forward. A few more days, tops. Also, I need to consume your blood for the twins to survive and mature."

I leave out the part where I'll collapse into a coma without it. No need to panic him. Yet.

Drake's thoughts hit me like a freight train.

'What the fuck? Soulmates? You need my blood? Twins? Oh my God. My parents are going to freak. I'm a dead man.'

Wow. So much for I love you. That's a knife to the heart. And he still hasn't realised I can hear everything.

"By the way, Drake — right back at you with *'what the fuck.'* And yes, we are soulmates."

I breathe in, trying not to let the disappointment drown me.

My head pounds. My heart races. I'm so angry I could punch something. Preferably Drake.

"This means — if you haven't figured it out — I. Can. Hear. Your. Thoughts. Yes, Drake. All of them."

His eyes bug out. Classic.

"Drake, you are a dead man walking when my parents catch up with you. You don't have to worry about yours."

I turn toward the window. And there it is — the castle. We've arrived. Didn't even notice. Usually, I'm more observant. Must be the rage fog.

The doorman opens the car door, waiting.

"Oh, by the way, Drake." I step out, tossing the final truth bomb over my shoulder. "That woman I was with earlier? She's my great-great-great-grandmother. And my great-grandmother — she's the Queen of Darshia."

I leave him in the car. Let him stew.

His thoughts echo in my head as I walk away.

'Oh shit. I'm in deep trouble now.'

Yes. Yes, you are.

It doesn't take long for him to scramble out of the car and follow me.

Smart man.

CHAPTER EIGHT

THE MOMENT WE STEP THROUGH THE CASTLE'S MAIN entrance, the doorman — butler — security guy — whatever he is — starts leading us toward the grand staircase. Not Grandma Ma's office. Not the war room. Not even the dramatic throne hallway. Straight to the stairs.

Okay. That's interesting.

Either Grandma Ma hasn't updated him, or I'm being deliberately left out of whatever post-attack debrief is happening. Which is cute. Because I only took down two of the henchmen myself. Pregnant. In heels. Where were her guards again?

This day just keeps getting better and better. If she tries to treat me like a child and keep me in the dark, I swear I'll kick down her office door and demand answers. Politely. Maybe.

Unease creeps in. I should've heard something by now. A message. A mind ping. A royal memo. Anything.

I study the back of the doorman as we walk. Over six feet tall. Built like a tank. Moves like a soldier. His suit might say "hospitality," but his posture screams "combat training." He's not just here to open doors and carry umbrellas. I'd bet my last mocktail he's part of the security detail.

I don't need an escort to my room. I stop walking.

"Excuse me."

He keeps walking. Seriously?

I raise my voice. "Excuse me. Can you stop? I want to speak with you."

Finally, he slows. Turns. Faces me. His expression? Mildly annoyed. Like I've interrupted his silent brooding routine.

"Yes, Miss Alexia. What do you wish to discuss with me?" His voice is low, deep, and very I could snap your neck but I won't.

"Hi. I don't mean to be rude," I say, raising an eyebrow. "But what name should I use when addressing you? I might be stuck in Darshia for a while, and I'd rather not keep calling you 'doorman guy.'"

His eyebrow lifts. Just slightly. I'm guessing he doesn't get asked that often.

"Thank you for asking, Miss Alexia. You may call me James."

"Nice to meet you, James. And what's your actual position here? Because something tells me you're not a concierge. If you are, the Queen is seriously underutilising your talents."

His other eyebrow joins the first one somewhere near his hairline. He pauses. Then replies, "You are observant, Miss Alexia. No, I am no concierge or butler. My position is in security here in the castle. If you need my services, dial thirty-three on your in-room phone."

Well. That explains the don't-mess-with-me energy radiating off him like heat waves. And the way he moves like he's always two seconds from tackling someone.

"And Miss Alexia," he adds, "you look a little flushed. How are you feeling?"

Concern flickers across his face before it vanishes behind the professional mask. Huh. So he's not a robot after all.

"Thank you, James. Drake and I will continue to my room. I need to lie down. It's been one hell of a night. If anyone's looking for us, that's where we'll be. Please pass on my message to the Queen. Good night."

I give him a curt nod and a small smile. He nods back, then turns and disappears like a shadow with a job to do.

I turn toward the staircase. Opulent marble. Grand. Dramatic. I start climbing, counting the familiar twenty-five steps like they're a countdown to sanity.

Because tonight? I've earned every damn one.

DRAKE'S THOUGHTS SLAM INTO MY SKULL LIKE A BATTERING ram. The urge to scream at him to shut up is almost unbearable. I pause mid-step, glance over my shoulder, and there he is — casually trailing behind me, hand gliding along the polished handrail like he's on a scenic stroll. He has no idea how annoying he is. None.

His thoughts keep coming. Loud. Repetitive. Whiny.

Shocked about the pregnancy. Shocked about the twins. Shocked about everything. It's like listening to a broken record narrated by a confused teenage boy. And I'm done.

I try to block him out. I really do. But my shields are shot, and his voice keeps bombarding my brain like a swarm of angry bees. The pressure builds. My head throbs. The headache of all headaches blooms behind my eyes. Great. Just great.

I massage my temples, hoping to ease the pain. No luck.

We reach my room. I kick off my shoes and head straight for the bed. Drake wanders toward the window like he's admiring the view in a luxury hotel. Meanwhile, I'm collapsing from exhaustion, pregnancy, and the emotional wreckage of today.

The doctor's warning echoes in my mind: I need Drake's blood. What I got in the club helped, but it wasn't enough. I need more. Soon.

I climb onto the bed, sink into the pillows, and feel instant relief in my feet — until I glance down and see they're swollen. Badly. My heart races. My breath shortens. Something's wrong.

I need to call the doctor.

Then — knocking. Soft at first. Then louder.

I glance at Drake. He's still lost in his own mental spiral, pacing and brooding. I slip into his mind. Yep. Still obsessing over how *I'm pregnant, how I'm in Darshia, and how I'm related to the Queen.* His thoughts are a chaotic mess.

The knocking continues.

"Who is it?" I call out, voice strained.

A male voice replies. The doctor. Of course. Perfect timing. Even though he looks twenty-five, he's probably pushing eighty. Vampire perks.

I look at Drake, silently begging him to open the door. He doesn't move. His eyes narrow. His thoughts spike.

'Alexia, we're not a couple right now, but why do you have a male at your bedroom door?'

Excuse me?

I replay his words in my head. *Not a couple? Oh, hell no.*

I scramble off the bed, one hand cradling my belly, the other gripping the edge of the dresser for balance. I head toward the balcony doors, needing air. Needing space. Needing to not murder Drake.

"Drake," I say aloud, voice shaking, "do you seriously think — after everything — that we're not together anymore?" I rub my belly, glaring at him. "Because you better not be saying that, mister."

Another knock. The doctor's still waiting.

"Go open the damn door," I snap. "That's the doctor. The one who's actually concerned about me and the babies. You know — your babies. And no, I'm not here in Darshia to hook up with someone else."

My heart pounds. Hard. Fast. Painfully.

My voice rises. "Is that what you think of me? Is that why you were dancing with those other girls? You were there to replace me, weren't you? I saw them, Drake. I saw their hands all over you. And you let them. You let them touch you."

My hands fly to my belly. "Do you really think you can

marry someone else after this? Just try it, mister. We are soulmates. Get it? Soul. Mates."

My heart slams against my ribs like it's trying to escape. My ears ring with the thunderous beat. I'm so angry I can barely breathe.

"Do you even know what that means?" I shout. Spittle flies from my lips. I'm shaking. I'm boiling. I'm unraveling.

I try to breathe. Inhale. Exhale. Nothing helps. My heart races faster. My feet — swollen. My hands — puffy. My body — overheating.

I glare at Drake. "Let the doctor in. At least he gives a damn. He probably knows about the attack. He's here to check on me. On the babies. Your babies."

Then I hear it — my voice. It sounds wrong. Muffled. Like I'm underwater.

I don't feel good.

Why am I here? The thought flashes through my mind like a warning.

I turn toward the window, needing to escape. Needing to breathe. Needing to not collapse.

Drake's words echo in my head. His attitude. His accusations. His immaturity. It's too much. He's too much.

I'm done.

A strange sound of breaking glass.

Then it hits.

A sharp pain. Radiating from my back. Like I've been stabbed. I stumble. My body seizes. My breath catches.

I blink. I'm on the floor. Staring at the ceiling. When did I fall?

Everything spins. My limbs feel heavy. My chest tightens. I need help. I need—

Darkness.

The lights flicker. Dim. Fade.

Drake's voice is distant. Muffled. White noise.

My eyes close. My body stills.

And everything goes silent.

CHAPTER NINE

'Alexia, wake up, baby. Please wake up.'

Ha... What? Who?

Who the hell is playing drums in my skull? The pounding is relentless. Loud. Obnoxious. Like someone's hosting a rock concert in my brain and forgot to invite me.

My head is killing me. Have I mentioned that? Because it's worth repeating. I don't even want to open my eyes. Nope. Not happening. I feel like I've been hit by a truck. Or maybe a bus. Or possibly a supernatural freight train.

Did I go out drinking last night? Would I? Could I? Because this feels like the worst hangover in history. Except... I'm pregnant. So, no. Definitely not a party night with Lucy Blachart, my ride-or-die bestie and professional bad influence. No vodka, no dancing, no regrettable karaoke. Just pain. And confusion. And a body that feels both freezing and boiling at the same time.

Mental memo: never party with Lucy again. Not that I did. But still — never.

Wait. Is that a radio? Or are people talking? I focus. Yep. Voices. Familiar ones. And none of them belong to Lucy.

'My Queen, Miss Alexia is safe for now. Thankfully, the poison is no longer spreading throughout her body. The follow-up blood work I had ordered should confirm the variety of poison used. And yes, I have my suspicions.'

'Doctor, I want my granddaughter and grandbabies safe and out of harm's way.'

'Yes, my Queen.'

Hold up. Poison? Blood work? Grandbabies?
Oh shite. I wasn't partying. I was… shot?
Okay. Time to freak out.

'Alexia, wake up, baby. We are all worried about you.'

That voice. Drake. Definitely Drake. And his words hit me like a slap.

Wake up? What do you mean wake up? I'm awake. Aren't I? I mean, I'm thinking. I'm hearing. I'm… not moving. Oh no.

I try to feel my body. Arms. Legs. Belly. Everything's fuzzy. My brain is wrapped in cotton. My heart's racing. I'm hot. I'm cold. I'm a mess.

Why am I unconscious? Why is everyone worried? What the hell happened?

Okay, Alexia. Think. Just think.

Mum. Yes — Mum was here. We're staying at the castle. With Grandma Ma. Alexettia. Right. That tracks.

What else?

Nightclub. Yes. Grandma Ma took me to a club. And then… fuzzy. My brain short-circuits. Again.

I rest. Try again.

Babies. Yes. I can feel them. Oh, thank the gods. They're okay. I send a mental message: Hello, my precious babies. Mummy loves you. And I mean it. Fiercely.

So I'm in Darshia. Met Dark Ones. Found Drake. Drank his blood. Got shot. Apparently.

My nose picks up his scent. He's close. Mum and Grandma Ma are here too. And someone else. I reach out with my mind.

'If we cannot keep her blood pressure down, we must admit her to the hospital. Alexia has developed preeclampsia, which can be dangerous for her and the twins. The bullet wound has healed and will not leave a scar. She is fortunate she had turned when she did. Otherwise, that bullet would have hit her heart. But…'

Excuse me — bullet wound? Scar? Preeclampsia? Was I shot? Like, actually shot?

Grandma Ma's voice cuts in: *'My Granddaughter is to have complete medical treatment and care right here, Doctor.*

Away from anyone else who is trying to assassinate my family and me. Do you understand, Doctor? Her safety has to be placed first. We have caught the shooter. One less thing to be concerned about.'

Okay. So someone tried to assassinate me. And Grandma Ma. And the babies. And I have preeclampsia. Whatever that is. Sounds terrifying.

'My Queen, while Alexia is resting, her blood pressure slowly decreases. The two babies are safe for now. But, I must inform Alexia's mother of Alexia's condition, and if she does not wake up soon, her life is still in danger.'

Wait — if I don't wake up soon? But I'm awake. Sort of. My eyes just aren't cooperating.

'I cannot determine if there is any other reason for her to be still unconscious. We know that the bullet was full of poison from the toxicology reports. I honestly cannot say if it is the poison or the amount of stress Alexia was under at the time of the shooting. Stress equals high blood pressure, which can equal death for her or her babies, most likely both.'

Well, that's just delightful. Death. Poison. Stress. All wrapped up in one neat little package.

Then Grandma Ma again: *'Doctor, the IV you placed on her arm. How much longer will she require Drake's blood? I have noticed he is starting to look a little pale. After all, he has been beside her for the last half hour.'*

Wait. What?

Drake is giving me his blood. Straight from his vein. Into mine.

Wow. That's… intense.

And probably not voluntary. I bet Mum guilt-tripped him into it. Or Grandma Ma threatened him with royal punishment.

Then it hits me. We were fighting. Drake and I. He didn't believe we were soulmates. His thoughts were slamming into my head like a wrecking ball. I was furious. My heart was racing. My hearing went fuzzy. Then — pain. Sharp. In my back.

I passed out.

That's why I'm here. That's why I'm unconscious. That's why my head feels like it's been stuffed with cotton and rage.

Then Drake's voice again. Soft. Guilty.

'Baby, can you hear me? I am so, so sorry, Alexia. I made you so angry with me. I know this is all my fault. If I did not make you upset and angry, you would not have placed yourself in front of the window and would not have been shot. You were right; the doctor was here to check on you and our babies.'

Wow. He sounds guilty. Good. He should be.

'What do you want, Drake?' I snap, my anger rising. *'You*

made it perfectly clear. You do not want to be with our children or me.'

His emotions slam into me — shock, guilt, love. *'Baby, please don't. I know I was a jerk. And that is not true about not wanting you and the twins. I love you and our babies. I have heard their little heartbeats and have seen them. The doctor brought a machine in, and we all saw the babies in 3-D. It was great.'*

Great. They all got the show. I missed it. Typical.

'Your mum even started crying when she saw them and heard their little hearts beating.'

Of course she did. And I missed that too.

'Alexia, the doctor printed out pictures for us to keep and had copies for your mum to take a few of the pictures home to show your dad as well. The doctor recorded it on a memory stick, so you can see our babies being measured.'

Okay. That helps. A little.

'Look, Alexia. I am sorry I hurt you so much. I know there is no excuse but look at it from my point of view. Everything was overwhelming when you said we would be parents and soulmates. While my blood has been intravenously fed to you, keeping me by your side, I have been giving everything a lot of serious thought.'

Good. He better have.

'About us, the part about us being soulmates — everything. It is a lot to take in. It did not help when Michael and Lucile saw me drinking your blood. They know I am turning into a Dark One now. That is why I am here in Darshia. My parents pushed the issue. They said it was time to pick a mate.'

Wait. What?

His parents — who faked a hospital stay for years — are here. In Darshia. And they want him to pick a mate.

Oh, hell no.

'That's why I was at the club,' Drake says, his voice soft, guilty. *'My... my heart wasn't in it. All I wanted was you, Alexia. You're all I've ever wanted. I've loved you for a long time. It's been hard keeping my family secret from you. Then I found out I'd been living next door to a Dark One all these years. I haven't told my parents about you consuming my blood or that you're here in Darshia. They're outraged I disappeared from the club. They've been sending me texts and voice messages — none of them polite. I spoke to your mum and the Queen. They both said I shouldn't talk to my parents right now. At least they can't find me here in the royal castle.'*

OKAY. SO HE'S BEEN THINKING. PROCESSING. PANICKING. BUT that doesn't erase the fact that he hurt me. Badly.

My mind stretches out over my body again. Still no movement. Not even a twitch. My eyelids are staging a rebellion. My limbs are on strike. What the hell is going on?

'Drake, let the doctor know I'm conscious but can't move. My head is pounding like a war drum. And by the way, how long have I been like this?'

He hesitates. That's never good.

'Ah, baby, please don't get upset.'

Oh, shite. That phrase is code for you're about to be very upset.

'You've been like this for eleven hours. I've given you three lots of blood. The doctor said your body needs it for the babies to survive. The pregnancy's advancing fast. He said you've reached twenty-eight weeks. I spaced out during most of what he said. Some of it went over my head. The rest freaked me out.'

Eleven hours. Out cold. And twenty-eight weeks pregnant. I've missed more than I even know.

'Drake, twenty-eight weeks means I'm seven months pregnant. There are forty weeks total. Can you please inform the doctor I'm awake?'

Out loud, Drake says, "Okay, baby. Just try and relax. I'll tell the doctor."

The room quiets. The others stop talking. Drake relays the message. And just like that, I become the center of attention again — except I still can't move. Can't speak. Can't even blink.

Apparently, Drake's been holding my hand this whole time. I didn't even notice. That's how disconnected I am from my own body.

The doctor confirms what I already know: preeclampsia. Dangerous. Stress is the enemy. If I don't stay calm, I'll be carted off to a hospital. Great. Just what I need — another sterile room and more needles.

Mum starts grilling the doctor. I wish he could just fix me. Snap his fingers. Make me normal again.

Half an hour passes. A phone rings. The doctor answers in hushed tones. When he hangs up, Mum jumps in.

"Doctor, have the test results returned? Have they named the poison?"

Oh, fantastic. I get shot, and now I'm poisoned. What's next? A cursed necklace? A haunted mirror?

"Yes," the doctor says. "That was the lab. The bullet was poisoned. Alexia is lucky to be alive. If she hadn't moved when she did, the bullet would've gone deeper. She would've died — either from the impact or the toxin."

Mum gasps. Drake mumbles, "I could've lost them all."

Someone out there really doesn't like me. I'm glad the doctor's sugarcoating things. He mentioned earlier the bullet nearly hit my heart. No one needs to hear that right now. Especially not Mum. Or Drake.

The doctor continues. "Whoever arranged this attack knew exactly what they were doing. Fortunately, I was able to administer immediate treatment using Alexia's Beloved blood. That likely saved her and the twins. The poison is what's causing her body to be non-responsive. She should improve with more blood and rest. But she'll need zero stress to reduce the preeclampsia."

He pauses. I hear Mum and Drake whispering.

Then: "What concerns me is that even though Alexia is a Dark One, her healing abilities are limited until she completes her transformation."

Another pause. "Let her sleep. The poison has worked itself out. But I must warn you — there is no cure."

No cure. Just what every girl wants to hear after being shot and poisoned.

Drake keeps talking to me. Narrating the room. Updating me on everything. It helps. A little. My eyelids still refuse to cooperate, but I finally feel something — my mum's hand in mine. Sensation. Progress.

Then Grandma Ma's voice slices through the fog.

"Doctor," she says, her tone sharp and regal. "I've been thinking about Alexia and her Dark One abilities. Don't forget — she and Drake haven't had the ceremony to make them official soulmates. That might be why her healing is incomplete."

Ceremony. Soulmates. Full transformation.

My brain short-circuits again. I can't process this. Not now. Not while I'm stuck in my own body like a prisoner.

I'm done. I need sleep. Real sleep. Not coma sleep. Not poisoned sleep. Just rest.

As the doctor's voice fades and Grandma Ma continues her royal theorising, I let myself drift.

Because right now, rest is the only thing I can control.

CHAPTER TEN

After a restless sleep that felt more like a coma with mood lighting, I finally wiggle my fingers. Then my toes. Then — miracle of miracles — I open my eyes.

Yay me.

Relief floods through me. I can move. I can feel. I'm not a limp, poisoned rag doll anymore. The sunlight slices through the gap in the drapes, warm and golden, like the universe is congratulating me for surviving.

The firm, warm pressure against my back and the delicious scent wrapping around me confirm what I already suspect — Drake is behind me. His arm is wrapped around my waist, protective and possessive. My head rests on his other arm, which is basically a sculpted slab of muscle. His body heat seeps into mine, soothing the ache that's been living in my bones since the shooting.

Everyone else is gone. Just us. Tangled together like we're the last two people on earth.

I glance at the wall clock. If I'm reading it right — and my brain isn't lying — I've been in Darshia for over thirty-eight hours. Thirty-eight hours of chaos, blood, betrayal, and near-death drama. And now? My stomach growls.

Or maybe it's not food I need.

Maybe it's blood.

Great. I'm officially adjusting to this whole Dark One lifestyle. Blood cravings, fangs, and all. At least I'm not freaking out anymore. The babies need it. I need it. Survival trumps squeamishness.

I glance at Drake's bare chest, rising and falling with each slow breath. My thoughts drift to the last time we were naked together — his bed, his blood, his body. That vein in his neck is practically glowing. Tempting. Pulsing. Begging.

My gums ache. My fangs drop. My mouth waters.

Okay. Cravings are officially here.

I shift, slowly, carefully, positioning myself for better access. My lips brush his neck. My tongue traces the vein. And then — I bite.

His blood floods my mouth, hot and rich and everything I need. It slides down my throat, filling me, healing me, feeding the twins. Drake moans softly, his hands moving over my body, grounding me in the moment.

"Hmm, baby," he murmurs, voice thick with sleep and pleasure. "Take as much as you need."

I seal the bite, lick the marks clean, and press my body against his. But the hunger isn't gone. Not completely. There's another ache. Another need. One only he can satisfy.

Drake shifts behind me, his body responding to mine. His breath warms my ear. His hands explore, gentle and reverent.

He touches my belly, my breasts, every inch of me like I'm sacred and fragile and his.

I arch into him, needing more. Wanting more.

His thoughts brush mine. *'Not yet, baby. Almost.'*

He opens me with careful hands, positioning me, preparing me. My body hums, ready and waiting.

'Drake, please,' I whisper into his mind. *'Now.'*

He enters me slowly, deeply, and everything inside me lights up. The pleasure is instant. Intense. Only for him to pause.

'Drake, baby, please...now. Enter me now, fill me.'

Drake thrusts hard and full. The air in my lungs whooshes out with the force of his impact. With one swift movement, he fills me. He was stretching and spreading me wide. The air eventually seeps back into my depleted lungs. We both let out a groan of pleasure at the same time with his next thrust.

We move together, bodies syncing, hearts racing. His touch, his rhythm, his presence — it's all I need.

And then — he stops.

What?

I try to move, but he holds me still.

'Drake, why did you stop? Is everything okay?'

'I need to ask you something,' he says, voice low and serious.

'Does it have to do with how hard I want you to move right now? Because that's the only question I'm interested in.'

'No, Alexia. It's more important than that.'

I groan. *'Nothing is more important than this.'*

'I'll continue,' he promises, *'as soon as you answer.'*

'Fine. What's the question?'

He kisses my neck, teasing me, distracting me. "Are you listening?" he asks aloud.

"Yes," I gasp. "More."

He moves again, slow and deep, and I'm drowning in sensation. His fingers find my most sensitive spot, and I'm spiralling. So close. So ready.

And then he asks, "Will you marry me?"

He thrusts his hips and tweaks my clit. I scream. Whether it's from the question or the pleasure, I don't know. Maybe both.

He thrusts again, harder, deeper, and I shatter.

"Yes," I scream, as my body explodes in waves of pleasure. Drake follows, his release crashing into me, his voice calling my name. Then my mind blank with sexual bliss.

And then—

A pinch on my shoulder.

His tongue on my neck.

And it hits me.
He bit me.
Oh no.
The poison.
The stupid, reckless idiot just drank my blood.

CHAPTER ELEVEN

I YANK MYSELF AWAY FROM DRAKE'S WARM, MUSCLED BODY like he's suddenly radioactive. The cool sheets slap against my skin, a jarring contrast to the heat still lingering between us. I roll to the far side of the bed, eyes locked on his face, searching for any sign of guilt, remorse, or basic survival instinct.

"What the hell?" I screech, voice sharp enough to cut glass. "Did you seriously just drink my blood? After everything?"

My blood. The same blood that was poisoned. The same blood that nearly killed me. And this idiot thought it was a good idea to take a sip like I'm some kind of post-coital smoothie bar?

"Drake, what do you think you're doing? My blood is poisoned! Do you have a death wish?"

I press my fingers to the spot on my neck where he bit me. It tingles. The puncture marks are already fading, healing under my touch. Great. At least my body's still got some fight left in it.

Drake, ever the king of bad timing and worse decisions, smiles like he's just brought me breakfast in bed. "Babe, it's okay. Your blood's back to normal. The doctor came in while you were sleeping. He checked you over again. You didn't even stir."

I blink. "I slept through one of Doctor Brean's exams?" I mutter, mostly to myself. "Are you sure, Drake? Because I'm not exactly in the mood to watch you convulse on the floor from a poison-induced blood seizure."

He nods, still smiling like a golden retriever who thinks he's done something good. I shake my head. I need to hear it from someone who didn't just try to turn our post-sex cuddle into a vampire buffet.

One phone call later, Doctor Brean walks into my room like he's arriving for afternoon tea, not a post-poisoning debrief. He's calm, collected, and carrying his medical bag like it's a briefcase full of secrets. I settle into one of the oversized armchairs, still wrapped in a robe, still trying to convince my body it's not broken.

He sits across from me, opens his tablet, and gives me that clinical smile that says, You're lucky to be alive, but let's not get dramatic.

"Good morning, Alexia," he says. "How are you feeling?"

"Like I've been shot, poisoned, emotionally wrecked, and stitched back together with vampire glue," I reply. "But hey, I can wiggle my toes now, so that's something."

He chuckles, nodding. "That's more than something. It's remarkable, considering what you've endured."

"Right. The poisoned bullet, the coma, the blood transfusions. All very glamorous."

"You're tougher than most. A lesser Dark One wouldn't have survived. But you're not just any Dark One. You're royal. Your grandmother's bloodline is strong."

"Yay for genetics," I mutter. "So what's the damage report?"

"You've developed preeclampsia. It's a condition that causes high blood pressure and can be dangerous for both you and the babies."

"Of course it is," I say. "Because being shot wasn't dramatic enough."

"Your pregnancy is progressing rapidly. You're now at twenty-eight weeks."

My eyes widen. "Twenty-eight? I was barely showing a few days ago."

"That's the accelerated gestation we see in Dark One hybrids. You could deliver in three days."

"Three. Days," I echo, deadpan. "No pressure."

"You're stable for now," he continues. "But you must stay calm. No stress. Keep your blood pressure down. And you'll need to consume small amounts of Drake's blood every four hours."

"Romantic," I say, raising an eyebrow. "Nothing says love like scheduled blood-drinking."

"It's what's keeping you and the twins alive."

I sigh, rubbing my belly. "Well, I guess we're officially past the point of normal. Thanks for the update, Doctor. And for not sugarcoating it."

"You're stronger than you realise, Alexia," he says. "Just keep resting. I'll check in again this evening."

He stands, nods, and exits, leaving me staring out the window, mind spinning.

Three days.

Three days until everything changes.

DRAKE, SENSING I NEED A DISTRACTION, HANDS ME HIS PHONE. "I've got a surprise for you," he says, grinning. "I've been taking photos. Keepsakes."

I scroll through them — me sleeping, me curled around my belly, me looking like a goddess in repose. One photo stops me cold. I'm on my side, naked, one arm and leg strategically placed, the other cradling my belly. My hair fans out like a halo. I don't even recognise myself.

"Drake," I whisper, holding up the screen. "Can you send me this one? I want it framed."

He nods, eyes soft. "Anything for you."

SOMETHING HAS BEEN BUGGING ME. THERE HAS BEEN NO mention of Lucile or Michael. Where are they? They've been Drake's guardians for fourteen years.

"Drake," I casually say. Before turning and facing my mate. "What happened to Lucile and Michael? I haven't seen or heard anything about them since my arrival."

Drake pauses his reading and meets my gaze with his.

"Ah. Um…" For once, I can see he is not sure what to say. I wait. I want the answer to my questions. "Um. You see, once we arrived here in Darshia, my mother dismissed them, and they were sent away."

Huh? "Why would they be sent away?"

"My mother had them leave before my father could question them."

"What are you not telling me, Drake?"

"My mother had kept my whereabouts secret. My father never knew where I have been living all these years. It was safer that way."

What kind of parents does Drake have? I am missing a big piece of the puzzle, and I'm determined to find out what it is.

THE SHRILL RING OF MY PHONE YANKS ME OUT OF THE moment. I'm curled in one of the plush armchairs by the window, watching the sun spill over Darshia like a golden promise. Drake grabs the phone, answers, and starts pacing.

I narrow my eyes. If my powers are growing, I might as well use them. I focus, tuning in.

And boom. I hear her.

Drake's mother.

And she is not happy.

She's ranting about him leaving Night Club 99 without permission. About how he still had "two more girls to meet." Excuse me?

Drake glances at me, sees the look on my face, and

mouths, "Sorry. My mum's being a control freak." He throws in an eye roll that would make Lucy proud.

I tune back in. Her voice is sharp, clipped, and full of judgment through the phone speaker. She's practically vibrating with disapproval. I don't even need to see her to know she's got a permanent frown and a pearl necklace clenched in one hand.

"Don't be foolish, Drake," she snaps. "Your father will never allow you to be with anyone other than a Red Royal. Not some unknown."

Drake's smile vanishes. His voice drops an octave, vibrating with power. "Mum, I'm going to say this once. Listen carefully."

I sit up straighter, the air in the room shifting. Drake's presence expands, commanding, electric.

"I'm with Alexia. I always have been. I'm staying by her side. She's carrying my children — your grandchildren. I love her. She's my soulmate."

Boom.

Silence.

Then her voice, annoying and disturbing. "Don't be absurd, Drake. You don't know what love is. This girl is not your soulmate. How do you even know she's pregnant? Let alone that they're your children?"

Oh no she didn't.

I grip the arm of the chair, knuckles white. This woman — this mother — is a piece of work. Every word from her mouth is a slap. A reminder that no matter what I do, some people will always see me as less.

Drake doesn't flinch. "Mother, even though it's no one's

business, Alexia and I have consumed each other's blood. We were both virgins until two weeks ago."

Oh gods. There goes our privacy. Right out the window.

His mother screeches. "What do you mean you were both virgins? And she's in the late stages of pregnancy? Drake, what have you done? Is this the girl — the one who lived next door? The human?"

There it is. The venom. The disgust. The bigotry.

I clench my jaw, fury simmering just beneath my skin. How dare she?

Drake doesn't miss a beat. "Mother, Alexia is no longer human. She's becoming a Dark One."

His mother loses it. "You turned a human into a Dark One — a vampire?"

Drake's voice is steel. "Get a grip, Mother. Alexia is from a long line of Dark Ones."

I smile, hand resting on my belly as one of the twins kicks. That's right, little one. We've got your back.

Drake turns to me, his eyes softening. He winks.

And in that moment, I know — no matter what his mother says, no matter what the world throws at us — we're in this together.

Me. Drake. And our babies.

Let her try to tear us apart.

She'll have to go through me first.

CHAPTER TWELVE

Less than two hours before the big showdown with Drake's parents, my nerves are doing Olympic-level gymnastics. I'm torn between punching a wall or watching my fists turn ghost-white from clenching. It's not just a meeting — it's a full-blown family summit. Grandma Ma, Mum, Drake, and yours truly. And the main topic? Me. Us. The scandalous soul-mated couple with twins on the way.

I already hate it.

My stomach's tying itself into knots so tight I'm surprised I haven't birthed a pretzel. The whole thing feels like a mistake wrapped in a disaster, sprinkled with a dash of why the hell are we doing this. Drake's parents have made it crystal clear they don't like me. Don't accept me. And definitely don't believe the babies I'm carrying are his. Charming.

I just hope I'm strong enough to stand my ground. Because if they come for my kids or my future, I swear I'll go full Dark One and burn the room down.

"Babe," Drake's voice pulls me out of my mental spiral. "Are you nearly ready to head downstairs?"

I turn toward him. He looks concerned. Sweet. Supportive. Completely unaware that I'm one sarcastic comment away from combusting.

"I don't want to see them," I admit. "But we have to. If we want a future together, we need to get through this circus."

I try to smile. It fails. Drake sees right through it. Of course he does.

"Look," I say, trying to sound like I've got my life together. "Grandma Ma already told us — you're a legal adult here in Darshia. Your parents can't boss you around unless you let them. You own the house back home. They can't take it. You'll always have a place to live."

Cue cold sweat and stomach flip.

Then — kick. One of the twins lands a solid jab to my ribs. I gasp, hand flying to the spot. Future footballer, clearly.

Drake drops to his knees, palms on either side of my belly, face close. His breath warms my skin through the fabric of my blouse.

"Hey, little ones," he murmurs. "Stop giving your mother a hard time."

My heart melts. Again. Every time he talks to them, I turn into emotional soup. They respond to him instantly. Me? Not so much. Unless I'm touching Drake's hand and eavesdropping through his mind. Cheeky little traitors. Daddy's babies, no question.

With a sigh, they settle. Thank the gods.

It's strange. With all the fresh blood in my system, my abilities have levelled up like I'm in a supernatural video game. I can read minds. Deep dive into memories. Slip past shields like they're made of tissue paper. Grandma Ma warned me my powers would grow once I became a full Dark One. What she doesn't know? They're already growing. Fast.

And I'm not telling her.

I don't trust her. Not fully. Not yet. She's sharp, calculating, and probably already suspects I'm hiding something. Let her. I'll play dumb and let her think my mind-speak at the club was a fluke.

She also told me not to tell Drake about my powers. Which, honestly, makes sense. If he's hiding things from me — and let's be real, with parents like his, he probably is — I need leverage.

I place my hands over Drake's and slip into his connection with the twins. It still blows my mind how this works. I can see them. Hear them. Feel their little thoughts. It's magic. And it's mine.

"Hello, my sweet little babies," I whisper. "I'm sorry if I upset you. Mummy's just nervous."

I rub the bump, tracing the curve of one tiny back and bottom. "We're about to meet your grandparents. So let's be strong, okay? No kicking. No chaos. Just calm."

They shift, settling into a comfortable position. Drake keeps talking to them, soothing them until they fall asleep. I exhale. Blessed silence.

Drake helps me onto his lap in one of the armchairs. His hands stroke my belly, then trail upward. I close my eyes, letting myself relax. His fingers undo the buttons on my blouse, freeing me from the bra. I stay still, watching him through our connection. He senses my emotions, leans in, and presses a kiss to my skin before taking my nipple into his mouth and begins to suck.

The sensation is electric. My body arches, craving more. Then — pressure. Tingling. A strange tightness in my breasts.

Drake reacts instantly, freeing my other breast. I glance down and — oh gods. Pale yellow liquid. Milk. My nipples are leaking.

Drake doesn't hesitate. He cups me, thumbs the nipple, and the liquid squirts. He drinks, gently, reverently, switching between both breasts until the flow stops. When he finally pulls back, he licks his lips and grins.

"Hmm. That was different. And yum. Must try that again real soon."

I blink. Still stunned. "Drake. What the hell was that?"

He shrugs, panty-dropping smile in full effect. "I don't know. It was like a little voice told me to help. Maybe one of the twins. But I enjoyed it. A lot."

His eyes flick to my chest again. I roll mine.

"Okay, enough of that," he says. "You need to drink from me before we go downstairs. Doctor's orders."

Ah. So that's what the hushed conversation was earlier. The how to *care for helpless, hormonal Alexia* talk. Lovely.

Drake interrupts my internal rant. "You need a blood top-up. For the babies. For your strength. Come on, my beautiful one, my soulmate, mother of my babies — drink. Or I'll strip you naked and have my way with you while the twins nap."

Tempting. Very tempting.

But I know what's coming. And if I'm going to face Drake's parents, I need to be strong. Calm. Ready.

My smile fades. "You're right. I need to drink. I have a bad feeling something's coming. Something big."

I bite into Drake's neck, drinking deeply. His blood is fire and silk, strength and comfort. It fills me, calms me, prepares me.

Whatever's waiting downstairs — I'll face it. And I won't back down.

Thanks to his blood, I hope to be mentally and physically strong enough to meet with Drake's parents. I will not hold my breath, though. I already have a horrible feeling something terrible is about to happen.

I just don't know what it is yet.

CHAPTER THIRTEEN

Walking side by side, Drake's warm, steady hand envelopes mine, his thumb brushing slow circles across my knuckles like he's trying to massage courage into my bloodstream. I squeeze back, mostly to keep myself from bolting. His thoughts about his parents — about their reaction to me, to the twins — are leaking through our bond like a broken faucet. I didn't mean to pick up on them, but here we are. Emotional overload, party of one.

We descend the grand marble staircase toward Grandma Ma's office, each step echoing like a countdown to doom.

Drake picks up on my nerves instantly. I must've let my shields slip. Rookie mistake.

"Oh shit, babe, breathe," he says, voice low and urgent. "Is that... really some of your thoughts flying through your head?"

I slam the mental door shut. Too late.

"Come on," he says, squeezing my hand tighter. "It's going to be okay. I'll stay by your side. I won't let them split us up. I love you. I love these two precious babies. Our babies."

His words help. A little. But the fact that he breached my mind shields without permission? Not great. He's not telling me everything about his family. Or his abilities. And if he's already stronger than me, what else is he hiding?

Pregnancy hormones are doing my head in. I swear I'm one mood swing away from launching myself off the balcony.

Drake's hand slides over my swollen belly, comforting and warm. One of the twins kicks his palm like they're saying focus, Dad. I flinch. Thirty-four weeks. The doctor's words echo in my head. I'm close. Too close. I could go into labour any minute now, and I'm about to walk into a room with two people who hate me on principle.

I turn to Drake, reach out with my mind. Kiss me, Drake. I need you and your strength to get me through this.

He doesn't hesitate. His lips cover mine, soft and grounding. One hand cradles my head, the other strokes the baby bump. His love wraps around me like armour, and for a moment, I forget where we are.

Then — the sound of a throat clearing.

Twice.

I snap out of it. My senses flare. Mum. Of course.

She's lucky I sensed her before I turned and accidentally knocked her into next week.

I pull away from Drake, lips still tingling. "Mum, don't sneak up on me like that. I could've hurt you."

She raises an eyebrow. "Alexia, I've been waiting for you two to stop kissing. We don't have time for this. Drake's parents have arrived. They're waiting in Grandma Ma's office. Come. We're late."

Her heels tap down the marble steps like a ticking bomb.

Great. Late. Another thing for Drake's parents to hold against me. Let's just get this over with. I'm tired of being treated like a mistake. I'm the next Queen of Darshia, damn it. If they don't like me, that's their problem. And if they push me, I'll make sure they never see their grandchildren. Ever.

We walk into Grandma Ma's office. The scent of lilac hits me like a floral slap. My nose twitches. Please don't sneeze. Please don't sneeze. Mucus bubbles are not the vibe I'm going for.

Drake greets his mother. I squeeze his hand, scanning the room. Time to test my Dark One tricks. Let's see what these new powers can do.

I slip into their minds without effort. No resistance. No warning. Just me, diving into their thoughts like a psychic ninja.

Drake's mother first. Her mind is a mess of judgment, fear, and denial. *She's clinging to the idea that I'm just a human girl who corrupted her son. Cute.*

I pull back.

One mind at a time.

My mind encounters a barrier similar to thick tar, yet I can effortlessly go deeper, like a hot knife slicing through butter.

Beyond the surface, Drake's father's mind hits me with full force.

Oh gods. Images. Fly fast and hard. Disgusting and hideous. His pathetic thoughts. His lies.

And then I see it.

The orders. The planning. The cold, calculated decision.

He's the one who arranged the assassination attempt.

The assassination attempt on me.

My blood turns to ice.

This creature — this smug, polished monster — is the reason I nearly died. And he's sitting here like he owns the room, ignoring me completely, eyes locked on Drake like I'm not even worth acknowledging.

My skin crawls. I want to scream. I want to run. I want to rip the truth out of his throat and shove it in everyone's face.

But I stay still. I breathe. I focus.

I study his features. The resemblance to Drake is uncanny. Same jawline. Same eyes — except his are colder, ringed with power. Drake has the same colour hair, too. Drake's lashes are the only softness he inherited.

From the corner of my eye, I spot Grandma Ma. Regal. Composed. Watching me. Waiting.

Crap. I missed the introductions. Missed the part where Drake helped me into the chair. I've been too busy playing psychic spy.

I reach out to her mind. *'I'm sorry, Grandma Ma. I missed the introductions. It's overwhelming.'*

'I understand, my Child,' she replies. *'Pay attention from now on. You've only missed the introductions. Your mother and I have covered for you.'*

I nod. Smile. Try to look composed.

But something's wrong.

Very wrong.

A dark cloud presses against my skin. Goosebumps rise. The air thickens.

I glance at Drake's father. Focus. Probe.

And then it hits me.

His aura is black. Not metaphorically. Literally. It pulses with hate, with power, with something ancient and vile. The vibration slams into me like a wave of filth. My body trembles. My skin recoils.

He's not just cruel.

He's evil.

And he's hiding something far worse than a failed assassination.

I glance back at Grandma Ma and offer a tight smile while she fills me in through our mind link. Servants glide in with refreshments like we're hosting a royal brunch instead of surviving a psychic ambush. I use the moment to pull myself together, smooth out my mental shields, and pretend I haven't just been mentally violated by Drake's father.

'Don't worry, my Child. We will talk. And I presume you require me to know that Drake's family is more dangerous than they appear. We will discuss this later. Now it is your turn to play a princess in waiting.'

Oh man. I really need to learn how she does that — listening, mind surfing, and still managing to look like she's posing for a royal portrait.

'Thanks, Grandma Ma.'

Time to play the role. I straighten my spine, plaster on a smile, and turn to Drake's mother with all the poise I can muster.

"Good afternoon, Mrs Smithlyn. I'm pleased to finally meet you after living next door to Drake all these years." I rest my hand on my belly, showcasing the bulge like a crown jewel. "I do hope we can become better acquainted before the babies are born. It would be lovely for both sets of grandparents to be part of their lives. Don't you think?"

Her eyebrows shoot up so high I'm surprised they don't detach and fly off her face. While I wait for her response, the pressure against my mind shields spikes. Hard. Sharp. Aggressive.

I glance at Grandma Ma, catch her eye, then shift my gaze to Mr Smithlyn. He's the one. I know it. I lock eyes with him and raise an eyebrow. Nice try, buddy.

The pressure intensifies. The twins squirm. I rub my belly, trying to soothe them.

"Do you mind, Mr Smithlyn?" I say, voice calm but cutting. "It's a bit rude to try to breach someone's shields."

His face flushes red, then purple. Classic. "Bla, ha, blah. What do you mean by that? I would never— You. You garrulous little human whore."

My eyes widen. My hands fly to my belly. The pressure in my head spikes like a migraine on steroids.

Drake is up in an instant, standing between me and his father. Grandma Ma rises, regal and furious. Two guards materialise beside her like summoned shadows.

Mum doesn't flinch. She grips her armrests, knuckles white, and unleashes her lawyer voice like a verbal blade.

"Mr Smithlyn, never call my daughter names. Alexia is carrying your grandchildren. And we all felt your pathetic attempt to breach our shields. Don't deny it. Even the Queen would agree. My daughter and I are not mere humans. Alexia is Princess Alexia, next in line — Queen of Darshia. Now sit down, shut up, and behave. You are in the presence of the Queen, and we have much to discuss."

I nearly choke on my laughter when Mr Smithlyn's face turns a shade of purple that should come with a medical warning. Well done, Mum.

I reach out and touch Drake's back. He kneels beside me, placing his hand on the baby bulge. I cover his hand with mine, watching him check in with the twins. His mind touches theirs, soothing them. Apparently, they hate their grandfather. Can't blame them. I do too.

Drake's parents go silent. His mother's mouth drops open when she realises her son is communicating with the babies.

"It's all right, little ones," Drake says aloud. "Mummy's okay. Go back to sleep for her... Yes, I'll stay right here."

He strokes my belly, calming the twin who's pressing against my blouse. His hand settles over the bump, and the baby relaxes.

Drake's mother gasps. "My goodness, Drake. Can you communicate with those babies?"

Drake looks up at me, winks, then turns to her. "Yes, Mother. I always have. I feel very close to both of them. My daughter was agitated because she felt her grandfather's attack. It hurt her head."

My breath catches. He hurt my daughter. If I'd known that, I would've had the guards drag him out by his smug, traitorous throat.

Drake senses my fury and gently caresses the bump again.

Mrs Smithlyn pales. Her eyes flick from the baby bulge to her husband. "Davelt. Is that true? Did you try to hurt our grandchild for your selfish arrogance?"

Her face shifts from ghost-white to rage-red. Even her eyes glow. Oh yeah. Mama Smithlyn's pissed. And terrifying.

Turns out the wicked mother has a conscience. And a backbone.

The energy in the room spikes. The hairs on my arms stand on end.

Davelt doesn't care. His arrogance thickens. "I will not stand by and allow this girl to be part of our lives, Mary," he growls, face contorting into something monstrous.

The pressure slams into me again. The twins kick. Hard.

I glance at Grandma Ma. She shakes her head. *'No, Child. It is not I. We will find it is Drake's mother wielding power now.'*

I boost my shields and dive into Mrs Smithlyn's mind. What I discover makes me slide back in my seat.

She's powerful. Dangerous. But not evil.

Her beliefs are strong. Her values solid. She doesn't know the full extent of her husband's betrayal — his mistresses, their children, the deaths. The secrets he failed to bury.

She married him for power. He married her for her gifts.

And he preferred Drake's twin. Sent Drake away. Hurt him. Wanted him dead.

Oh gods. Drake has a twin. And he never told me.

The room pulses with heat. Pins and needles crawl over my skin. I slump in my seat, dizzy.

Something's wrong. Very wrong.

I feel it — an attack against my mind shield. Is someone trying to kill me? At the same time, it seems someone else is trying to protect me.

I probe their minds. It soon becomes obvious. Davelt is trying to destroy me. And yet, Mary is trying to save me.

I reach out to Grandma Ma. *'Grandma Ma, you must stop Drake's father. He's trying to kill me and the twins with some powerful mind stuff.'*

I hope she hears me. I hope it's enough.

To Drake, I whisper through our bond, *'Drake... Baby, get us out of here before it's too late.'*

He looks into my eyes. His eyes widen. He knows.

He turns to his father and roars, "Father, stop it! You're killing my babies and my fiancée!"

Fiancée. That word hits me like a punch and a promise.

Davelt laughs. Cold. Cruel. "That is my plan..."

"Nooo!" Drake screams. "You low-life bastard!"

He scoops me into his arms, pressing me against his chest, and bolts for the door. The pressure crushes me. My ears fill with white noise. My vision fades.

Something is wrong.
Very wrong.
I need help.
My last thought before the darkness swallows me—
My twins are in danger.

CHAPTER FOURTEEN

GEEZ, WHAT HAVE I BEEN UP TO THIS TIME? DID I GET HIT BY
a bus? A psychic freight train? A rogue Dark One with a
vendetta and bad aim?

Whatever it was, it hurts.

I try to wiggle my toes. Nope. They protest. My legs?
Same story. My back feels like I've been folded in half and
left in a dryer on high heat. My body curls in on itself like it's
trying to shield me from the world. Or from whatever the hell
just happened.

I feel like I've gone ten rounds in a martial arts tournament
I didn't sign up for. Did I fall down stairs? Get into a fight?
Did Lucy drag me into another one of her *"this'll be fun"*
disasters?

Oh man. Lucy Blachart. My best friend since school. The
human hurricane with waist-length dark hair, violet eyes, and
a body that defies physics. Five-foot-six of pure chaos

wrapped in cheeky charm and a magnetic pull toward trouble. Big trouble. Capital T. That's my Lucy.

If she's involved, I wouldn't be surprised if I woke up in a nightclub wearing someone else's shoes and a tiara.

But this? This feels different.

My eyes are still closed. I'm not ready to open them. The throbbing in my skull is doing a drum solo, and I'm not in the mood for an encore. My nose twitches. Something smells… awful. Acrid. Chemical. Like burnt plastic and despair.

Where the hell am I?

I listen. Carefully. There's a slow, rhythmic beeping. A machine. A monitor. The kind that screams hospital.

Oh gods. Am I in a hospital?

Why would I be in a hospital? Did I collapse again? Was it the twins? The psychic attack? Did Drake's father finally succeed in turning me into a cautionary tale?

The pain. The confusion. The smell. The beeping. It all adds up to one thing: I'm not okay.

My brain tries to shut down again. Drowsiness creeps in, wrapping around me like a weighted blanket. Maybe if I sleep a little longer, reality will be less painful when I wake up. Maybe the nurse will have answers. Maybe I'll wake up to Drake's voice and not the sound of machines keeping me alive.

Maybe.

For now, I let the darkness pull me under again.

Because facing reality?

That's going to hurt.

"HA." WHAT THE...?

Is someone calling me? Saying my name?

My brain feels like it's booting up in slow motion. I must've been sleeping like the dead. Again. The pulsing noise in my ears is back, and the smell — ugh, that smell. Burnt antiseptic and despair. Oh, crap on a stick. I know that combo. I'm in a hospital.

But why?

Someone better start explaining before I rip out these wires and demand answers with fists and sarcasm.

I crack my eyes open. Blurry. Great. I blink a few times, but everything still looks like a watercolour painting dunked in bleach. I close my eyes again, regroup, then try once more.

Fluorescent lights. A TV on the wall. Wires. IV drip. Private room. Fancy. Still smells like misery.

My bladder chooses that exact moment to scream for attention. Of course. How am I supposed to escape this bed with tubes and wires like I'm some kind of science experiment?

"Babe, come on, it's time to wake up."

That voice. That voice is familiar. Drake. Definitely Drake. He sounds worried. I must've drifted off again, because now the room's darker and his voice is closer.

I turn toward him, force my eyes open.

"That's it, babe. Please open your eyes and try to keep them open for me. I want to look into your beautiful eyes."

Okay, what is he on about? Beautiful eyes? I'm pretty sure I look like roadkill right now. But before I can snark back, my eyelids betray me and droop shut.

My head is blank. No memories. No context. Just

confusion and a vague sense of something's wrong. Why is Drake here? Why am I here? Why does everything hurt?

"Drake?" I croak, voice scratchy like I've swallowed sandpaper. I force my eyes open again. His smile is soft, but it doesn't reach his eyes. There's sadness there. Deep. Heavy.

"Drake, what's going on?" I manage. "Why am I in... hospital?"

Ow. My throat. Talking feels like a workout.

Drake's eyes widen, then quickly mask whatever emotion just slipped through. Okay, something big happened. And I'm not in the loop. Not even close.

"Drake... tell me," I whisper, impatience bubbling under my skin.

He touches my fingers, and it's like electricity dances across my hand. He lifts it to his lips, kisses it gently. His breath warms my skin, and my spine tingles like it's trying to remember something my brain won't give me.

Okay, what is happening? Why am I having weird sexual feelings toward my next-door neighbour? And why is he calling me babe?

I stare into his eyes, searching for answers. All I get is concern. Great. Super helpful.

"Babe," he says gently, "I can see you're confused. What's the last thing you remember?"

I dig. Hard. But my brain's a blank slate. I remember Drake. I know I'm in a hospital. That's it. No timeline. No context. No clue.

"I know your name is Drake," I say slowly. "I know I'm in a hospital room. My body hurts. But before waking up here?

Nothing. Zip. No memories at all. And… why do you keep calling me babe?"

Drake's face shifts. Sadness creeps in like a shadow. What am I missing?

"Alexia," he says softly. "Baby, we're a couple. We're engaged to be married. Actually… we're parents. Parents to twins."

I blink. Then blink again.

Engaged?

Parents?

Twins?

I gulp. My eyes want to pop out of my head. This has to be a joke. A cruel, elaborate, Lucy-level prank.

"What… are… you… talking about?" My voice cracks under the weight of disbelief.

Engaged. Parents. Twins. I mean, come on. Drake and I are a couple? We're getting married? And we have twins?

I glance down at my body. Hospital bed. Wires. Flat belly. Very flat. Like, no way I just had twins flat.

But then — my boobs. Hello. Since when did I get upgraded to the deluxe model? They're bigger. Rounder. Definitely not how I remember them. Assuming I remember anything at all.

I stare at my chest, then back at Drake. "Drake, how are we a couple? Let alone parents. And parents of twins! When did this all happen? What is going on, and what is wrong with me?"

My eyes mist up. What the hell? I don't cry. I'm not the crying type. At least, I don't think I am. Great. Now I'm second-guessing my own personality.

I need answers. Real ones. And I need them now.

Because if this is my life… I want to know what the hell happened to it.

My focus snaps back to Drake as he moves toward the little table in the corner. He picks up an empty glass and fills it three-quarters from the water jug, his movements slow and deliberate — like he's trying not to spook me. Honestly, I feel like a feral cat right now, so fair enough.

He walks back, holding the glass like it's sacred. I reach out with trembling fingers, half expecting to drop it and baptise myself in cold water. But no — miracle of miracles — I manage to grip it and take a sip without wearing it.

Oh, Gods, yes.

The water hits my lips and floods my mouth like salvation. Cool, wet, glorious. It rolls over my tongue, coats my throat, and settles in my belly like a peace offering. I take a few more slow mouthfuls, savouring every drop like it's the elixir of life. Which, let's be real, it kind of is right now.

I pass the glass back to Drake, who places it gently on the table. His attention shifts to the hospital door. He walks over, pauses, then opens it.

Huh? Who's here?

I wait, nerves prickling. The sound of creaky wheels and footsteps echoes down the hallway, growing louder. Someone's coming. And judging by the way Drake's smiling over his shoulder, it's not just a nurse with a clipboard.

"Baby," he says, voice soft and warm, "I'd like to

introduce you to two very special little people who've been demanding to see you."

Demanding? What — like fans? Royal subjects? Mini assassins?

My eyebrow shoots up. Drake steps aside, revealing what looks like a plastic tub on a wheeled cart. Inside — oh gods. A baby. A real, actual baby, wrapped up like a burrito in a clear plastic bassinet.

Before I can process that, another cart rolls in. Another baby.

My brain short-circuits.

I stare. One baby. Then the other. Then back again. My head's doing a carnival game swivel, and I'm one step away from asking someone to throw a ping pong ball at me.

"Alexia, good to see you're finally awake. How are you feeling?"

The voice snaps me out of my stunned trance. I turn my head and see my mother standing beside the bed, smiling. Thank the gods — I recognise her. Amelia Steele. My mum. At least that part of my brain still works.

"Mum," I croak, "what is going on? Can you tell me why I'm in a hospital?"

My gaze shifts to Drake, who's now approaching one of the fussing babies. He picks the child up with practised ease, cradling them against his chest like he's done it a hundred times. His face softens, eyes full of adoration.

My mouth drops open. Drake Smithlyn is holding a baby. And not just holding — loving. Like this tiny human is his whole world.

I turn back to Mum. "Tell me what in the world is

happening. I know you're my mother, but who are these babies? Why are they in my room?"

Drake looks up, meets my eyes. His smile fades. He gently rubs the baby's back, voice low and sad. "Amelia... Alexia just woke up. She has no memory."

Mum's face crumples. "Alexia, are you saying you remember nothing before waking up?"

I nod, still watching Drake with the baby. His tenderness is surreal. Like I've stepped into someone else's life.

"Oh, my baby," Mum whispers, more to herself than to me. "What did that man do to you?"

That man. Okay, someone really needs to fill me in on who the villain of this story is.

Drake's voice pulls me back. He's still holding the baby, eyes full of pride and love. "Leave it for now, Amelia."

Wait — Drake calls my mother by her first name? Since when? I remember their names, but not where I live. Not what happened. Not why I'm here.

"Drake, can you contact her via your connection?" Mum asks.

Connection? What connection? Are we talking psychic hotline or vampire bond?

Drake shakes his head. "No. Nothing at all."

I glance at Mum. Her face is pure sadness. What are they talking about?

Drake's gaze returns to the baby. "Alexia, I'd like to introduce you to our daughter, Alley. And over there, still sleeping in his little bed, is our son, Damien."

My jaw drops. My eyes widen. My head swivels again. I'm officially a carnival attraction.

Twins?

I'm a mother?

Oh. My. Gods.

Pressure on my hand draws my attention. Mum's comforting me, her touch grounding. "Alexia, it'll be okay. We'll help you sort everything out. We'll answer your questions."

Confusion. Shock. Hold me. That's all I've got right now.

Mum wraps me in a warm embrace. Her breath brushes my ear as she speaks. "Come on, love. It's time to meet your daughter. She looks so much like you did as a newborn. You're going to love her. We already do."

She releases me and moves to the other side of the bed.

Drake's smile lights up his face as he walks toward me, baby Alley in his arms. "Alexia, your mother and the nurse will help you sit up so you can hold our daughter."

Nurse? What nurse?

My eyebrow shoots up again. I glance around and — oh. There she is. Standing behind the baby tubs on wheels, like she's been there the whole time. My senses must be on a delay.

Her smile reaches her eyes. I instantly feel calmer.

She steps beside me, checks my tubes and leads, then picks up a remote.

"Good afternoon, Alexia," she says, voice firm but kind. "My name is Sharonia, and I'm your nurse. Your mother will help rearrange your pillows. We'll raise the bed to support your back so you can hold your baby and try to feed her. Your breasts must be overfull by now. It's time to relieve the pressure again."

Ha. Say what now?

My face must scream confusion, because she continues.

"While you were unconscious, we used a lactating pump to collect milk for the twins. The doctor recommended it to prevent mastitis."

Mastitis? What fresh hell is that?

She sees my panic and smiles gently. "It's an inflammation of breast tissue. Can lead to infection. When your breasts are overfull, they get tight, hot, and lumpy. Expressing milk helps relieve the pressure."

Okay. Freak-out level: moderate. I force a smile and nod.

Mum and Nurse Sharonia help maneuver me upright, stacking pillows behind me. I try not to yank out any tubes. Especially the one between my legs.

Oh great. A catheter. Just what I needed. At least I'm not wetting the bed. But yeah, that thing can go.

"When you're ready, Alexia," Sharonia says, "I'll remove the catheter and leads. How about a shower?"

Yes. A shower sounds like heaven.

But first — I'm about to hold my daughter.

And I have no idea who I am anymore.

ONCE I'M PROPPED UP AND REASONABLY SURE I WON'T PASS out or rip out a tube, Drake moves in beside me, cradling the baby like she's made of starlight and spun sugar. His expression is soft, reverent. I've never seen him look at anything — or anyone — like this.

Our eyes meet, and I study him. Really study him. There's

love there. Adoration. Fierce, unshakable devotion. And it's not just for the baby. It's for me, too.

Gods, what did I miss while I was unconscious?

Before I can process that, Drake gently places the squirming bundle into my arms. My heart leaps into my throat. I freeze, terrified I'll drop her or break her or do something catastrophically wrong. But the moment she's in my arms, she settles. Just... melts into me. Her tiny face turns toward my chest like she knows exactly where she belongs.

What is she doing?

Her little mouth opens and closes, rooting around like she's searching for something. Then I feel it — a wet patch on my gown. My breasts tighten, feeling heavy and tingling.

Oh no.

Drake's voice cuts through my rising panic. "Alexia, our little Alley recognises you. She's hungry. She's looking for your breast so she can feed."

Breastfeed?

I look down at the baby, then at the damp spot on my gown, then back at Drake like he's just suggested I juggle flaming swords.

The baby lets out a tiny, frustrated noise. Her mouth keeps opening and closing, her little fists waving like she's trying to file a formal complaint.

I glance up at Drake again. He's smiling, calm, like this is all perfectly normal. "If you want," he says gently, "I'll help you with your gown. You can try to feed her."

Say what now?

Before I can launch into a full-blown meltdown, Mum

steps in. "Alexia, I'll leave you with Drake. You can practice feeding the twins."

I must look like I've been hit by a truck. Emotionally and overwhelmed doesn't even begin to cover it.

"Alexia," she says, her voice soft but steady, "it'll be okay. The nursing staff explained everything to Drake. He's been learning how to help you. He didn't want to miss a thing. He's been a fantastic father to the twins."

Wow. That's all I've got. Just... wow.

I'm still blank. My memory is a black hole. Nothing. No flickers. No flashes. Just this weird, aching emptiness where my life used to be.

Why me?

Why now?

I don't want to live like this — adrift in a life I don't remember. But something deep inside me whispers that I have to get those memories back. Not just for me. For Drake. For these babies. For something bigger. Something important. Something I can't name yet, but I feel it thrumming beneath my skin like a warning.

I look down at the baby in my arms. She squirms again, her tiny face scrunching in frustration. Okay. Time to woman up.

I take a breath. "All right, little one," I whisper. "Let's figure this out together."

I fumble with the gown, awkward and unsure, but determined. Drake helps, his hands gentle, his presence grounding. I shift the baby closer, guiding her tiny mouth toward my breast.

She latches.

Oh.

Oh.

It's strange. Foreign. Intimate. But not painful. Her little mouth works rhythmically, and I feel the pressure in my chest ease. A warmth spreads through me, not just physical but emotional. Like something inside me is clicking into place.

I look down at her — at Alley — and for the first time since waking up, something feels right.

I may not remember how I got here.

But I know this matters.

And I'm not letting go.

CHAPTER FIFTEEN

I LOOK DOWN AT THE GORGEOUS SLEEPING BABY IN MY ARMS, and my brain is still doing laps around the chaos track. Thoughts race. Emotions swirl. My head slowly shakes side to side like I'm trying to physically reject the reality I've woken into.

What am I doing here?

How did I end up in a hospital?

And most of all — what the hell happened to me?

No one's told me what town we're in. No one's explained why I woke up with zero memories and two babies. I feel like I've been dropped into someone else's life and told to play along. Spoiler alert: I suck at improv.

I glance down at the baby's features — her perfect little button nose, her soft cheeks, her tiny lips — and my heart melts. Again. It's becoming a habit.

At least my boobs are less swollen now, though they still feel like someone inflated them with a bicycle pump. Tingly, heavy, tender. And don't get me started on the nipples. Are they sore? Are they numb? Are they plotting against me? The jury's still out.

The leaking milk situation is a whole other drama. My hospital gown is soaked, cold, and clinging to me like a passive-aggressive ex. I close my eyes and try to convince myself this is a dream. A weird, hormonal, milk-soaked dream.

But then my breath catches. My eyes snap open.

Oh. My. Gods.

I breastfed a baby.

A baby I don't remember conceiving, carrying, or giving birth to.

While my hormones are throwing a rave in my bloodstream.

Breathe, Alexia. Just breathe.

Thankfully, with Drake's help, I managed to hold, feed, and burp baby Alley without dropping her or crying. He said with practice, I'll be able to feed both babies at the same time.

Both. Babies. At the same time.

Oh, gods. That might be pushing it. Baby Damien is still asleep, and I'm grateful. One newborn at a time, please. That's all my scrambled brain can handle right now.

My brain must've taken a sabbatical. I swear I'm living in an alternate reality. While Alley sleeps, I gently run my fingertip from her forehead down to her chin. She's mine. This little angel is mine. And something inside me shifts — a pull, a bond, a tether forming between us.

I'm a mother.

Of twins.

It still doesn't feel real.

I glance back at Alley's cherub face, cataloguing every tiny feature. Her hand reaches up in her sleep and rests on my breast. My heart squeezes. The attachment is already forming, and I don't know what to do with it.

I'm still waiting for answers. What happened to me? Where did my memory go? How did Drake and I end up together? Engaged? When did this happen? And who the hell is "he"?

Drake and Mum aren't exactly rushing to fill in the blanks.

If Mum's here, where's Dad? I know I have one. I just don't remember where my parents lived. Or where I lived. Or anything useful, really.

A soft noise pulls me out of my spiral. Damien. The little guy's waking up. Probably hungry. At least I know what to do now.

Drake stands, moves to my side, and gently lifts Alley from my arms. I instantly miss her warmth and baby smell. He kisses her head and places her in her plastic bassinet. She stays asleep, looking like a tiny, contented queen.

Drake turns to Damien, speaks softly to him, and lifts him with practised ease. Damien's little noises melt my heart. He settles against Drake's chest, mouth open, head bobbing like he's searching for a buffet.

I laugh. I can't help it. The kid's hungry. Time to do the mum thing.

I prep my other breast, trying not to overthink it.

"Drake, bring Damien here. I might as well meet him and feed the little guy."

Drake smiles, walks over, and passes me the baby. My

arms adjust automatically, supporting him as I guide him to my leaking nipple.

Damien's mouth opens wide. His head moves side to side, searching. I help him latch, and he starts suckling like a pro.

The tingling starts again. My breath hitches. Hind milk, Drake said. The good stuff. Damien drinks like he's been waiting his whole life for this moment.

"Geez, what a little piggy," I say, watching him guzzle. "Boy can this kid drink."

"He sure can," Drake replies, stroking Damien's head with gentle fingers. "Look at him go."

Damien's hand reaches out, kneading against my breast like his sister did. I touch his tiny fingers, tracing the soft skin, the delicate nails. He grabs my finger and holds on tight.

Then he looks up.

Big, bright baby eyes lock onto mine. A gasp catches in my throat. He's looking straight into my soul.

My eyes mist up. My chest tightens. What is this feeling? Is it love? Is it something deeper?

Damien keeps holding my finger, staring into my eyes until he falls asleep, still nursing.

"Babe," Drake says gently, "if you want, I'll arrange for a nurse to escort Damien and Alley back to the nursery. You probably need time to yourself. Maybe even a shower."

I turn to him, raise an eyebrow. Great. He thinks I stink. This is his polite way of saying it. Thanks, Drake.

My face shifts into a frown. I look down at Damien. At least he wants to be near me — stink and all.

Drake chuckles. "Oh, babe, don't take it the wrong way.

You've been unconscious for over three days. The nursing staff and I gave you sponge baths while you were here."

Wait. What?

Three days?

I've been unconscious for over three days.

Oh my gods.

What happened to me?

BEFORE DRAKE LEAVES FOR THE NURSERY, A QUESTION FORMS in my foggy brain and tumbles out of my mouth.

"Drake, do I own a mobile phone? And does it work?"

He blinks, then walks over to the drawers and pulls out a sleek touch phone. "Oh, sorry, Alexia. I forgot all about your phone."

He holds it up like it's a sacred relic. "Battery's dead. I'll plug it in while you're in the bathroom."

Something inside me clicks. That phone — it's mine. I know it. I don't know how, but I do. Maybe it holds answers. Maybe it's just full of cat memes and old texts. Either way, I need to see it.

The nurses remove all the tubing from my body, and I finally feel like a human again. A sore, confused, milk-leaking human, but still. Freedom.

They help me to the bathroom, and I take stock of the damage. My body's changed. My breasts are two — maybe three — cup sizes bigger, and they leak like broken faucets. But the real shock comes when I see my reflection.

There's a fine pink line across my lower belly, right where

my underwear would sit. The nurse explains it's from an emergency caesarean. She says I had a blood transfusion from Drake, and that's why I've healed so quickly. The scar will be gone in a day or two.

Gone?

How can a scar vanish?

How can my stomach be this flat after carrying twins?

What the hell is in Drake's blood?

I stare at my belly, trying to reconcile the facts. I gave birth. I had surgery. I was unconscious for three days. And now I look like I just came back from a yoga retreat.

The warm water pelts my back, and I let myself sink into it. It feels divine. Or at least, I think it does. My memory's still a black hole, so who knows what divine used to feel like.

I sit on the shower chair, the plastic cold against my skin. It slowly warms, and I feel like I'm sitting in a puddle of my own confusion. The chair's here in case I fall. Which, honestly, feels likely.

Also, it's the only way to keep Drake from "helping" me in the bathroom. Boundaries, dude. Learn them.

Yes, I feel attracted to him. Yes, there's a pull. A sexual tension that makes my skin buzz. But I don't remember our relationship. I don't remember falling in love. I don't remember anything.

He needs to back off.

Of course, now I feel guilty. He's been here the whole time. Looking after me. Looking after our babies. Mum said he's been amazing. That he's a good father. That he refused to be left out of anything.

And I believe her.

But I don't remember our life together. I don't remember where I live. Where I went to school. My dad. Do I even have siblings? Cousins? A dog?

I need to talk to Mum.

Drake should mean more to me. He should feel familiar. But there's nothing. Just flashes of emotion. Odd feelings. And confusion.

When I look at him, he's gorgeous. Sexy as sin. Polite. Caring. And when I look into his eyes — those beautiful eyes framed by ridiculously long lashes — I see love.

Real love.

But I also see secrets.

And that's what I hate most.

Secrets.

CHAPTER SIXTEEN

THAT'S BETTER.

Clean. Refreshed. Slightly less like a walking science experiment. I didn't realise standing upright and showering could feel like a full-body workout. My legs are jelly, my arms ache, and I'm pretty sure my boobs are plotting a mutiny. But I'm upright. I'm clean. And I didn't pass out. So… yay me.

While I was in the bathroom, the nurses snuck in and changed all the bedding. Bless them. At least my short-term memory seems to be working. I recognise Nurse Sharonia as she walks back in, smiling like she's about to deliver a tray of miracles.

My belly grumbles at the sight of food. The tray rolls in on one of those wheeled hospital tables, dome lid hiding whatever mystery meal lies beneath. The moment she lifts the lid, the aroma hits me like a warm hug. My stomach growls again, louder this time. It's officially hangry.

I don't waste time. I inhale the food like it's my last meal on earth. My taste buds throw a party. Flavors. Textures. Actual joy. I wipe my mouth with a paper napkin, already wondering if I can bribe someone for seconds. Or juice. Definitely juice. My body's screaming for fruit juice like it's a life-or-death situation.

I mean, I'm expected to produce enough breast milk to feed two babies. Surely that earns me extra snacks.

Speaking of breast milk, Nurse Sharonia returns with a portable breast pump. She explains everything with calm efficiency, like she's done this a thousand times. Within ten minutes, I've successfully filled two small baby bottles. I'm weirdly proud. Like I've unlocked a new achievement in the "Motherhood Without a Manual" game.

She tells me the more I practice, the more confident I'll feel. I nod, pretending I'm not still mildly freaked out by the fact that my body is now a milk factory.

Before she leaves, I ask her to bring me the touch phone Drake had been charging. She hands it over, and I surprise myself by turning it on without help. No signal. Of course. But I can still poke around inside.

Excited, I scroll through the apps. Nothing triggers a memory. Not a single flicker. It's like someone handed me a stranger's phone and told me it was mine.

Then I find the photo gallery.

I tap it open, and there I am. Heavily pregnant. Belly out to here. I scroll through the images, studying each one like I'm trying to recognise a version of myself I don't remember becoming.

The last group of photos stops me cold.

I'm naked. Tastefully covered. Fast asleep.

Someone took these while I slept.

Drake?

I stare at one of the images — soft lighting, peaceful expression, belly cradled by my own hands. It's beautiful. I set it as my screen saver. Until I can replace it with photos of the twins.

Scrolling further, I find something else.

Operating theatre photos.

I enlarge one. My eyes nearly pop out of my head. There's a blood-covered shape being pulled from… something. I scroll again. Another image. Then another.

It's my caesarean.

I'm watching my own surgery. My own babies being pulled from my body, cleaned, wrapped, and held.

Proof.

Undeniable proof.

I had the babies.

I gave birth.

Even if I don't remember it.

Nurse Sharonia returns with a tray — tea and cupcakes. My belly grumbles again. I eat the sweet confections slowly, savouring every bite. The tea is warm, comforting. My body relaxes. My eyelids droop.

The room is quiet. No visitors. No chaos.

Just me.

And the whispering thoughts that won't shut up.

I yawn, let my head sink into the pillow, and decide to sleep while I can.

Because when I wake up?

I want answers.

BABY, WAKE UP. WE NEED TO TALK WHILE NO ONE ELSE IS here…

The voice is soft, urgent, familiar. Drake.

Pressure wraps around my hand — warm, steady. Someone's holding it tight.

My eyelids flutter open, heavy and reluctant. Drake's face comes into focus, sitting on the edge of my bed, eyes locked on mine, full of something that looks a lot like love.

"Drake?" My voice is groggy, my brain still rebooting. "What's going on? Is something wrong?"

He doesn't answer right away. Instead, he leans forward and brushes his lips against mine. Just a whisper of contact. Warmth blooms across my mouth, then spreads — down my throat, through my chest, into my limbs.

Then he kisses me again.

Harder this time.

His tongue slips past my lips, and I don't even have time to think. My body responds before my brain can catch up. I kiss him back, hungry, desperate, like I've been waiting for this without even knowing it.

If I were wearing socks, they'd be halfway across the room by now.

This kiss is… wow. Capital W. It's fire and silk and something else — something deeper. Something that feels like it's rewriting my DNA.

Then I taste it.

Metallic.

Not blood. Not quite.

It's sweet. Sharp. Familiar in a way I can't explain.

I suck on his tongue, chasing the flavor. It intensifies —
richer, deeper, like liquid gold laced with starlight. Ambrosia.
That's the only word that fits. It's addictive. Euphoric. I want
more. I need more.

Another mouthful, and my body lights up like a circuit
board. A strange tingling spreads through me — my skin, my
spine, my scalp. My head spins. My limbs go weightless.

Something's happening.

Something's wrong.

My breath catches. My vision blurs. The room tilts.

"Drake..." I try to say his name, but it comes out as a
whisper.

Everything goes dark.

OH MAN, IT'S DARK.

Why is it so dark?

Wait — hang on. I think my eyes might be closed. My
body feels weird. Floaty. Detached. Like I'm made of mist and
bad decisions. What was I doing this time? Trying to make
sense of it all?

Nope. Not happening.

I might still be asleep. That would explain the weight in
my limbs, the fuzz in my brain, the complete lack of
coordination. My eyes are too heavy to open, and nothing's
responding when I try to move. Might as well keep dreaming.
This sensation — this surreal, drifting weirdness — it's too
strange to be real.

What a dream.

"Babe, can you hear me?"

A voice. Male. Familiar. Sexy.

"Alexia, it's time to wake up, Baby."

There it is again. That voice. That Drake voice.

"Babe, open your eyes. It's time to wake up. Come on, Alexia, can you hear me?"

Is he moving toward me? Or am I still dreaming? Maybe I'm stuck in some weird limbo between sleep and consciousness. Maybe I'm just losing my mind.

"Babe, come on. You can do it. Wake up. That's it, start waking up."

Why do I have to wake up? Did I oversleep? Miss the alarm? Am I late for school?

School...

Oh, crap on a stick — school. I can't be late. I have to hand in my assignment. Then we're reviewing work before practice tests. End-of-year exams. Deadlines. Pressure. Panic.

"Alexia, open your eyes, babe. That's it. Open those beautiful eyes. Let me see them."

I fight against the heaviness. My eyelids lift, slow and reluctant. I blink. Once. Twice. And then I see him.

Drake.

His face is right there, gorgeous and glowing like he's carved from moonlight. My lips twitch, then stretch into a full-blown smile. I know that face. I know that man.

I stretch out my tired body, and it hits me — we're not in my bedroom. Not in Drake's either. My eyes scan the room.

Hospital.

We're in a hospital.

Why?

A sharp pain blooms behind my eyes. I squeeze them shut, trying to block it out.

And then it hits.

A flood.

An avalanche.

An information overload that slams into my brain like a psychic tsunami. Images. Sounds. Feelings. Memories.

Too many.

Too fast.

I can't breathe.

Are these mine?

Are they real?

If they are, then everything I thought I didn't know — I suddenly do. And it's too much. The panic builds, clawing at my chest, threatening to drown me.

I open my eyes again, wide and wild, staring at Drake. My heart races. My mind spins.

I remember.

Everything.

And the better question is — do I want to?

I focus. Clear my mind. Reach out with my thoughts.

Drake, can you hear me? Please say something. I want to know if this is real.

CHAPTER SEVENTEEN

I SLOWLY OPEN MY EYES AGAIN, BLINKING AWAY THE HAZE, and focus on the face in front of me. That face. The one that's haunted my dreams and now floods my memories. Drake.

He's watching me, waiting, and then — buzz.

A familiar pressure builds behind my eyes, like someone's gently knocking on the inside of my skull. Then I hear him. Not out loud. In my head.

'Babe, I can hear you in my head again. I love you so much. How are you feeling? Do you remember anything? Stupid question... You must have some memory if you're speaking to me like this. Because before, you had no recollection of anything. It was scary and worrisome.'

Oh boy.

I can hear Drake in my head. And he's responding to my thoughts. That means the connection is back. The soulmate bond. The psychic soulmate link. Whatever you want to call it — it's real. And it's strong.

And the memories? Yeah. They're back. All of them. The good. The bad. The risqué.

Oh gods, the risqué.

More images flash through my mind — Drake and me, tangled in sheets, skin on skin, lips on lips. Heat floods my cheeks. My face must be glowing red by now. I can feel it radiating like a furnace.

My eyes meet his, and I swallow hard. I can't believe it. Drake Smithlyn — the guy next door, the walking embodiment of male sex appeal — is mine. We're lovers. Soul-bound. And I'm the one who gets to run my hands down his sculpted body, feel his lips on mine, taste him, claim him.

Oh my gods, I love him.

Drake's face flushes pink, and he gives me that panty-dropping smile that could melt steel. "I love you too, babe. I love you so much, it hurts."

Before I can respond, his lips are on mine — warm, soft, demanding. His arms wrap around me, pulling me close, and suddenly my body's on fire. I don't know if the hospital room's heating is on, but I'm burning from the inside out.

The kiss deepens. Hot. Scorching. Mind-erasing.

My thoughts fade away, and my mind becomes fuzzy. I lose track of our conversation and forget everything except the sensation of his lips, his taste, and how perfectly my body aligns with his, as if we were meant to be together.

Time loses meaning. Seconds? Minutes? Hours? I don't care. I just want more.

Drake pulls back slightly, lips brushing my ear, sending shivers down my spine. His voice is low, rough, full of need.

"Baby, bite me. Bite me now. I want to feel you. Your teeth piercing my flesh, your tongue sweeping against my skin. I want to feel my blood leave my body while you drink it. Do it, Baby."

You don't need to tell me twice.

My gums tingle. My incisors lengthen. Instinct takes over.

I run my tongue along his neck, tasting the salt of his skin, feeling him shiver beneath me. Then I bite — deep, precise, perfect. My lips seal around the wound, and his blood floods my mouth.

Hot. Thick. Divine.

He's mine.

I grip his shoulder and the back of his head, holding him close, refusing to let go. Drake moans, the sound vibrating through my chest, fueling my hunger. His blood is ambrosia — rich, intoxicating, electric. It rushes down my throat, coating me in warmth and power.

Time disappears.

I drink.

And drink.

Until something in my brain whispers — enough.

I seal the wound with a sweep of my tongue, then press a kiss to his skin. "Thank you, baby. I needed that."

Then—

Pain.

Sharp. Blinding. Instant.

"Aww, ow. Oh my gods, this hurts."

My hands fly to my head, clutching my skull, but it does nothing. The pain is inside. Deep. Twisting.

Drake's voice breaks through the fog, panicked and raw. "Alexia, what is it? What's wrong?"

But I can't answer.

Because something is happening.

And it's not good.

The pain builds like a storm behind my eyes — black, smoky fireworks exploding inside my skull, each one louder, sharper, more violent than the last. I clutch my head, gasping, as the pressure crests and then — light. A dull, flickering glow that grows until it becomes a blur of images, too fast to catch, too jagged to ignore.

Then they slow.

And I see him.

No. No, no, no.

Drake's father.

His face twists and morphs through the haze — smiling, snarling, commanding. The blood drains from my face. I try to look away, but the images keep coming, faster now. Horrors I never wanted to remember. Faces I'll never forget.

Women. Children. Screaming. Bleeding. Dying.

The pain finally recedes, but my mind is a battlefield — confused, scorched, and raw. If I can speak to Drake through our mind link, then everything I've seen — everything I've remembered — is real. The Dark Ones are real. The monsters are real.

And Davelt Smithlyn is the worst of them.

Oh gods. Drake.

He's going to be shattered.

I shake my head, trying to dislodge the memories, but they cling like thorns. I suck in a breath, grounding myself in the present. My hometown. The drive to Darshia. Meeting Grandma Ma. Finding Drake in that nightclub. The poisoned bullet. The coma. The twins.

The assassination attempt.

Drake's father tried to kill me.

And not just me — our babies.

My heart slams against my ribs. My hands fly to my belly, flat and empty. Panic claws at my throat.

Where are they?

Where are my babies?

My eyes dart around the hospital room, wild and searching. No bassinets. No tiny cries. No warm, wriggling bundles.

Then — memories. Feeding them. Holding them. Their tiny hands on my skin. Their sleepy sighs.

They're alive.

They're okay.

'Alexia, the twins are well and fast asleep in the nursery. They are nearly due for their next feed. And yes, you are still in Darshia. You are in a private room here in the hospital.'

Drake's voice in my mind is calm, steady. He's answering my panic before I even speak. His hand finds mine, warm and grounding, his thumb brushing over my knuckles in a silent promise: I've got you.

But then his voice shifts.

'I cannot believe my father is behind the assassination attempt on your life. But then again, I had firsthand experience of what that man tried to do to you and our babies... What were those images of all the other children and women? They looked like they were being slaughtered or something. Do you know who they are, Alexia? What was going on?'

No.

No, no, no.

He saw too much.

I slam my mental shields up, blocking the worst of it. He doesn't need to see that. Not yet. Maybe not ever.

Davelt's crimes go deeper than anyone knows. Affairs. Experiments. Children bred and discarded like failed prototypes. Women used, experimented on, and slaughtered when they didn't meet his twisted standards. All in pursuit of power. Of creating a superrace. Of becoming the most dominant Dark One in existence.

He used Mary — Drake's mother — for her bloodline, her name, her magic. He tricked her into believing they were soulmates. They weren't. It was all a lie. A glamour. A manipulation wrapped in dark magic.

How do I tell Drake that everything he's ever believed about his family is a lie?

I need Grandma Ma.

But she hasn't come.

And neither has my dad.

Where is everyone?

I close my eyes and focus, reaching out with my mind.

Grandma Ma, are you there? Can you hear me? Excuse me, Grandma Ma, I am awake and starting to remember.

I wait. Count to ten. Nothing.

Eleven.

Still nothing.

Fine.

I sever the link and reach for someone else.

Mum, can you hear me? I am awake, and I can remember everything. Can you bring Dad? I would love to see him here. I want him to meet the twins. Where are you?

A familiar pressure brushes against my mind. I open my shields just enough.

'Alexia, is that you?'

Oh gods. It worked.

'Mum. Yes. I can hear you.'

'How are you doing this? Can you hear me?'

Tears prick my eyes. *'It's so good to hear your voice, Mum. Drake is here with me. He saw some of my memories... about his parents. Horrendous things. I don't want him to know everything yet — not until I speak with Grandma Ma. But she's not answering me. Do you know where she is?'*

'Grandma Ma has gone back to our town. She's following up on something. She didn't think I needed to know the details. After all, I'm not a Dark One. Just her

granddaughter. Just the mother of the next Queen of Darshia.'

Ooo. Mum's pissed.

And honestly? I don't blame her.

Grandma Ma better start talking. Because what I saw in that office — what I felt — can't be ignored. And if we're going to survive what's coming, we need to be united. Not divided by secrets and power plays.

I glance at Drake.

His jaw is tight. His eyes are narrowed. He knows.

He knows I've been talking to someone else.

And worse — he knows I blocked him out.

"Alexia," he says, voice low and sharp, "don't smile at me like that and think we're not going to talk. I felt you block me. Don't even try to deny it. You know that hurts me. I thought you loved me. But here you are, hiding things from me again. What are you keeping from me? What don't I deserve to know?"

Oh no.

Here we go.

I've just gotten my memory back, and now I'm about to lose the one person who's been my anchor through all of this.

I take a breath. Count to ten. Exhale.

I meet his eyes, steady and calm, even though my heart is pounding.

"Drake," I say softly, "first — thank you. For staying. For protecting me and the twins. For not giving up on me."

I place my hand over his, squeezing gently.

"Second… I'm the Princess of Darshia. I'm going to be

Queen. And that means there are things I can't share. Not yet. Not without the Queen's approval. What happened in her office — it's not just about me. It's bigger than us."

Drake's expression hardens. "Are you serious right now? Alexia, don't bullshit me." His voice is sharp, wounded. "I was there. I felt what my father did. I saw what he tried to do to you and our babies. So no — you don't get to shut me out. I'm your soulmate. You're not getting rid of me that easily."

He leans in, eyes blazing. "Now start talking. Because right now, I'm this close to dragging that bastard into the light and making him tell me what I saw. Why I saw him with other women. Why I saw children. Blood. Death."

My stomach twists.

Oh shite.

He saw too much.

And now?

Now I have to decide how much truth he can handle.

CHAPTER EIGHTEEN

OH, CRAP ON A STICK. DAMN THESE MIND SHIELDS — OR should I say, the total lack of them. My memories keep clawing their way back, piece by piece, like a horror movie marathon I didn't sign up for. Flashes of images, some bad, some beyond horrendous, slam into me. And now Drake is glaring at me like I just stole his favorite blood bag. Fantastic. Where is Grandma Ma when I actually need her?

Speak of the devil... I feel her presence pressing against my mind, and I let her in. Alexia, it is good to know you are finally back with us. I will arrive at your room shortly. We have much to discuss, and I will have my head of security with me. Is Drake with you at the moment?

Finally, Grandma Ma decides to respond. Grandma Ma, it is good to hear your voice. How far away are you from the hospital? And yes, Drake is right here with me.

I glance at Drake's annoyed face. He knows I'm mind-talking again. Well, tough luck, buddy. He better get used to it.

I'm the Princess-in-waiting, the next Queen of Darshia. Royal perks include telepathic conversations whenever I damn well please. Still, guilt gnaws at me.

Footsteps echo down the hallway, snapping my attention. Nurse Sharonia marches in, armed with a tray of empty bottles. Great. Showtime.

"Oh good, Alexia. I am here to collect milk. It should only take a few minutes." Efficient doesn't even cover it — she's practically a machine. In seconds, she hooks me up to the breast pump. Milk flows down the hose into the container like I'm a dairy cow in a vampire soap opera.

I'll give it to the nurses — personal boundaries vanish the second they're handling your naked body parts. Sharonia works fast, fills several bottles, and packs everything away. I sit there stunned, clutching my gown back over myself. Geez, woman, warm your hands next time. Expressing milk is now officially part of my life, along with breastfeeding the twins. Motherhood: glamorous edition.

Not long before I sense Grandma Ma and two others outside the corridor. Wow, my abilities are levelling up. I focus on Drake. Let's see if I can sneak into his mind without him noticing. He tilts his head, already aware who's approaching. And he's not thrilled. At least my Dark One powers are sharpening.

When I'm sure he hasn't noticed me poking around, I dive deeper.

'Why is Alexia leaving me out of her conversations? She knows more and refuses to acknowledge those horrific images. They're about my parents — especially my dad —

but she hides it from me. It hurts. Why doesn't she trust me? I love her so much; Alexia is my world. I bet her grandmother told her to keep secrets. Bloody Blue Royals. Secretive buggers. Great, her grandmother is coming. Just what I need — the old Dragon showing up right when Alexia remembers. Shit, I better crank up my shields before the hag tries to read me. I don't trust her one bit, especially after she groped me while Alexia was unconscious...'

My heart twists. I'm hurting Drake. But then his words echo — Grandma Ma groped him?

My mind screams: *'What? Grandma Ma touched my man?'*

Oh hell no. He's my soulmate, and she tried to move in while I was unconscious? What kind of woman does that? Think, Alexia. Don't go nuclear yet. I trust Drake, but Grandma Ma? Not so much. I don't even know what happened to her husband. Fine. I'll keep quiet for now, but I'm watching her like a hawk.

I stare at Drake, catching the hurt in his eyes. I send him my thoughts. *'Drake, if you can hear me, remember I love you. Come kiss me before my visitors walk in. I want to feel you — I want your sexy lips on mine.'*

The hurt vanishes. He flashes that devastating smile, and my belly flutters. Lower too. Dampness pools between my thighs.

He leans in, scent flooding my senses, arms wrapping me

tight. His whisper tickles my ear, sending shivers down my spine. "I love you too, Alexia. Never forget that. Now give me your lips. I need to taste you."

You don't have to tell me twice. I turn my head, lips locking with his. Firm, hot, intoxicating. This is what I need — Drake and his kisses, the kind that make the world disappear.

Oh, Babe. I do love you. Please be patient with me. I have things to sort out, and I need to do it myself first. When I know what's happening, I'll include you. It's confidential. Just be patient. Now, increase your shields. Grandma Ma is about to walk in with the head of security and one of his team members.

Drake and I keep kissing, hot and steamy, like the hospital room is suddenly auditioning for a Dark One soap opera. Erotic sparks race through me, and honestly, if this weren't important, I'd tell Grandma Ma to come back later.

'Drake, we have to stop. I don't want to be loving you like this in front of Grandma Ma...'

'Oh, Baby. Your grandmother must learn that we love each other, and nothing is coming between us.'

Ha — wha... what does that even mean, Drake?

Before he can answer, Grandma Ma sweeps into the room, cutting off our make-out session like the world's worst chaperone. My mind is already primed, so I dive straight into hers. If she's hiding something, I'm going to find it. I skim her surface thoughts, then push deeper.

Her irritation slams into me. *'Oh my, how dare they behave like this before me? Soon, Drake will be mine, and Alexia cannot stop me. Just because they are soulmates will not interfere with my plans. Oh no, I will prevent them from joining, and soon, Drake will want nothing to do with Alexia. He will be mine for the taking.'*

Well, isn't that just peachy. Grandma Ma plotting to steal my man.

At least Drake follows my mental nudge and sits on the bed, thigh pressed against mine. He murmurs, Alexia, you don't have to tell me twice. I was going to do that anyway. Plus, this...

His arms wrap around my shoulders, squeezing gently, and he plants a kiss on the top of my head. We snuggle close, united front activated, and both turn toward the intruders. My face is all smiles, shields locked tight.

"Hello, Grandma Ma. It's good to see you again. It's been frustrating not knowing or remembering. At least I don't have to worry about that now."

Oscar-worthy performance, if I say so myself. I pout just enough, tilt my head, and let my eyes go wide and innocent. Sad but sweet. And there it is — the flicker in her eyes. Barely a twitch, but I catch it. Gotcha. If I weren't looking, I'd have missed it.

She still hasn't figured out that I can hear her thoughts. Silly child, you should still have no memories. How you seem to have them back is a hindrance to my plans. Damn her. Alexia's mind shields are too strong to get through.

Thanks for the commentary, Grandma Ma. Now I know

exactly where we stand. One step at a time. I'll keep skimming minds, sorting allies from enemies, and never let her suspect I can slip past anyone's defences. As the old saying goes: keep your friends close, and your enemies closer.

AFTER FIFTEEN INTENSE MINUTES OF BACK-AND-FORTH WITH the head of security, Jones, and one of his team members, Riley, Grandma Ma keeps chiming in with her royal "I'm still in charge" commentary. Subtle reminder, Nana, but I can already tell her security isn't one hundred percent behind her. What did she do to earn that scorn?

My eyelids droop, and I yawn. Wow. I'm more exhausted than I thought. I need a break. A break from the lying, two-timing woman who also happens to be my grandmother and the Queen of Darshia. Queen of the Dark Ones — vampires, if we're being blunt. Note to self: watch every word, every move around her and her staff. Keeping what I know about Drake's parents to myself feels risky, but I don't trust Grandma Ma. She's scheming, and I know she wants Drake. I have to figure out her plan for my fiancé before she makes her move.

Nurse Sharonia strolls casually into my room, startling Grandma Ma. Ha. Nana's too busy trying to worm her way into my mind and Drake's to notice anything else. Finally, she clocks my exhaustion. Her thoughts confirm she's planning to continue this little meeting back at the castle in a few days.

Well, at least she knows when I'll be released from the hospital. Funny, since the doctor hasn't even bothered to show up. Suspicious much? Maybe Grandma Ma is playing mind games.

"My child, you are looking fatigued," she says in that condescending tone that makes me want to yawn harder. "We will leave you for now. We'll speak in a few days back at the castle." Oh, sure. Is she trying to look concerned? Because she doesn't sound it. Her eyes keep darting toward Drake. Lucky for him, he avoids eye contact. Her thoughts betray her annoyance anyway.

I shoot a quick mental message to my soulmate. Drake, keep your eyes on me. Don't give Grandma Ma the satisfaction. She's fishing for your attention — don't bite.

My gaze locks with hers. "Thanks, Grandma Ma, for stopping by. As I said, about Drake's parents — there's not much to tell. We must stop Davelt at all costs. He's evil." My lips twitch as I glance at Drake, then back at her. "Drake will help me to the bathroom, and after that, I need sleep before the twins wake up for another feed."

I tilt my head up at Drake, smiling. His arms tighten around me, and he kisses the top of my head.

"Are you ready, Alexia? Don't forget you haven't been on your feet for a while. We better take it slow."

I nod, sliding my legs to the side, bracing myself to stand. With his help, I shuffle to the edge and rise carefully. My balance wobbles, but I steady. Together, we shuffle to the bathroom.

As soon as the door closes, I focus on Mum and send a quick message. *'Mum, can you hear me? Next time you speak with*

Grandma Ma, act jubilant and relieved about my progress and memories returning.'

'Yes, Alexia. I've already come to that conclusion.'

Really? That's good to know.

'Thanks, Mum. There's something about Grandma Ma. I don't trust her.'

'Yes. There is something not right about her. Anyway, enough about the woman. Your father should be with me the next time you see me.'

'That will be awesome, Mum. Keep safe.'

'You too, Alexia. I better go. Love you with all my heart.'

'Love you with all my heart too, Mum.'

At least I can hide my ability in the bathroom. Grandma Ma still lingering in my hospital room is annoying. Didn't she say she was leaving?

I savour the ability to slip into others' thoughts, eavesdropping on conversations. Speaking of listening…

'Can you believe our queen?'

That voice — Jones. Oh, this is going to be good. I can

already tell they've left my hospital room. Finally, someone actually goes. Time to pause and eavesdrop.

She will cause a security risk to the young woman. This kid is our next Queen of Darshia, and our current queen does not like the competition of a new replacement.

Ha, you picked up on that, Jones. Did you see the way Alexettia's eyes kept watching that boy? It was disgusting the way she kept eye-fucking the kid. What's his name? ... Oh, yes, Drake.

Yes, Drake Smithlyn. His father — that son of a bitch who thinks he's the king — didn't want the kid. They took Drake from Darshia as a baby and dumped him among the humans.

I don't know why the Queen hasn't stopped that overbearing idiot. Davelt Smithlyn will keep trying to assassinate our little princess. We better place extra guards on her, because we know the Queen won't sanction it. Riley, call in three extra guards and place them around the hospital grounds. We'll go from there when I find out what our Queen plans.

You're right, Jones. We have to protect the kid, especially now Alexia has given birth, continuing the Queen's dynasty. Alexettia has been queen for far too long. It's time for a new queen — fresh ideas. Someone who's seen the real world outside our borders.

Be careful what you say, Riley. We don't need anyone listening in, or we'll be the ones rotting in a prison cell. Just to be safe, we better go. I haven't felt the Queen merge into my mind. I feel safe for now, but we must leave and clear our thoughts, just in case.

Wow. With any luck, I've got two more allies here in

Darshia. But let's be real — these two just confirmed what I already know: Grandma Ma is hiding things from me. And then there's the little matter of her wanting my soulmate.

I glance around the cramped bathroom, eyes settling on the closed shower curtain. At least it gives me a shred of privacy while I pee. I'm not nearly confident enough to empty my bladder while staring into Drake's eyes. It's bad enough he can hear everything — embarrassment level: maximum.

I press the metal square pad on the wall, and the toilet flush roars like a stadium cheer. Great. Now the entire hospital floor knows I've been to the loo. My cheeks burn as I slide the curtain open and meet Drake's gaze.

I wash my hands quickly, drying them with a paper towel, and send him a message. I'll fill you in when Grandma Ma leaves. Just remember — I love you. Time to face the old dragon again.

Drake nods, fighting hard not to laugh. His grin spreads across his face, and his laughter echoes in my head, making me smile despite myself. He moves to my side, kisses the top of my head, and opens the bathroom door.

Back to my bed. Time to say goodbye to Grandma Ma and finally shove her out of this hospital.

THINKING BACK OVER ALL THE DISCUSSIONS WITH GRANDMA Ma today, I realise she never once mentioned her trip to my hometown or gave me anything useful about Drake's father. Surprise, surprise — she's still hoarding secrets like a dragon with a treasure chest. The only thing she wanted was to pry into what I remember about Davelt. Typical.

How dare she play her mind games? I feel it every time she tries to breach Drake's shields. Credit where it's due — he blocks her as best he can. But I still have to step in, reinforcing his defenses like the world's sassiest psychic bodyguard. Honestly, if she keeps poking at him, I might just bite her. And not in the polite vampire way.

When I push deeper into her thoughts, one name keeps surfacing: Zalend. I don't know who he is, but he matters to Alexettia. She guards him in her mind like a secret weapon. Whoever Zalend is, he's important enough that she won't let anyone near the truth. Which means I need to dig harder.

I lean back against the pillows, exhaustion tugging at me, but my mind refuses to shut down. Every piece of this puzzle feels heavier than the last. Grandma Ma wants Drake. Davelt wants me dead. Zalend lurks in the shadows of her thoughts. And I'm stuck in a hospital gown, pumping milk like a dairy cow while plotting royal conspiracies. Fabulous.

Drake squeezes my hand, grounding me. His warmth cuts through the chaos, and for a moment, I let myself breathe. He doesn't say anything, but his eyes tell me everything: he's with me, no matter how twisted this gets.

I smirk because sarcasm is my armour. Fine, Grandma Ma. Keep your secrets. Keep your Zalend. Keep your creepy obsession with my fiancé. I'll play along. But I'm watching you. And when the time comes, I'll be ready.

The thought settles in my chest like steel. I'm not just Alexia, the tired patient in a hospital bed. I'm Alexia,

Princess-in-waiting, Dark One, mother, and future Queen of Darshia. And no one — Grandma Ma, Davelt, or mystery-man Zalend — is going to take that from me.

CHAPTER NINETEEN

THE SUPREMACY BUZZ CREEPS ALONG MY SKIN FROM A powerful Dark One.

Grandma Ma.

I stay calm, sitting in my hospital bed as best I can. The radiance of her authority crawls over me, making it feel like hot ants are marching across my flesh as she finally departs from the hospital building and drifts out onto the grounds. I wait, patient but tense, until I sense her completely leave the area. Only then do I feel safe enough to speak with Drake.

Oh boy, my Dark One abilities are levelling up fast. I'm amazed I can still sense her from this distance. Impressive, but also annoying. I wonder how I can block this feeling before it drives me insane.

One look at Drake tells me it's time to come clean. His annoyance radiates like a storm cloud, and then anger slams into me. His attitude is not something I will tolerate.

Okay… it's time to talk.

Before he can speak, I hold up my hand, signalling him to wait. I push my senses outward from the hospital room, sweeping through the surrounding halls and rooms, making sure no one is close enough to overhear or interrupt.

Drake's voice cuts through my concentration, sharp and frustrated. "Alexia, I will not wait any longer. I need you to explain what is happening because I am sick of being left out of the loop. Your grandmother made sure the information she shared about my family was hurtful and damaging. And she did it in front of me, knowing it would confuse and hurt me."

He's right. Alexettia has played with my life enough, damn it. Hearing the pain in Drake's voice, seeing the raw hurt in his eyes, nearly brings me to my knees if I were standing. I will not hurt him again if I can help it. Enough is enough. I will no longer play by Grandma Ma's rules or her twisted games.

I take a slow, deep breath, bracing myself for what I'm about to say. I hope he doesn't hold it against me. What I'm about to reveal will hurt him, maybe even shatter his family's memory and beliefs. I pray to the goddess he can see in my eyes how much I love him.

Here goes. "Drake, just remember — I love you."

His eyes snap to mine, confusion and hurt flashing across them. His eyebrow arches before he turns his back to me, staring out the window like it holds answers.

"I know that," he says, voice tight, "but come on, Alexia, it's time to tell me what is happening. Stop hiding things from me. Fair's fair."

Fair's fair, he says! Oh, please. What about him?

"Yes, Drake, it is time. But it's only fair you do the same with me. Remember, I'm new to all this Dark One stuff. I only recently found out Dark Ones exist. As for you… well, it's part of your history. You've known about Dark Ones for years. Give me the benefit of the doubt and let me speak."

Annoyance toward Drake rises inside me, and I fight hard not to snap. It's difficult, staring at him while we balance on the edge of civility. He's biting back words, I can see it. Gee, how gentlemanly of him to let me talk first. Well, here goes.

"Drake, how much do you know about the Dark Ones and their individual powers and abilities — apart from the basic mind reading and shielding?"

Drake raises an eyebrow, then turns his head away from me. Hmm. Not the reaction I was expecting. He keeps his face turned, delaying his reply far too long. If he doesn't start talking soon, I'll breach his shields myself. He's not the only one annoyed about being kept out of the loop, especially after how I've been treated since arriving in Darshia.

Finally, he turns back, meeting my eyes as he walks toward me. He gently picks up my hand, his gaze steady but shadowed with concern.

"Alexia, I understand you've had a lot to learn since arriving here in Darshia, finding out you come from a long line of Dark Ones. The information dump can overwhelm anyone when learning about Dark Ones and soulmates. As for abilities, yes, I know of some." He pauses, choosing his words carefully, taking a deep breath. "My mother has more abilities than my father, but they are both extremely proficient in their powers. They kept me in the dark about their abilities. My father banished me from Darshia to live in your town and hid certain Dark One details from me. In time, I will learn more, and my power will increase. Now that we are here in Darshia, my mother has informed me I must learn about Darshia, its people, its rules, and most of all, how to keep my abilities secret and under control."

My eyebrow lifts slowly as I process his words. Okay, so Drake just admitted his mother is stronger than his father. His powers will increase. And he's keeping secrets. Interesting. I wonder what abilities he really has — ones he might even be hiding from me. Can he penetrate my mind? For now, I keep my shields locked tight.

"Drake, what do you know about the history of our Dark One families? Did you know my grandmother's daughter was supposed to marry one of your family members? But instead, she fell in love with another and left Darshia, never to return."

Drake's reaction tells me he didn't know. His face is a mix of shock and confusion. Okay, next question.

"Did you know your father is not your mother's soulmate?"

His eyes widen, his mouth opening and closing as he struggles to form words. Yes, it's cruel of me to tell him this way. But it's time. The truth has to come out.

"What do you mean, my parents are not soulmates? That's impossible." His voice cracks with hurt and disbelief. "They are soulmates."

I cut him off, sharp and unflinching. "Your father is powerful, but don't forget — he's not as powerful as your mother. He's been using her for her powers and her family's wealth. And he's been having affairs for as long as you've lived next door to me... if not longer."

The words hang heavy in the air, slicing through the fragile trust between us.

His thoughts brush against my mind — he's annoyed. *'What now? Surely there cannot be more?'*

I SLOWLY NOD, HESITANT TO INFORM HIM THAT HIS FATHER WAS really a monster. "He stooped low, trying to create his own race of Dark Ones. Only to find they weren't to his liking and killed off the babies and their mothers. Those are the visions you've seen. He is using your mother. As far as I know, she doesn't know about your father's extracurricular activities."

Drake quietly sits down on my bed beside me. His hands grip the edge, knuckles turning white. The images of the atrocities swirl in his mind, and he refuses to comprehend what his father has done over the last decade — or more.

Gently stroking his hand, I push the images back into his head for him to see while I fill him in with more details. "Drake, the images you're seeing are of your father. These are what I obtained from him before he tried to kill me."

Drake stiffens beside me, his hand sliding away before he stands, moving across the room, leaving me cold.

"Oh, Gods no. Why did he do this? These things?" His voice cracks under the strain of the vile images. He stops, leaning against the wall, forehead pressed to the surface as if the solid barrier is the only thing holding him up. "Alexia. Stop the images; I've seen enough... I don't need to see any more."

I quickly finish the images, clearing my mind, watching him struggle with the overload. He turns, face pale, voice slow. "And what do you mean you were able to obtain...?

How...? Just exactly what powers do you have, Alexia? Should I be concerned about our children? Should I be concerned about my safety?"

What? Oh, hell no. That's enough. I stand, cutting him off before he can continue. "Stop right there."

I force myself to breathe. If I don't calm down, Drake and I will end up fighting, and Grandma Ma would love that. Deep breath in. Slow release.

"Drake. Don't. Do not turn me into something bad when your dad is the evil one here, not me. I'm still learning about Dark Ones and their individual powers. Someone already warned me I must keep my new and increased powers hidden. As Princess of Darshia, it's wise not to let anyone know what I can do, or the Queen's enemies will use it against me."

Drake opens his mouth, but I push on before he can interrupt. "I've kept some of my talents away from Grandma Ma. Because I don't trust her. Not yet. Little things she's done — or hasn't done — tell me she's hiding something. And then there's her obsession with you... Trust and Grandma Ma are not happening."

I wait, watching him, gauging his reaction. If he doesn't admit what she did, I will.

"Alexia, I have something to tell you regarding your grandmother. Alexettia doesn't care who you are. She thinks she can have anything she wants because she's the Queen, and no one will go against her."

He pauses, fidgeting, clearly uncomfortable.

"Alexia, while you were unconscious, Alexettia had a bad habit." He hesitates, eyes pleading with me to believe him. "She would continue to flirt. It made me uncomfortable."

His hand reaches for my arm, but his touch doesn't comfort me. He takes a deep breath, bracing himself. "Alexia. Grandma Ma was trying to crack onto me without regard for you or us as soulmates."

I pull my arm away, legs swinging to the other side of the bed. I need to pace. My hunger for his blood stirs, dangerous and insistent. We need to clear the air properly, or we won't survive this.

Damn you, Grandma Ma, and your Dark Ones.

"Thank you for telling me, Drake. I already picked it up in your thoughts when I let you into my head, without thinking about the consequences." I pause, letting the words sink in. "Yes, Drake, I can delve into your mind. All your thoughts. I have access whenever I want. That's why I blocked the connection — to give you privacy. I don't need your thoughts and images running through my head on top of everything else running through my mind. It's already overcrowded in my skull. Even when Grandma Ma was here earlier, I had to help you block her from bypassing your shields. This time, she failed. She thinks you're becoming stronger."

I raise my eyebrow, watching his reaction. I don't need to read his mind to know what he's thinking.

I shrug my shoulders and carry on, "Yes, you're getting stronger. But not quite enough to fully defend yourself from her. And before you ask, yes — I can get past anyone's shields. I can access their thoughts, memories, and secrets. Even Grandma Ma isn't safe from me."

Surprise flickers across his face. I keep mine neutral.

"Drake, remember — this is top secret. Grandma Ma doesn't know how far I can go. She thinks I can only skim the basic surface stuff. I've convinced her your father's thoughts were too close to the surface, allowing me access. She doesn't know I can go deeper. I didn't have time to investigate fully, but I learned enough to know he wants me dead."

My body shudders at the memory of what that monster tried to do to me and the babies.

Next time I'm near him, I'll dig deeper. Same with Grandma Ma. I've had enough of living in the dark.

Speaking of her, it's time to do something about this Joining Ceremony. I've heard bits and pieces, but I know there's more. And I think I've just had a lightbulb moment. If I'm right, joining with Drake will strengthen his shields and mine. Our health, our Dark One powers, our survival — it all improves when we're joined soulmates.

I glance at Drake. In the short time I've been thinking, he's already trying to break through my shields. Poor guy. He really doesn't want to believe I can keep him out. I bypass his shields easily, ignoring his thoughts.

'Drake, stop trying to break through my mind shields. Call my doctor here. I have an idea that should solve many of our problems.'

He startles, narrowing his eyes. *'What idea? What can the doctor do, Alexia?'*

His thoughts drip with attitude. Oh yeah, Drake doesn't like my doctor.

My senses flare. Two nurses are approaching in the

corridor. But then… Something about them feels… wrong. The urge to move overwhelms me. Danger is coming.

I slide out of bed, grab Drake's hand, and pull him toward the bathroom.

"Come on, Drake," I whisper harshly. "There's danger approaching, and it's coming from the two nurses heading this way."

"Huh? What nurses?"

I close the door behind us. "Chances are, they're not actually nurses."

I turn the tap on, water rushing loud enough to mask us. Anyone listening will think I'm in the bathroom. "Stay here, remain quiet. I'll be back in a minute." And squeeze Drake's hand.

"Alexia, no. I'll go," he hisses back.

I shake my head and press a hard kiss to his lips, and shove him back as I slip back through the doorway, closing the bathroom door in his annoyed face.

I press my back against the wall beside the hospital room door, every nerve on edge, ready for the two strangers to enter.

Drake's voice interrupts my thoughts, muffled but sharp. *'Alexia, I'll confront th—'*

BEFORE DRAKE CAN FINISH HIS SENTENCE, THE TWO FEMALE nurses barge in through the hospital room doorway, my foot stopping the door from colliding with me. Instinct kicks in. I breach their minds fast, gathering the information I need before it's too late to protect myself.

With the last lot of Drake's blood still running through my system, I move faster than usual. Within milliseconds, I size up my opponents, distinguishing the difference between the two, calculating the best way to bring them down before they even realise I'm right behind them. Their mind chatter is loud, sloppy, and full of murderous intent. Perfect.

Who hired these two idiots?

I surge forward, hands snapping out to disarm them. The gun and a syringe clatter across the floor, the noise loud enough to summon guards from the other end of the hospital. My foot connects hard with the first nurse, then the second, sending them both crashing to their knees.

But they're not down for long. The first one snarls, swinging a fist toward my ribs. I twist sideways, catching his wrist mid-air, and slam my elbow into his jaw. The crack echoes through the room. She stumbles back, dazed, but still conscious.

The second nurse lunges, trying to grab me by the throat. Oh, please. Amateur hour. I duck low, sweep my leg out, and hook her ankle. She crashes to the floor, but I don't give her time to recover. My knee drives into her chest, knocking the wind out of her.

The first nurse recovers enough to charge again, but I'm already moving. I pivot, spin, and drive my heel into his stomach. He folds like a cheap deck chair, collapsing against the wall.

Quick jabs, sharp thrusts — my fists and feet strike with precision. I hammer blows into their ribs, their shoulders, their temples. The final strike lands at the back of their heads, knocking them both out cold.

Geez. I'm getting better at this Dark One power stuff. Cool. My breathing is steady, not even out of breath.

Within seconds, Drake bursts back into the room, eyes wide as he takes in the scene. His gaze flicks from me to the unconscious bodies sprawled across the floor.

"Alexia…" His voice is half awe, half horror. "What the hell did you just do?"

I crouch beside the assassins, carefully moving the gun and syringe away. "What does it look like? I redecorated the floor with their faces. You're welcome."

Drake kneels beside me, his jaw tight. "What the hell… who are they? And what were they planning?" His voice is sharp, angry.

"Quiet down, Drake. Quick, use the room's phone and call security." I would like to know why the Royal security is not here. The noise level should have attracted both the hospital and Royal security to the room.

He hesitates, still staring at me like I've sprouted double fangs. "You didn't even break a sweat."

I smirk, brushing imaginary dust off my hospital gown. "Yeah, well, I'm a Dark One princess. Perks of the job. Now stop gawking and call security before Tweedle-Dumb and Tweedle-Dumber here wake up."

Drake finally moves, grabbing the phone and punching in numbers with more force than necessary. His voice drops low as he informs someone of the situation, requesting immediate backup.

I stay crouched, slipping into the unconscious assassins'

minds. Their thoughts are fragmented, but the truth is clear — they're not nurses, which I had discovered quickly. They were sent here to kill me. Well…that is obvious. And the orders — straight from Drake's father.

My stomach twists. He's supposed to be locked up in the castle's holding cells? So how the hell is he still pulling strings?

I glance at Drake, my voice low but firm. "Drake, phone the nursery now. Make sure the twins are safe."

His face pales instantly. He dials, knuckles white, until relief washes over him. "These two idiots are here to kill me. Why am I always the one attracting assassins? Do I have a neon sign over my head that says *Target Practice?*"

I double-check their minds to ensure they're still unconscious and slip further into their minds.

I grit my teeth. Enough of this crap. Why is Drake's father still trying to kill me?

Drake's voice brings me back when he says, "Can you wait one moment, please? I'll let her know."

My stomach twists. His look tells me something's up.

"Alexia, your parents have arrived."

What? My heart lurches. Excited? Worried? Both.

"Drake, tell my parents to stay in the nursery."

He relays my words. "Alexia, the twins are safe and still sleeping. Your parents said they are not going anywhere. They want to spend some quality time with their grandchild. And no, the Queen hasn't spoken to your mother since they arrived in Darshia. I don't think she even knows they're here."

Relief floods me. My dad is finally here. It feels like years since I last saw him, even though it's barely been a week. I've missed him so much. But Grandma Ma not speaking with Mum? Something is off.

He glances at me, smiles faintly, and nods.

But the relief doesn't last. My senses flare again. A familiar buzz creeps along my skin — Grandma Ma's authority pressing closer.

Great. Just what I need. Another fight

Her presence is like nails on a chalkboard.

"Drake, guard your mind. Grandma Ma is almost here. Let my parents know."

With a quick update and goodbye to my parents, Drake hangs up and steps beside me.

Within seconds, hospital security and Royal security arrive. Grandma Ma sweeps in like a storm, her authority pressing against my skin. I step back from the unconscious assassins.

"What is going on, and who are these two people?" she demands, voice sharp.

"Grandma Ma, these two idiots came to assassinate me with their gun and syringe." I point to the evidence, forcing the security personnel to acknowledge it.

The guards glance at me, then at her. I slip into their minds, breaching their shields with ease. The truth slams into me — Drake's father has escaped.

Did Grandma Ma allow this?

I casually move away from the window, not eager to become target practice again. To keep my hands busy, instead of hitting someone, I lift my glass from the table, draining the contents in two gulps, masking my fury.

Looking at the guards, I tilt my head. "What are your

names again, gentlemen? Forgive me, my memory is playing tricks. I've been through a lot."

They glance at Grandma Ma instead of answering. Typical. I hear her mind whispering to them, testing me. Does she really think I can't hear?

I set the glass down, turning back to them, still waiting. Geez, how rude.

My eyes lock on Grandma Ma. I keep my expression innocent, unaffected, while listening to their secret chatter. Finally, I move back to Drake's side. He wraps his arms around me, lips brushing my forehead.

'Drake, don't react, but I just heard your father escaped a couple of hours ago.'

His grip tightens painfully. *'What in the hell is going on at the castle? Your grandmother is incompetent. She's losing control of Darshia.'*

I force myself not to react. *'Drake, calm down. She's testing me right now, waiting to see if I slip. She wants proof I'm stronger than I've admitted.'*

More security arrive, wheeling in gurneys. The assassins are tagged, bagged, and hauled away, along with the gun and syringe.

Grandma Ma remains, flanked by her guards.

I seize the moment. "Grandma Ma, when I'm cleared to leave the hospital and return to the castle, Drake and I want to interview his father. We have questions."

Her eye twitches. Gotcha. Lies incoming.

I keep my face neutral, but inside, I'm done playing her games. It's time to play by my own rules.

I close my eyes slowly, repeating the motion, feigning exhaustion. Operation Tired Alexia begins. Honestly, I don't even have to act — I am drained.

All I want is to curl into Drake's warm, muscled body, sink my teeth into his enticing neck, and sleep in his arms, safe. Nice thought. Doubt it'll happen.

CHAPTER TWENTY

I MOTION FOR DRAKE TO ESCORT ME BACK TO MY BED. Reaching into his mind, I inform him of my intentions.

'Drake, can you play along, please? Grandma Ma is watching closely. Help me back into bed and hold me. I will start being sleepy and nod off against you while you're holding me tightly against your body.'

Drake turns us toward my bed, guiding me to the side where the sheet and blanket are already pulled back.

'Alexia, what are you up to now? Yes, I'll go along with what you're saying for now as long as you inform me of what is happening — however, I can see you look exhausted. You need sleep, baby.'

I sit down, the cool sheet brushing against my thin hospital gown. I give Drake a sleepy smile, knowing Grandma Ma is watching every move I make. At the same time, I keep my eyes diverted from hers and yawn into my hand.

Out loud, Drake says, "Tired, baby?" His voice is soft, but I catch the steel beneath it. Looking back into his smiling face, I nod. "All this excitement has exhausted you," he continues smoothly, playing his part, "but you still haven't had the chance to have a good afternoon's rest with all these interruptions."

I shake my head no, but truthfully, he's right. I am tired. Worn out. My body aches, my mind feels stretched thin, and I've missed my afternoon's sleep.

Drake picks up the water jug and a clean glass. Wise man. Even I forgot to keep my fluids up. I have to drink to keep my milk supply strong for the twins. My hand drifts to the side of my warm, swollen breast, reminding me of them.

Drake's voice interrupts my thoughts. "Baby, what is with the face?"

Startled, I glance up and smile faintly. "I was just thinking of the twins and how much I miss them. It's time to feed them again."

I wonder if Grandma Ma and her two security men have taken the hint to leave. Somehow, I doubt it.

Drake passes me the glass of water. I drain it quickly, then hand it back. "Drake, can you refill the glass? I must be thirstier than I realised."

He pours another and places it in my hand. I drink again, the room-temperature water sliding down my throat. "Ah, that's better."

Drake sets the empty glass beside the jug, then moves back

to my side. His arms wrap around me, pulling me close. I rest my head against his chest, breathing in his intoxicating scent. Gods, I'll never get enough of that — Drake and his scent.

Once again, Grandma Ma tries to breach my mind shields. Pathetic. At the same time, I'm busy protecting Drake's mind from her. Her power surges, pressing harder, but she still fails. Big fail, Grandma Ma.

I close my eyes, snuggling deeper into Drake. By slipping past his shields, I can see everything he observes. He glances up at the security team and Grandma Ma. All three continue talking as if we're not even in the room.

Yep — feeling the love, Grandma Ma. The rudeness is unbelievable. The attack happened right here in my hospital room. I apprehended the assassins myself. And yet she leaves me out of the conversation, like I'm some fragile doll.

'Drake, keep your shields up. I want to check on something.'

'What are you up to, Alexia?'

'As soon as I know, I'll tell you. Okay, Drake. Now increase your shields, please.'

Drake's embrace tightens around me. His eyes close, and I sense his shields rising, stronger than before.

I let my mind drift outward, brushing against the edges of Grandma Ma's thoughts. She's irritated — her focus is split between me, Drake, and her guards. She's testing me, waiting to see if I slip, waiting to confirm how strong I really am.

I smirk against Drake's chest, hiding it from her view.

Keep testing me, Grandma Ma. You'll find out soon enough that I'm not the weak little girl you think I am.

I REACH OUT WITH MY MIND TO TRACK DOWN THE DOCTOR. Within twenty seconds, I find him still busy attending to his other patients.

'Excuse me, Doctor? Doctor Brean, this is Alexia.'

Sensing the doctor's reaction, his body stiffens, hearing my voice. His head whips around in search of me, eyes darting like he expects me to materialise in front of him.

I reassure him quickly. *'Please don't be alarmed.'*

'Alexia, wow. Your Dark One powers are increasing,' the doctor pauses, his thoughts buzzing with curiosity. *'Hmm. This is...interesting. Fascinating indeed, that we can communicate like this.'*

I roll my eyes mentally. I don't have time for his scientific commentary. *'I need to speak with you.'*

'If I'm not mistaken, Alexia, you do not wish your Grandma Ma to know about our private chat?'

'That is correct, Doctor. Grandma Ma is still standing in my room with her security, and they are not leaving yet.'

'What is it you wish to speak to me about?'

'How do I arrange for Drake and myself to have our soulmate Joining Ceremony? And to be officially married. Who do I need to discuss this with? And please do not say Grandma Ma, because Drake and I would like to complete the Joining Ceremony as soon as possible without her knowing or attending if possible.'

The doctor's thoughts ripple with surprise. *'Alexia, you are in luck. The authorising ceremony priest is here in the hospital. Your timing is impeccable, as he has been busy with another couple who wished to Join today. Plus, I have the documentation required on my desk. Sometimes, we must perform the ritual here at the hospital, as we had to for this other couple.'*

I cut him off, sharp and urgent. *'Doctor, my parents are in the nursery with the twins. Can you give them the paperwork to fill out on our behalf?'*

'That is great, Alexia. We should not have any problems. Once I have the completed documentation, with your parents and the ceremony priest signing off on it, we should be set to go. Thankfully, Drake is an adult under Darshia law and doesn't need his parents' approval.

'Good. One less thing to worry about. My major concern is Grandma Ma. Oh, and what about a wedding ceremony?'

'Alexia. By law, the Queen is not required to attend. However, most Dark One couples feel it is part of the ceremony to have the Queen attend their ceremonies. We should be able to perform the wedding and Joining Ceremony ritual after your grandmother leaves the hospital.'

My mind floods with relief. Finally — good news. Drake and I can be married, complete our Joining Ceremony, and finish becoming Dark Ones, all without Grandma Ma interrupting. Once everything is complete, I will finally be able to embrace my full powers. Stronger. Faster. Able to heal quicker. And maybe, just maybe, less of a target for assassins.

I refocus on the doctor. *'Doctor, how soon do you think you will hand the documentation to my parents and speak privately and confidentially with the authorising ceremony priest?'*

'I'll finish my rounds in five minutes. Get all the required paperwork and meet your parents in the nursery. I will also contact the ceremony priest to inform him I wish to speak to him regarding another matter.'

Surely it cannot be that easy to organise? My paranoia whispers otherwise.

'Okay, that would be great if you could arrange the necessary documents with my parents. I feel Drake and I need to move quickly on this matter. Thank you, Doctor. Keep in touch.'

'Alexia, I will go to your room to assess your medical status soon. I have heard there was another attempt on your life. Your grandmother contacted me, recommending the rest of the medical staff, including me, to stay clear of your room for a certain amount of time. We have been waiting for her to give us the all-clear to continue our duties on your level.'

What? Geez. Alexettia really over-dramatises everything. The assassins were dragged out ten minutes ago, and she's still playing queen of theatrics.

I bite back a sarcastic laugh, keeping my face neutral against Drake's chest. Of course, Grandma Ma wants the staff to stay away. Less chance for anyone to notice her little power games. Less chance for me to get help without her interference.

But now I have a plan. And if Doctor Brean moves quickly, Drake and I might just outmaneuver the Queen herself.

'Doctor, I give you my permission to continue. My grandmother is standing here talking to her security; nothing else is happening. I feel fatigued, but apprehending two assassins can do that to you.'

Another yawn escapes me, and I cover my mouth, slowly opening my eyes again. The movement stirs Drake, and I sense him opening his eyes as well.

I quickly say goodbye to the doctor, then scan my surroundings. Grandma Ma and one of her security men are still here, while another castle Royal guard has slipped away.

Oops. My bad. I really need to pay closer attention to my surroundings.

Tilting my head back, I look up at Drake's face and give him a sleepy smile. "Hey, baby. Have I missed much?"

With my mind, I ask him, *'Babe, when did the other guard leave?'*

Drake squeezes me gently, brushing his lips against my hair. "Hello, sleepyhead. No, you haven't missed a thing. Unless you call one of the Royal Guards leaving... something to miss?"

He kisses my head again, and my eyes flutter closed at his touch. Gods, I'm more tired than I thought. My body demands sleep — before the twins wake for their next feed.

Drake's voice slides into my mind. *'Alexia, they're up to something. I just don't know what yet. These three rude people refuse to tell us about my father escaping. I feel like a sitting duck with no protection.'*

I agree. It's time to update him. *'Drake, I've spoken to the doctor. He will arrange for a ceremony priest to attend us and perform the wedding and Dark One Joining Ceremonies as soon as Grandma Ma leaves the hospital.'*

Drake's lips linger against my head, his arms tightening around me. *'Oh, Alexia. That is fantastic news. I cannot wait to marry you and call you my wife. The four of us will be a*

family — living together: you, me, and the twins. And the
twins can have my surname as well.'

Ha. I was going to put his surname on their birth
certificates regardless. Drake senses my reaction.

'Alexia, according to Darshia law, the babies can only have
my name if — and only if — we are legally married.'

Well, okay then. That answers that. Harsh, but it forces
responsibility. Time to deal with the old dragon.

I force my heavy eyes open and peer at Grandma Ma.
"Grandma Ma, what is happening? Where did the other
security man go?"

She stops mid-conversation, raising her manicured
eyebrow. "Alexia, you look tired, little one. I think it is time
for you to sleep before the twins wake for their next feed." Her
condescending tone grates on my nerves. "It is time for us to
depart and leave you alone to rest."

She flicks a glance at her head of security, then at Drake.
Oh no. I can already hear her thoughts directed at him —
annoying, possessive, and dripping with entitlement.

"Drake, I would have thought you would be down at the
nursery by now and give Alexia a break from your
presence."

The words leave my mouth before I can stop them, loud
and sharp. "That is rude to say, Grandma Ma. Drake knows I
sleep better when his arms are holding me. Plus, the nursery
staff will either phone us when the twins are awake or bring
them here for feeding."

She's not used to anyone talking back. She takes a step back, startled. Geez, was I that loud?

Drake's mind brushes mine, amused. *'Alexia, wow. That was… wow! And great all at the same time. It hurt her to hear the bit about you being wrapped in my arms.'*

I stare down at Grandma Ma, waiting for her venom. I know she wants to lash out. But no — she keeps her mask elegant and poised, though I can feel her seething underneath. Her thoughts are nasty, vicious, aimed squarely at me.

The woman doesn't even know if she wants Drake as her lover or locked in the dungeon. Geez, can she give it a rest?

"Grandma Ma, I reckon it's time you filled me in on what's going on. My life's becoming the target for assassins. Why are they after me? No one should know I'm here in Darshia — or that I'm your granddaughter."

I lift my eyebrow, keeping my face passive. Meanwhile, her inner commentary is so foul it makes me want to hand her a bar of soap.

"Come on, Grandma Ma. I want to hear your reasons for the assassins targeting me, and the interrogation with Drake's father. I'm becoming a Dark One and a princess of your royal family. Therefore, I request you keep me informed."

I take a slow breath, steadying myself. "Oh, and I'm not bothering to mind talk with you. Drake has a right to hear what's happening. This affects him too. He is my fiancé and the father of my babies."

My lips curve into a smile at the thought of the twins.

Grandma Ma snorts, dragging my gaze back to her. "Oh,

please, Alexia. Do you think I will believe you have not tried to gain access to my thoughts while I've been in this room?"

Ha. I like how she said tried. She's fishing. Testing me. I won't bite.

"Back off, Grandma Ma. Even if I could gain access to your thoughts, why would I right now? I need time to recover and heal from the ordeal I've been through. That's why I asked you verbally. I want answers. Otherwise, leave so I can sleep, and I'll see you tomorrow."

I turn my head, cuddling back into Drake's chest, closing my eyes as I inhale his scent. It calms me, steadies me.

Her constant pressure against our shields is a pain in the butt. Annoying, but useless. She's not as strong as she thinks. Compared to some of my Dark One abilities, she's already falling behind.

Reminding myself of the doctor's visit to the nursery, I reach out with my mind. It doesn't take long to find my parents. Each attempt gets easier. Breaching Mum's shields, I quickly update her on the doctor's plan and the documents they must fill out.

Once everything is complete, the ceremony can go ahead. And as far as I know, Grandma Ma is still blissfully unaware that both Mum and Dad are here in the hospital with the twins. That's exactly how I want it to stay.

CHAPTER TWENTY-ONE

SHE FEELS SMUG, CONVINCED SHE'S HIDING HER THOUGHTS from me, when in reality she's broadcasting them loud and clear — every slip, every suspicion leaking through her so-called shields, and I catch them all. What I get from the annoying woman's thoughts is that she's determined to catch me out, like I'm some naughty child sneaking cookies. Grandma Ma thinks she's clever, but her mind is basically a radio station I can tune into whenever I want.

I listen to a few of her thoughts as she leaves my hospital room. She'll be busy for the next few hours — questioning the two would-be assassins and meeting with one of her lovers, Zalend. Geez. Too many visual images of the two bombard my mind, and I would have preferred not to know who Zalend was...well, his naked self and the sexual acts he performs. Some things should stay in the "*do not picture*" category. At least I know she'll keep away from Drake for a while. Unfortunately, the obtuse woman refuses to discuss anything with Drake or me. She just walks out, not even bothering to say goodbye. Rude. I follow her energy pattern until she's clear of the hospital grounds.

I speak out loud to Drake in a groggy voice, "She's gone, Drake. I still cannot believe Alexettia will discuss none of this with me. It's as if she doesn't trust me or something?"

Drake laughs at my words. I raise my head and move away from his warm chest, his arms releasing me as I slide down on the bed, snuggling into my pillow, feeling the heaviness of my tired body.

With my back facing the door, I hear someone entering my room. My senses pick up my intruder to be none other than Nurse Sharonia. More exhausted than I thought, I didn't detect her while she was still out in the hall. Her voice captures my attention: "Alexia, before you nod off to dreamland. I'm here to attach the breast pump to extract your excess milk before you come down with mastitis. You're producing more milk than the twins are drinking."

Fantastic. Just what every girl dreams of — industrial suction cups before bedtime. The last thing I want or need is mastitis, so I roll onto my back into the pillows and slowly open my eyes to watch Nurse Sharonia set up the equipment and attach the device to my breasts, then turn it on.

This is the second time Nurse Sharonia has done this today. Okay, now I know why she was here earlier — it was to get everything ready to express milk. Or maybe it was another excuse for Grandma Ma to leave. Chances are, it had more to do with the woman's booty call instead. Priorities, right?

"Drake, I'm going to take a little nap." Another yawn escapes as I feel his warm hand glide gently over my head, then firm, mild pressure on my shoulder, comfort in a small gesture. "Can you go to the nursery and speak with my parents and ensure they've correctly filled out our paperwork? Plus, the twins should wake soon. Can you bring them back here when they do, please?"

Not bothering to open my eyes, I can already sense what Drake sees while he leans forward and kisses my head.

"Alexia, I'll go this time because we have much to do before the ceremonies. Plus, I need to see our babies with my eyes to ensure they're safe." His lips brush my head again. "But I'm not looking forward to seeing your father. That meet and greet — awkward."

My lips curve into a small smile, and a giggle escapes at the thought of Drake and my parents. "Good luck, Drake." Another giggle slips out. "You're going to need it."

Oh boy. When my father first found out I was pregnant… let's just say he wasn't impressed with Drake. Finding out your teenage daughter is pregnant doesn't exactly earn you the "Father of the Year" award. Dad wanted to track down Drake himself and give my lover a good telling off for being so irresponsible. Hopefully, his temper has cooled enough for Drake and me to marry later today without any bloodshed.

"I'll be back soon, baby. Try to get some sleep when you finish expressing." Drake's warm lips press against my head again, followed by his footsteps leading out of my room and down the hall. I hear the whoosh and firm clunk echo around my hospital room as the door closes.

Several minutes later, Nurse Sharonia announces eight filled bottles. She quickly packs away the express pump, gathers the full milk bottles, places them in an insulated bag, and picks up the rest of the equipment for cleaning. With her hands full, she quietly exits my room with everything balanced on the portable trolley. Once again, I hear the whoosh and firm clunk echo around my hospital room as the door closes behind her.

Alone, at last. Silence fills my hospital room, giving me quiet time for a much-needed sleep before everyone arrives for the ceremonies. My thoughts fade off as I fall into a deep sleep.

"Babe, it's time to wake up. Our twins are eager to see you." Ha, what? Drake's voice drags me out of a sound sleep. I roll and stretch, sitting up while I battle to pry open my sleepy eyes. Hearing one of the twins makes me turn my head in that direction.

A smile spreads across my face as soon as my eyes focus on my little boy. "Hey there, handsome. What are you up to?" My voice instantly catches Damien's attention. His big, beautiful eyes open wide, and his baby smile forms like sunshine.

Yep, my boy knows my voice. Talented little man I've got. Damien's gorgeous eyes leave mine and flick back to Drake. Oh yeah, this kid has it all figured out. I can already see his tiny mind at work — knowing full well he can have his father pick him up and deliver him straight into my arms.

Sure enough, Drake leans forward, lifting Damien from his crib and settling him against his muscular chest, carefully supporting his little head. He whispers to our son until he gently places Damien into my waiting arms. A feeling of home and belonging settles inside me the moment I hold him. His baby weight feels comforting, grounding, like he's the missing piece I didn't know I needed.

"Hey there, my little man. I'm so happy to see you. Are you ready for your next feed?" Damien doesn't waste time — he roots around for my bare nipple, and within seconds he's guzzling milk like a champion, releasing the pressure in my breast. I watch him for a while, soaking in the moment, until my eyes lift and start searching for Alley, my daughter.

I frown when I realise she's not in the room. Drake notices my reaction immediately. "Babe, your parents are bringing Alley to your room. The little monkey needed a bath after her nappy change."

Listening to Drake talk about our daughter makes him glow. He's practically bursting with pride as he explains her antics in the nursery.

"Our little girl overflowed her nappy, and it went everywhere. It was a big mess, right down to her adorable, tiny toes. Don't even get me started on the smell." A laugh escapes him as he shakes his head. "I was lucky to escape with this little guy."

Ha, what a cheeky male — dodging the messy stuff while the getting was good. "Is my dad helping Mum with bathing our daughter? Did you take a picture? I would have loved to have seen that."

Drake pulls his phone from his back pocket. After tapping the screen a few times, he moves closer to the bed, holding the screen out so I can zoom in on the photo.

Oh, my... wow. My eyes mist up at the scene before me.

My father is holding my squirming, naked baby daughter over the bathwater in the nursery. His face is lit with love and adoration, smiling down at her like she's the most precious thing in the world. A smile tugs at my lips as warmth floods my chest. Oh my, I love my dad. Just look at him — one very proud grandpa, already wrapped around his granddaughter's tiny fingers.

And here's the kicker: this is the same man who once wanted to wring Drake's neck for knocking me up. The same man who stormed around like a raging bull when he first found out his teenage daughter was pregnant. Now look at him — grinning like a fool, cradling his granddaughter like she's spun from gold. Talk about a turnaround. If I didn't know better, I'd say my dad's already forgotten his threats and traded them in for grandpa bragging rights.

I can't help but laugh softly. "See, Drake? My dad might have wanted to kill you once, but now he's too busy being in love with our daughter, Alley, to remember."

Drake smirks, leaning closer with that panty-dropping grin. "Good thing, too. I'd rather not fight your father in the nursery while holding a baby. Babies are the ultimate get-out-of-trouble card. You can't strangle a man when he's holding their grandson, right?"

I roll my eyes, but the laugh escapes anyway. "Cheeky male. You dodged the messy nappy, and now you're dodging my dad's temper. You're getting far too good at this."

Drake chuckles, brushing his lips against my temple. "Survival skills, babe. You've got to know when to fight and when to hide behind a baby."

CHAPTER TWENTY-TWO

I<small>T ISN'T LONG BEFORE BOTH OF MY PARENTS ARRIVE WITH MY</small> baby daughter, all happy, dry, and clean. Drake continues casually walking back and forth with Damien in his arms, trying to convince the baby boy to go back to sleep after being fed and burped. As soon as baby Alley hears my voice, she demands to be given to her mother. Geez. This kid already has my parents wrapped around her baby fingers — demanding little thing.

After several minutes of feeding, Alley starts to nod off until the little bugger hears my father speak. Instantly awake again, she continues to feed until her belly is full. As soon as Alley finishes, my dad reaches for her, wanting to hold her again.

"Alexia. Here, I'll take Alley. I am mastering the technique of burping her. Wait and watch." His voice is full of pride, like he's just unlocked a new level in the grandparent game. With coolness instantly coating my arms, much too fast, my dad has my daughter upright and snug against his shoulder. Sure enough, a windy burp escapes near his ear. Well, he did say he's mastering the technique of burping Alley.

"Oh, Amelia, I still cannot believe these two gorgeous babies belong to our daughter. I have to keep pinching myself to remind me we are grandparents. Grandparents, Amelia. Grandparents!" Okay, I can understand Dad is still in awe and shock over everything. My mother leans over to him and kisses his cheek, followed by a quick kiss on Alley's head. With the phone in her hand, Mum snaps a few more photos for her growing collection. Dad quietly places a sleeping Alley back in her little portable bed, looking smug like he's just won a medal.

Mum has updated him on everything, so no hidden secrets are ready to jump out at us. No misunderstandings. Even though he hasn't met Grandma Ma yet, he's already informed us he doesn't trust the woman. Well — Dad, that applies to both of us, even though she's technically my long-lost relative. I still haven't figured out if it's just her or all the Dark Ones.

"Dad, believe it or not, I'm having just as hard a time as you. However, these beautiful babies are your grandchildren and my twins. I wasn't contemplating children for a long time, but life can be unpredictable." I look back over both of my sleeping twins with a big, silly grin plastered across my face.

I wonder what Drake is thinking. I've blocked him from my thoughts and me from his, giving each other's minds a break from the constant chatter. Drake catches my eye and taps his head slightly with his finger. Okay, I get it. He wants to talk to me.

Smiling up at Drake, I nod, reaching out with my mind to his. *'Yes, Drake. I'm sorry I blocked you. I thought you'd like some privacy from me, plus I also wanted to give you some time to your thoughts while my parents are in here with us.'*

Drake presents me with one of his panty-dropping smiles — sending erotic tingles through the lower half of my body.

'Thank you, babe, for that. I appreciated the mind-free time to myself. I've been busy thinking and trying different things regarding our future. First off, we need to discuss a few things. One of them is our Joining as Dark One soulmates, a joining to unite us as husband and wife. The doctor will be back here soon and discuss some of the Joining Ceremony with us while your parents take the twins back to the nursery. I love you so much, Alexia. I look forward to our wedding ceremony and finally completing the Joining Ceremony.'

My hormones must be playing up, because my eyes want to mist up.

'I love you too, Drake. I cannot wait until we're finally wed and complete the Joining Ceremony. And stop whatever Grandma Ma has planned.'

Over the next twenty minutes, Mum has Nurse Sharonia take several family photos — different shots, with or without the twins. Nurse Sharonia, thankfully, takes a few of all six of us together. I lose count of how many photos we take, but judging by Mum's grin, she's already planning to wallpaper the house with them.

WHILE MY PARENTS ESCORT THE TWINS BACK TO THE NURSERY, the doctor and priest arrive to discuss what they expect regarding the necessities for both the Wedding Ceremony and — most of all — the shock of what we have to do in the Joining Ceremony.

My first thought? This priest is nothing but a pervert. But after searching his mind first, followed by the doctor's, it becomes apparent they're actually telling the truth. Great. At least with the Joining Ceremony, we'll have a large ceremonial cape draped over and around our naked bodies. But seriously — barbaric doesn't even begin to cover it. Being watched while having sex? That's not a ceremony, that's voyeurism dressed up in fancy robes.

And then there's the condom. Or rather, the Condeam. Outrageous doesn't even begin to describe it. The Condeam doesn't prevent pregnancy — it's basically a magical receipt of our lovemaking. Proof we've done the deed. Drake's orgasm breaks the tip of the Condeam, releasing his semen, and voilà: evidence of our Joining. Followed by the both of us biting, taking, and consuming one another's blood. Romantic, right? Nothing says "soulmates forever" like bodily fluids and ceremonial paperwork.

Once we finish, the Ceremony Priest approaches us, collects the broken, wet Condeam like it's some sacred artifact, and announces, "The Joining has been completed." He then leaves the room with the other witnesses, leaving Drake and me alone. At least we'll know — we're officially joined as Dark One soulmates, which is the main thing.

So basically, no pressure! Just perform under a cape, break a magical condom, bleed a little, and smile for the priest. Easy.

Honestly, I wouldn't be surprised if this priest has a drawer somewhere full of *"holy used Condeams"* he's collected over the years. Imagine him cataloguing them like trophies — "Ah yes, the 200th Joining, still sticky with destiny." Ugh. The thought alone makes me want to gag.

The doctor assures me that because of my Dark One nature and the amount of Drake's blood I've consumed so far, my body has already recovered from the twins' pregnancy and birth. Doctor Brean says my body is equal to a woman's postnatal six-month body. Thank goodness for small mercies. At least I won't collapse mid-ceremony.

When I scan their minds before the doctor and priest leave my hospital room, I discover that my Dark One powers and new unique ability will only be fully activated on the condition that I conceive the next Princess of Darshia. Funny how they conveniently left that part out during their little lecture — no mention that I'll have to carry the next heir to inherit my full and any extra Dark One abilities. Only the next queen gets the full package, apparently.

So while they're busy droning on about capes, Condeams, and ceremonial blood-sharing, they skip the fine print: Congratulations, Alexia, you're not just a bride — you're also the designated baby factory for Darshia's future queen. Typical. Men in robes always forget to mention the part that actually matters until I dig into their minds myself.

That little hidden clause will transform me into one of the strongest beings in Darshia. Okay, if I end up even half as powerful as Grandma Ma, I might actually survive living here one day. But still — would've been nice if someone had said it out loud instead of leaving me to play psychic detective.

CHAPTER TWENTY-THREE

AFTER A QUICK SHOWER IN THE PREPARATION SUITE NEAR THE
hospital chapel, I apply light makeup, and Mum styles my
hair. Once I'm ready, she assists me into my knee-length satin
sheath dress with a high laced neck and sleeveless appliqué.

I love it. The bodice hugs my ribs and chest, framing my
high, full, milk-laden breasts and showing off my slim waist.
The back of the dress, even though it's lace, is see-through
enough to flaunt the low cut down to the rise of my backside
— my back exposed through the gap in the lace.

The whole dress feels light and wispy, like I've been cast
as some fairy princess. We gather most of my hair up in the
back, leaving a few twirling wisps at the sides to frame my
face. My veil sets everything off: elbow length, two layers of
tulle edged with lace appliqué, short in the front and long in
the back. Mum keeps wiping her eyes, happy tears spilling at
the sight of me in bridal finery.

Before we leave the preparation suite and walk the short

distance through the hospital gardens to the chapel, Mum asks me to sit down. The look on her face worries me, but soon I realise she's just nervous.

"Alexia, I wanted to show you something. I've had something that belonged to our family since before Allasett ran away from Darshia to start her new life with her human husband."

Okay, Mum has my full attention now. What could she have that belonged to my great-grandmother Allasett? Is it something old? Something borrowed? Something blue? My excitement spikes. Come on, Mum, show me.

Without another word, Mum rifles through her handbag and draws out a small black leather jewellery box. Placing her bag on the table beside me, she meets my eyes with a sparkly smile.

"Alexia, what I'm about to show you has been in our family for a long time. Each generation is told what this box contains. It hasn't been worn since before Allasett escaped Darshia all those years ago. The items in this box belong to the rightful Princess of Darshia and can only be worn by the next in line for the throne. The next Queen, the Queen of Darshia."

Mum slowly picks up my left hand, raises it before her, and smiles again. Geez, now I'm nervous. "Once you're wed and the items in this box are on your body, followed by the Joining Ceremony with your soulmate, the items cannot be removed until your daughter is ready to wear them. You must decide if you can take responsibility for such items. The ability of your Dark One powers will increase and enhance with these items. Do you think you can handle the responsibility that comes with it?"

Oh, wow. That sounded straight out of Spiderman. With great power comes great responsibility. Do I feel scared or privileged right now? Both. But I've come too far to back out. This opportunity is my birthright, and I'm here to stay. Well… after I finish high school, of course.

"Mum, you're just about scaring the crap out of me. But saying that, I'd be honoured to wear whatever's in that box. To wear it until my daughter is ready to wear it."

Slowly, Mum opens the box. Inside are two beautiful gold jewelled rings. One is a wedding band with diamonds and sapphires inlaid in the band. The other is an engagement ring — not ordinary at all. This one carries the royal crest among the stone settings, crowned with a huge princess-cut white diamond. Antique, immaculate, and breathtaking.

Looking back up at Mum's misty eyes and radiant smile, I see how proud she is just to show me these rings.

"Alexia, someone told me the diamonds and surrounding stones were charmed with special powers for the rightful wearer." Huh? Charmed? Special powers? Is it even safe to wear them? "When I returned home after leaving here, I had the rings professionally cleaned and valued. These two rings contain authentic, rare precious stones. So don't lose them."

She digs into her handbag again, pulls out another ring box, and opens it. Oh, my… wow. Inside is another antique-looking ring, a matching male band to the princess set.

"This is the ring for your husband. Allasett took them when she left Darshia, but she never sold them. She wanted one of her female descendants to wear them one day. Alexia, that day is today — with you."

I'm speechless. All I can do is nod, eyes misting, throat tight.

Mum must realise I can't speak, so she closes both boxes and places them back inside her handbag. Wow. That's all I can manage right now.

Then my mind flashes to Alexettia — how she questioned us about her daughter, how she checked our hands, running her thumb over our fingers while holding them. Oh my gods. She was checking to see if we had worn these rings, or if the stones had been reset elsewhere. My mind races. What are her motives?

I bet she was searching for them when she went to my hometown. No wonder Grandma Ma was unsuccessful in finding them — the rings were at the jeweller's. Drake and I better get this wedding ceremony underway, because something tells me Grandma Ma wants these rings back, and she'll try anything to get them.

For Allasett to leave, something big must have happened. What is my grandmother really up to? And most of all, what does it mean for Drake and me?

Okay, Alexia. Focus. Wedding and Joining Ceremonies. With my next breath, I inhale deeply, hold, and exhale.

DETERMINED TO CHANGE THE TOPIC, I THINK OF SOMETHING silly, and my old friend Lucy comes to mind — what she would say right now. I picture her here with me, in one of her light-flowing dresses with a low-cut V in the front and a split running up the side, right to her naked thigh. Her long dark hair frames her high, perky breasts and tiny waist. Her violet eyes sparkle while she talks with that cheeky smile.

One of her annoying sayings from the few weeks before she left echoes in my head: "What in the world, girl, are you craz-zy. But then, if I had myself some of that Drake boy, I would shine him like a new penny." Yep, that girl needed a filter for her potty mouth. Still, I love her like a sister.

It broke my heart when her family sent her away over a month before we finished school for another term. I don't know what really happened — one day she was here, the next, poof. Gone. I never even got to say goodbye. It's just sad I can't have her here by my side today. Our old motto — Live Your Dream — repeats in my head. All our dreams for the future are gone now. My old life is forever gone, and my new paranormal one has begun.

Smiling up at Mum, I reach out to her with my hand. "Come on, Mum, we have a wedding to attend, and I have a bridegroom to Join with."

Mum has her phone busy with the camera feature, snapping two quick photos of me, then one of us together. She reaches forward, grabs my hand, and helps pull me up from my seat on the padded stool. We walk out of the preparation suite, nervous in anticipation of what's about to happen.

The hospital gardens stretch before us, trimmed and perfect, but my stomach is a mess of knots. Every step toward the chapel feels heavier, like the air itself knows what's coming. Mum squeezes my hand, her smile brave but her eyes still misty. I force myself to breathe, to keep moving, because this is it — the moment everything changes.

THE HOSPITAL GARDENS AND CHAPEL COULD NOT BE MORE beautiful. Roses bloom alongside other flowers I can't even name, their foliage lush and magnificent. Some type of large dark green leafy shrubs — plants I've never seen before — line the path. At least the fragrance isn't overpowering; the last thing I need is sneezing my way down the aisle.

Dad meets us at the open double doorway of the chapel, dressed in a black three-piece suit, looking very handsome. Sure enough, Mum snaps a few pics of him, dashing in his suit. As she walks up to him, I notice her pass both ring boxes to him, followed by a quick, passionate kiss.

"Never. Never give up," Mum says with a smile and a wink toward me. "You can still live your dream, Alexia." I frown, wondering what she's trying to say.

She quickly snaps more photos of Dad and me. "I'll see you both inside." Then she turns and walks into the chapel, leaving Dad and me alone.

"Well, my gorgeous little princess, your mother is correct. Never give up, and you can still live your dream. As an eager eight-year-old, I remember you telling me how you would marry Drake one day. Now look — today is the day I get to give you away. So if you want to change your mind, let me know now, and we can get out of here and never come back, or we can make our way inside and put Drake out of his nervous, worried misery."

Hearing Dad laugh, I think he enjoys seeing Drake sweat. "Daddy, don't be mean. I love him, and don't forget he's the father of your grandchildren."

Uh-oh. The happy look on Dad's face shifts instantly. "Do not remind me of what Drake has already done, Alexia. He has much to make up for. I will not forgive him in a hurry for his carelessness. And yes, I know it takes two, but he is the male. After all, he should have used protection every time."

Oh boy. Awkward conversation alert. "Yes, Daddy, we both know that. But as you know, things happen. And it just happened to be twins for me. Come on, let's go. We have a wedding to attend, and you have a bride to give away."

With that, I lean toward my handsome father and place a quick kiss on his smooth-shaven cheek. He gathers himself, pulls down the front of my bridal veil over my eager face, and offers his arm. I take it, and together we step into the chapel — toward my new husband-to-be, and toward my new life.

CHAPTER TWENTY-FOUR

THE SOFT SOUNDS OF DIAMONDS AND PEARLS BY PRINCE sweep through the cathedral ceilings from the speakers positioned high above. Hearing the lyrics reinforces just how much I love Drake — and how much he loves me.

Dad sets the pace as we slowly walk from the entrance past the long twin lines of hardwood bench seating. Walking down the aisle, I glance up toward the front and lock eyes with Drake. He stands tall in a black tuxedo, and my mouth waters. Yum. How did I manage to end up with this sexy specimen of a man?

Drake flashes me his panty-dropping smile. The space between my thighs overheats. Damn the man. He should not do things like that to me in front of my parents.

We join Drake, my mother, the doctor, and the priest of ceremonies at the front of the altar. The music lowers in volume, and my father turns, lifts my bridal veil, kisses my cheek, and places my hand into Drake's larger one. His palm is cool and clammy. Dad moves to stand beside Mum, reaching for her hand.

Whatever the priest is saying goes right over my head. I'm too busy drowning in Drake's eyes to pay attention.

Pressure brushes against my mind shields. Drake wants to speak to me. *'Hey, baby, are you even listening to the priest? Because your beauty blinds me, and anything else seems irrelevant. I want to lift you, place you upon that stone altar, and make love to you with my mouth.'*

Moisture pools awkwardly between my thighs. *'Drake Smithlyn. You have to stop doing that. You're making me wet, and everyone is going to know.'*

Right. Two can play this game. I smile back at him. *'Drake, baby. I want you between my thighs, filling me…'*

His eyebrow lifts, his smile widens. *'Oh yeah, I can go for filling you up right now.'*

Grrr. Drake. My imagination runs fast and hard, especially with him between my thighs, enticing my body to fly to the moon. My lungs expand slowly, my breathing calms, and the visions fade. He's pushing every sexual button I have, making me react unladylike in front of my parents.

'Sto… stop it, Drake. We're here to be married. We need to save all this pent-up frustration for the Joining Ceremony. Which I still feel this priest guy is a pervert!'

Drake's face shifts slightly at the priest's comment. *'Yeah, I agree with you there. I'm keeping an eye on this priest guy.'*

A throat clears. Our attention snaps back. Everyone is watching us.

Oops. Busted.

I glance toward the ceremony priest. Uh-oh. He does not look happy. His glare is pure reprimand, like we're misbehaving children.

What did he just say? Something about vows? Oh wow. Are we already up to the vows? Oops.

Dad passes the rings to Drake. I see him nervous, trying to smile his thanks to Dad before turning his head toward me, throat busy swallowing. Hmm. Drake is more affected by this wedding ceremony than he lets on. After today, we'll be Mr and Mrs Smithlyn.

The ceremonial priest speaks to Drake in a loud, clear voice, asking him to repeat the words after him. Meeting Drake's eyes, I see his love shine from their depths. His lips move, forming the words I love you with a smile. I mouth back, *I love you, too.*

I focus on Drake, watching his handsome face transform with his trademark panty-dropping smile. The priest's voice fades into background noise. I keep my eyes locked on my best friend.

WITH A WINK, DRAKE PROCEEDS TO REPEAT THE WORDS required for our vows. "I, Prince Drake Davelt Smithlyn of

Red Darkness, take you, Princess Alexia Amelia Brioni Steele of Blue Darkness, to be my wife, my partner and best friend for now and for eternity. To have and to hold from this day forward. I give you myself and my unending love and devotion. I always promise to be true to you, cherish you, and share my thoughts, hopes, and dreams."

Lifting my left hand, Drake slides the rings onto my finger as he speaks. "Wear this ring as a symbol of my love for you. I will love you until my last breath. You are my life, soul, blood, and heart. I look forward to spending the rest of my life with you, my best friend. I will continue to love you until my last day."

That was so romantic. Oh... wow. Hang on a minute... What the? Drake — a prince? What...? Since when? Confusion overrides my brain; nothing makes sense. Trying to process this little bombshell is not happening. Prince — since when? Prince of Red Darkness? Oh, crap on a stick.

Looking up into Drake's face, I see the concern written there, feel his presence in my mind.

'Babe. Are you okay? You seem a little stunned. Much to my so-called father's disgust, I thought you knew I was a Prince.' Hurt and anguish wash across his face with each word. 'My lineage comes down from my father's side of the family. Didn't your grandmother explain all this to you when she was filling you in on the failed wedding attempt between our families with her daughter Allasett and my great-great-great-grandfather Devialyn?'

Drake, a prince from his father's side!

Oh boy. Does this change anything? No. I still love Drake. His father doesn't want him, so I know he won't be able to influence Drake. The main thing is that Drake is our twins' father, and I want the four of us to become a legal family.

Shaking my head slightly, I reply through our mind link, *'Drake, no, I knew nothing about your father's side of the family being part of a royal family or you being a prince. Something else my so-called grandmother has kept from me. At least we both know we're part of a prominent royal family!'* I try to smile, to prove to him everything is still okay. *'Just remember, Drake, I love you.'*

Turning my head, I listen to the Ceremony Priest carefully.

My father passes me the ring for Drake. I smile in thanks at my dad before I turn and face the man I love, my soulmate, meeting his eyes as I repeat my vows. "I, Princess Alexia Amelia Brioni Steele, Princess of Blue Darkness, take you, Prince Drake Davelt Smithlyn of Red Darkness, to be my husband for now and eternity, to continue to be your best friend. I promise to be true to you, cherish you, and share my hopes and dreams with you and a royal throne."

Smiling at Drake, I lift his hand and slide the wedding ring onto his finger, repeating, "Wear this ring as a symbol of my love and my decision to join my life with yours until death should ever part us. I will love you until my last breath. You are my life, my soul, and my blood. Stand by me as my equal." And I add, "Assist me to guide and teach our children to be the best they can be. We'll raise them to be kind and respectful to each other and toward other people. For that one day when they will follow in our footsteps."

Smiling at Drake, I hear him quietly say, "Right back at you, babe. My love, my beloved, we'll try to be the best parents and teach our children to be considerate and thoughtful and not to hate. We'll be there for their milestones and to help them through all their problems."

Drake smiles back at me once again. I nod in agreement, and then we both turn our faces toward the ceremony priest.

"Today, we stand here to witness as Princess Alexia and Prince Drake have spoken their vows and declared their love for one another. We have seen them place a ring on each other's hand, symbolising their love and commitment while declaring to one another. I will now declare them husband and wife."

Seeing the ceremony priest smile at us is a little unnerving. I glance back at Drake and hear the priest say, "Prince Drake, you may kiss your bride."

My thoughts — exactly, and about time — as my lips meet Drake's warm, moist, tender ones in a kiss that grows into a heated, passionate kiss, sending erotic sensations throughout my body. Everything around us fades. Oh no. My mind is going blank again. Damn Drake and his highly passionate, toe-curling, panty-soaking kisses.

AFTER SIGNING ALL THE NECESSARY WEDDING CEREMONY paperwork, we can finally say that Drake and I are legally married. Mum keeps herself busy taking photos. The way she keeps clicking, I think she's just about filled the memory card on her phone. At least we'll have photo proof of everything: the ceremony, the rings, the kiss, the registry, the chapel. Mum has taken a picture of almost everything.

I love my mum.

Big, strong, warm arms wrap around me from behind, and warm lips brush against my nape.

"Babe, it's time to go. We have a Joining Ceremony to complete." Drake's voice quietly fills my ear, sending little shivers down my spine.

"Okay. Just let me say goodbye to Mum and Dad. They might as well take the twins back to the castle for us. Doctor Brean said before I came here, the twins are thriving. He doesn't see a problem with them leaving the hospital and has signed off on their release paperwork." Turning in Drake's arms, I look into his gorgeous eyes. "Drake, do you know where we're meant to go for the Joining Ceremony?"

Drake brushes his lips against mine, tempting me for more. "Yes, Babe. I spoke with the doctor and the ceremony priest before you arrived at the chapel and had everything organised and prepared. Everything is waiting for us to arrive in an undisclosed location. We'll go to a different part of the hospital as soon as we leave here."

What? Undisclosed location? Before I can question him, Mum and Dad walk up with huge smiles, giving us more hugs and congratulations.

"Welcome to the family, Drake," Mum says, smiling at him. "Now we understand we're to go back to the nursery. The twins are going to be released today. Brian and I will take them back to the castle with the expressed milk and wait for you to arrive. I understand the Joining Ceremony will start soon. We better let you both go. Happy Joining Ceremony, and good luck."

Sure enough, Mum has to give us another hug each, lingering her tight hold on me with whispered words in my ear: "Never forget, Alexia, your father and I love you."

"Thank you, Mum. Now go — Dad is eager to get back to the twins. I think he's missing them as much as I am." I smile at Dad, knowing he listens to every word I say. Instead of talking, he gives me a wink, reaches for Mum's hand, and walks off, just about dragging her behind him.

I watch them disappear down the hall, my heart tugging toward the twins even as anticipation coils in my stomach. The wedding is done. The vows are spoken. Now comes the Joining Ceremony — the part that will bind Drake and me forever, body and soul.

CHAPTER TWENTY-FIVE

It isn't long before Drake and I emerge into a part of the hospital reserved primarily for the Joining Ceremonies. Even though this section is kept low-key, each suite is tucked away in an undisclosed area. I'm not sure if that's a good thing or a bad thing. My mind struggles to come to terms with something so serious being held in a hospital — why here? Can something bad happen?

We enter our suite for the ceremony. I glance around the room, taking in the fancily dressed bed piled with red, black, and gold-coloured pillows. Black silk covers the bed, rose petals sprinkled across it like some honeymoon suite from a high-end hotel. There's even a kitchenette tucked in the corner. The only difference — the large framed mirror opposite the bed, curtains pulled to either side. I bet that's where the ceremony priest and doctor will watch us to confirm the Joining.

Drake notices the direction of my gaze and moves quickly,

shutting the curtains over the mirror by hitting a red button on the wall.

Ha. My lips twitch as I mentally laugh at his action. That'll stop the old perv from sneaking a peek before he's supposed to.

Before this Joining Ceremony goes any further, I reach out with my mind to check on Mum and the twins. Relief washes over me when I sense they're safe and fast asleep again. Next, I scan for Grandma Ma. Drake and I don't need any surprises from her. For once, she's busy — entertained by her lover in her room. That leaves us free to continue.

Something catches my attention, and I glance back toward the mirror. Above it, a flash of red light starts blinking. A crackling noise follows, then the booming voice of the ceremony priest fills the room, making me jump. Shite. Is he trying to scare the crap out of me?

I look at Drake. His face shows pure annoyance, one hand balled into a fist. Yep, he's not happy either.

"Princess Alexia, and, Prince Drake, you will have thirty minutes to shower and dress in the ceremonial gown. Once you are both on the bed and ready, and the Condeam in place, hit the green button on the wall beside the bed to open the curtains and allow us to witness you both in the process of the Joining. Once you have completed the joining, Drake, we will require you to place the Condeam on the ceremonial plate for our inspection."

How far-fetched is this whole situation? I swear this guy gets off on watching. He probably believes he has the right to turn Darshia's young couples into his personal porn show. He's sick. Mentally sick. My body shudders at the thought. Oh

Gods. How embarrassing and stressful it is to be watched having sex by this man and the doctor.

The aggravating voice continues: "If everything is the way it should, we will acknowledge by saying out loud, 'The Joining of Princess Alexia and Prince Drake is now complete.' We will complete the last part of the Joining Ceremony documentation, and the doctor can lodge it on your behalf."

My eyes meet Drake's, eyebrow lifted. So, the doctor submits the paperwork, not the priest. Hmm. Interesting.

"The two of you must stay here in this suite for at least twenty-four hours for your Dark One powers to come into full effect. After this time frame, the doctor will return to perform some tests on you, Princess Alexia. He will give you both a copy of your documentation and your certificate of marriage and joining. When you are both given the go-ahead, you will be free to leave the ceremony suite."

Geez. The urge to climb onto the bed, cover my head, and hide from this bloke grows stronger with every word. Seriously, can he waffle on any more or be even more embarrassing? At least Doctor Brean explained everything earlier today, but hearing the priest drone on and on... Grrr. He's wasting our thirty minutes.

I reach out with my hand to Drake, glance toward the open bathroom door. He slips his fingers into mine, and I tug him behind me as I walk to the bathroom.

SHUTTING THE BATHROOM DOOR BEHIND US, DRAKE SIGHS AT the quietness of the tiled room, finally freeing us from the aggravating drone of the priest. I slip off my high-heeled sandals, relieving my aching feet of the pressure they've been under, wiggling my toes to get the blood pumping again. Carefully, I disentangle my veil from my hair, dropping the white fabric against the wall. It slides down the tiles into a pile of tulle and lace.

Looking back at Drake, my smile grows wide as I watch this handsome hunk of a sexy specimen slowly, enticingly undress in front of me. Hmm mmm. He's mine — all mine — and only mine. And he's my sexy, brand-new husband. Ha. That's going to take some getting used to my new title — Mrs. Smithlyn.

Each movement, each removal of clothing, is in rhythm with his own beat of music, most likely playing inside his head. I watch his gorgeous, muscle-toned body and remember exactly what Drake can do with it. Oh yes, how well indeed.

Okay, enough of my fantasies. We don't have time to waste. I turn and present Drake with my back — the fun task of untying my dress. I try to sound seductive over my shoulder. "Drake, baby, can you untie my dress for me, please? I cannot see what I need to do…"

I smile when I feel him come up behind me, wrapping his arms around me. His warm lips press against my shoulder, followed by gentle kisses upon my bare skin, goosebumps rising instantly.

"I can do more than that, babe. Have I told you today how beautiful you looked walking down the aisle? You are one hot bride, Alexia. If we didn't have to worry about this Joining Ceremony, I'd have you stripped naked and pressed against this tiled wall, with your legs wrapped around my waist, while

I fill you up balls deep. Hearing you moan and scream your pleasure when I make you orgasm over and over again."

If my underwear was dry before, they definitely aren't now. Gods, I want this sexy-as-sin man to fill me up and take me every way possible. It might be possible to orgasm from his words alone.

"Oh Gods, Drake. Please hurry and undress me. We need to be in that shower and on the bed, ready. If I turn around before then, I'll jump your gorgeous, sexy body."

I glance over my shoulder toward his face and catch his panty-dropping smile, the up-to-no-good twinkle in his eye. Oh no. I know that look.

"It is time for your shower, Mrs. Smithlyn. Now, be a good girl, and I might wash your hair and make you cum with my mouth."

My eyes want to roll back in my head, my knees debating whether they'll keep me standing. My panties are far beyond wet now. Oh yeah, I'm looking forward to his talented tongue.

DRAKE'S EYES LOCK ON MINE, HUNGER BURNING THERE, AND for a moment I forget the ridiculous ceremonial gown, the ticking clock, and the priest waiting behind the curtain. All I feel is him — his presence, his heat, his focus entirely on me.

My breath stutters as he lowers himself between my thighs, not touching yet, just hovering, teasing, making me ache with anticipation. The gown pools around my waist, heavy fabric contrasting with the vulnerability of my bare skin.

The absurdity of it all hits me — rose petals, silk sheets, a hidden audience waiting for proof of our Joining. My sarcastic inner voice mutters, 'Congratulations, Alexia, you're starring in the priest's favourite reality show.' But then Drake's hand slides up my thigh, grounding me, reminding me this isn't about them. It's about us.

"Babe," he whispers against my skin, voice low and rough, "forget them. Forget the mirror. This is us, and our time to Join to be together forever."

And I do, especially feeling Drake's warm tongue glide through my folds. Each enticing swipe sends me higher. My breathing quickens with each suck of his mouth, each nibble from his teeth, and every thrust of his tongue. His mouth is a talent for any gold medal performance. My eyes roll back as my orgasm shatters my mind, my knees buckle, and Drake catches me. My knight. My protector. And now my legally wedded husband.

AFTER OUR EROTIC SHOWER AS HUSBAND AND WIFE, DRAKE and I step out of the bathroom wrapped in the ceremonial gowns. The heavy satin fabric clings to us, concealing nothing but our bare skin underneath. My eyes flick to the clock on the wall — my stomach tightens — only a few minutes left before the priest demands the curtain be drawn for his inspection. The thought makes me shudder. The old pervert.

Drake assists me on the bed, my back pressing against the mattress, my damp hair pooling around my head. My toes are barely touching the floor. I turn my head to the side and notice the turned-down bedding on one side of the bed, exposing the fresh sheets. Great, someone has been in here while Drake and I were in the bathroom. Geez, this place is annoyingly frustrating and has boundary issues regarding someone's privacy. Talk about overstepping the privacy rule.

Leaving the ceremony gown on, I lift the front of it up over my open legs, exposing my thighs as the gown slowly makes its way up to my naked waist. Allowing Drake to see my bare pussy, he has reminded me a few times how he prefers the feel of my smooth, hair-free skin. Personally, I prefer to have it waxed, clean, and smooth. Not having to worry about my bikini line or anything hanging or poking out, or making sure it is kept trimmed when wearing skimpy or lace underwear. Plus, I find it is more hygienic this way as well.

Drake's eyes zero in on my eager, naked pussy. His tongue brushes his lips, and a sexual hunger increases in his eyes.

Before I can breathe in a breath, he makes his way between my naked thighs, lifting and spreading them wide, the heat of his breath washes over my sensitive skin. His warm, moist tongue slowly swipes between my folds. My breath catching in my throat, my back arching off the bed and my centre reaching for his mouth, seeking his deliciously talented tongue with each manipulative swipe, spreading my sensitive, inflamed wet folds, opening them up like petals of a flower.

"Oh, my Gods, Drake. Don't stop; this feels far too good, baby. Oh, yes. Right there. Harder... More of that. Yes." Okay, my brain is about to fail on every level. Coherent thoughts have left the building.

With Drake sending my body into a utopia overload,

nothing else matters; nothing else exists. Oh, my Gods, I am about to… "Drake, I'm …cumming," I scream.

Drake quickly moves his body over mine and thrusts forward. With my heart racing and the air rushing out of my lungs, all my brain function ceases; it no longer exists. My quivering flesh is pulsating around Drake's hard, thick steel length, not wanting to let him escape my pulsing, wet flesh.

The next thing my brain finally registers is the room moving. Or maybe that is me. As for when I open my eyes, I'm staring straight into Drake's. Nearly level with his eyes, feeling my long damp hair loose down my gown-covered back, which means I am sitting up. Quickly surveying what had just happened, somehow I am straddling Drake's lap. Both of our ceremony gowns were positioned in a way, that no one, would be able to see what was going on underneath.

Rolling my hips a little, I confirm for myself, that Drake is fully embedded inside me and filling me whole with his engorged heated flesh. With a quick roll of my hips again, I notice something feels slightly different. Then it hits me, *the Condeam*. Drake must be wearing the Condeam. Drake lifts his eyebrow, at the same time I feel his length start to pulse. Okay. He is ready for action, but am I?

He rolls his hips. My back arches, my fingers clutch at the sheets, and I force myself to breathe. The ceremonial gown may be meant to hide us, but right now it feels like nothing can hide the intensity between us.

Drake's arms tighten around me, his forehead resting against mine. For a moment, the world shrinks to just us — the pounding of my heart, the heat of his body, the weight of what we're about to do.

The ceremonial gowns hide everything from view, but the truth presses between us. The Condeam is in place, the ritual demands are waiting, and the priest's voice still echoes in my head like an unwanted intruder.

"Alexia," Drake murmurs, his voice low and steady, "we'll get through this. Forget the mirror. Forget them."

I nod, though my stomach twists. Ours, yet not ours. Tonight should belong to us alone, but instead it's a performance, a ritual, a test. My sarcastic inner voice mutters, Congratulations, Alexia, you're starring in the priest's favourite reality show.

Still, Drake's words ground me. His hand slides to mine, fingers entwining, and I feel the strength of his resolve.

"Remember," he says softly, "the bite is what seals it. They need to see it, but they don't control it. We do."

I swallow hard, my mind racing. He's right. The bite is dangerous, but it's also sacred. It's the moment that will bind us forever.

I lift my eyes to his, determination sparking through the haze of nerves. "Then let's make it ours. Even if they're watching, even if they're waiting — we'll own this moment. Tonight, we become one. Soulmates forever."

Drake's smile is faint but fierce, his eyes burning with the same defiance I feel. Together, we turn toward the mirror, toward the inevitable opening of the curtains, ready to face the ritual that will mark us as soulmates.

My body trembles, every nerve alive, but beneath the haze of desire another awareness pushes through — the ritual, the Condeam, the mirror, the priest waiting to confirm what should be ours alone.

Drake's lips press against mine again, his kiss deep and consuming, but his voice slips into my mind, steady and grounding. *'Alexia, I love you, baby.'*

I cling to his words, even as my body quivers with the intensity of the moment. The ceremonial gown slips further, exposing skin, exposing vulnerability, but I refuse to let the priest's shadow steal this from me.

The pressure builds, not just in my body but in my chest, in my soul. This isn't only lust — it's power, it's union, it's the moment that will mark us as soulmates.

I lean closer, my lips brushing his ear. "Do you feel it? Something big is happening."

Drake's eyes blaze, his hands tightening on my hips. He nods in agreement.

Together, we move in rhythm, not for the priest, not for the doctor, but for ourselves. The ritual demands proof, but what it cannot demand is the love that pulses between us, the bond that no mirror or curtain can contain.

It isn't long before a strange sensation sweeps over me. I don't know what it is or where it comes from — all I know is that I have to speak, the words spilling out with urgency I cannot control.

"Drake Davelt Smithlyn of Red Darkness.

With my body, I give freely to you.

With my blood, I give freely to you.

With my soul, I give freely to you.

I, Princess Alexia Amelia Brioni Smithlyn, accept you above all others.

To join our bodies and souls together as one.

With our combined powers, we shall join as one.

I am yours, and you are mine for eternity.

Forever, we are true Dark Ones."

Strange lights shine around us. Gold, red, silver and bright blue.

My gums twitch as my incisors descend, my top lip lifting to expose sharp vampiric teeth. My mouth opens wide, pulled by a force I cannot resist, toward Drake's bare, enticing neck. Within seconds, my teeth pierce his skin — like a hot knife through butter — sinking deep and unleashing a rush of ambrosia. His blood floods my mouth, exploding down my throat, igniting every nerve.

A sharp pinch high on my shoulder follows, and a surge of endorphins implodes through me. Drake pierces my skin, his pull at my vein sending me spiralling into a haze of sensation. My teeth withdraw from his neck, leaving behind twin marks, and I swipe my tongue over them, savouring the taste of his free-flowing blood.

With another roll of my hips and a hard thrust from Drake, something immense erupts inside me. I don't know whether to feel ecstatic or terrified. My body burns with a high, erotic fire, spreading through every fibre of my being.

Then — fireworks. Full-blown, colourful explosions burst across my mind, dazzling and overwhelming. The climax crashes through me, the most powerful I've ever known, before everything fades into blackness.

CHAPTER TWENTY-SIX

I OPEN MY EYES AND WAKE TO FIND MOONLIGHT FLOODING through the window. A bright glow illuminates the room, and the essence of our sex-filled marathon still lingers thick in the air. Taking another deep breath through my nose, I catch the scent I've fallen in love with.

The delicious, irresistible fragrance fills my nostrils — Drake. Mmm — yum. With my head still down, my eyes glance around the room from my horizontal position on the bed. My resting place, my body, is half lying across the man I love. The man I married. In this strange but beautiful location — Darshia. I would nearly give anything to walk around and tour the countryside of Darshia.

Instead, we're locked in this ceremonial suite until I conceive. I keep reminding myself that soon I'll have my full Dark One abilities.

Excellent. What in the world are these Dark Ones really up to? Why do we have to be locked inside this room? I don't have to be kept in bed to conceive another baby. Drake and I have already proven — with our twin babies — that unprotected sex works just fine. Oh Gods. Speaking of the twins, my breasts feel like they're about to burst. I need to express some of this milk before I leak it all over the bed.

Moving slightly, I realise it's too late. A puddle of milk has already formed on Drake's muscled chest, one river running toward his belly button, and another line of milk rolling to the side and soaking into the sheets. He's still fast asleep, completely unaware of the mess I've made. Oops. My bad.

Carefully, I get up and reach for one of the folded towels at the end of the bed, wrapping it around my chest to prevent more leaking. Checking around the room, I find the extra baby bottles with the breast pump and set everything up on the dining table, ready for expressing.

Returning to the bathroom, I pull a washcloth from the pile under the sink and run it under the hot tap. I make sure to clean around my breasts and nipples before I attempt to express any milk for the twins.

After cleaning up and carefully drying each breast, I wrap another towel around my waist before returning to the bed. I place a spare towel beside Drake to use when he wakes. Turning, I move toward the dining table and sit on one of the dining room chairs.

I check that the main milk holding tank is clean before turning on the expressing machine, with the lever tap pointing over the table's edge. Everything looks ready. I make myself comfortable before hitting the on switch.

The machine's distinct noises fill the room, and I feel the suctioning pull on each breast. It brings back memories of visiting a cow dairy farm years ago, helping the farmer with his cows at milking time. Now I know how the poor cows felt, putting up with the pulsing vacuum extracting milk from them.

I scan back over the machine and down the hoses, watching the milk emerge through the clear tubes, travelling quickly into the holding tank. Within minutes, the milk builds up fast, the levels rising steadily.

Leaning to one side, I reach for an empty bottle. Sitting upright, I unscrew the top, place the bottle at the tap on the bottom of the tank, and start filling. I quickly fill two bottles, screw the tops back on properly, and set them aside. Then I repeat the process, waiting until there's enough milk before filling the next bottle.

Looking back toward the bed, I watch Drake slowly wake. It doesn't take him long to notice the puddle of milk on his body. He runs his finger through it a few times, then uses the towel near him to soak up the cooling liquid before climbing out of bed.

It doesn't take him long to strip the wet bedding and find clean sheets in the linen cupboard. Within minutes, Drake has fresh bedding back on our temporary bed, with the wet sheets tucked away in the bathroom laundry hamper.

FINALLY RELEASING SOME PRESSURE, MY BREASTS FEEL LESS bulging and lighter. I wonder what the twins are doing right now. I miss my twin-loving little babies. That's it — I decide to reach out to Mum.

With my mind, I call to her, hoping she's awake. *'Mum. How is everything, and how are the twins?'*

A startled squeak answers me. Oops. I just scared her.

Sounding a little annoyed, Mum replies, *'Oh boy, Alexia. Try warning me next time!'*

'Sorry, Mum. I woke up leaking milk. I'm expressing at the moment and miss the twins. How are they? Are they sleeping—'

Mum cuts me off. *'Alexia, the twins are fine. They woke an hour ago. Your father and I fed and bathed them, and now they're back in bed, fast asleep. They're okay, but they miss you and Drake. How much longer do you have to stay in the ceremony suite?'*

I sigh, shaking my head. *'Oh, Mum. Don't ask. This suite is a joke. We have to stay here for twenty-four hours. After that, the doctor has to perform some tests, and if I pass, then Drake and I can leave.'*

The thought of the what-ifs annoys me. Stupid tests.

'Alexia, what happens if you do not pass the tests?'

Right at his minute, I do not want to contemplate it.

'Mum, we are not thinking along those lines. I will pass them; that is all there is to it.'

No way am I going to tell her that her little girl is expected to conceive again.

Leaning forward, I fill the next bottle. It doesn't take long before it's full, and I can fill another. Two more bottles are quickly done with the quantity of milk I'm expressing.

Drake picks up the filled bottles and places them in the little bar fridge to keep them cold. Before closing the fridge door, he grabs two water bottles and passes one to me.

"Thank you, Drake."

"I miss them too. We'll be back with the twins before you know it." His warm lips brush against my bare shoulder, sending chills down my spine. Then he leans near my ear, his voice low and teasing. "Alexia, I'm going to shower. You should join me once you're finished expressing, of course."

With a pout, I watch him walk naked into the bathroom, my eyes glued to his high, tight, muscled butt. My body reacts in all sorts of funny ways, and I'm stuck here until I finish expressing. Damn that sexy man.

Then I remember Mum.

Oh, crap on a stick. Reaching out again, I hear her annoyed voice. She's telling me off, noticing I wasn't listening anymore.

'Alexia Amelia Brioni Steele Smithlyn, you better still be there, and nothing bad has happened to you. Now start talking with me, young lady.'

Oops. I know I'm in trouble when Mum uses my full name.

'Sorry, Mum. Drake was helping me. I'm stuck here, attached to this annoying machine, busy expressing. It wasn't fun waking up with a wet bed and overfull breasts. Thankfully, Drake changed the bedding while I sit here connected to the express pump, resembling a dairy cow and filling bottles.'

Laughter fills our link — it's good hearing Mum laugh. At least her mood shifts. *'That is good regarding the expressing. We need more bottled milk, Alexia. The twins guzzle it down as quickly as they both can.'*

'Okay, Mum. Leave it with me. I'll arrange with the doctor for someone to collect the bottles and bring them to you. I want to hold my babies again. I'm missing them. This breast pump makes me feel like a cow more than ever.'

Mum laughs again, which is not funny, even though it's good to hear.

'Oh, Alexia, it will only be for a short time. You'll be back here before you know it. By the way, your father and I brought the twins home. He received an urgent phone call and has to sort out some business issues first thing in the morning. Now go; I'll talk to you later in the morning at a reasonable hour. Night, Alexia — we love you.'

'Thanks for letting me know about the twins, Mum. Please give them a big hug for me. Love you, too. Good night.'

It isn't long before I've expressed three more bottles. I remind myself to arrange later in the morning for the bottles to be collected and delivered to Mum at their home.

Before heading to the bathroom, I contact the doctor. We arrange for the milk to be picked up and delivered to my parents. He reminds me to keep my fluids up and rest as much as possible — and that I should lie down on the bed, rest my feet high against the wall, and place a pillow under my butt to elevate my lower half, increasing the chances of conception. Great. That's exactly what every new bride wants to hear on her wedding night.

Once I finish expressing and washing the different parts of the machine, I leave the equipment out beside the sink. There's no point packing it away; I'll need to express again in a few hours. It's not like I'll be anywhere else by then. Most likely still locked in this room.

I drink over half the bottle of water in one go, realising I'm thirstier than I thought. With a few more mouthfuls, I empty the rest, crush the bottle, and drop it into the recycle bin.

Deciding I might as well freshen up, I head toward the shower for a hot, soapy wash. After all this messy milk-expressing business, I feel a little milky and grimy. Hearing the water still running, I hope Drake hasn't used all the hot water.

CHAPTER TWENTY-SEVEN

My red sock-clad foot taps to the beat of the background music while I sip coffee and read the dusty old family journal. The black satin robe I pulled on earlier slips from my shoulder, exposing bare skin.

The journal has kept me engrossed until my eyes blur — pages filled with Dark One history, law, customs, and behaviour. It's time to focus on something else. With a snap, I close the book and drop it onto the side table with a thud. I know I've missed out on a lot. Not attending school or growing up here in Darshia means I need to learn as much as I can if I decide to stay. Once my school holidays end, I'll return to the human realm to finish the last three months of high school alongside Drake and my old classmates.

Now, where is my husband? The sound of running water reaches my ears. So that's where Drake disappeared. I lean back into the propped-up pillows against the hard bedhead, take another mouthful of coffee, and debate making a fresh cup. The bathroom door clicks open, and steam curls out like smoke toward the ceiling.

Heat spreads through me at the sight of Drake stepping out, droplets cascading down his taut muscles. My tongue sweeps across my lips. Hmm-mm. I could lick every drop of water from him.

Drake's voice interrupts my fantasy. "Alexia, if you keep licking your lips like that while staring at me, I might find another use for your talented tongue and sweet mouth."

Um, yeah. That sounds interesting. His words wrap around me, but I'm too busy devouring the vision of him. My hormones spiral into hyperdrive.

I catch only fragments of what he says next, my mind too distracted by the sight of his body. His smile tells me he knows exactly what effect he's having.

"Huh, what?" I bite my bottom lip, eyes tracing every inch of him before meeting his gaze again. "Sorry, Drake. I only caught the part about licking my lips and you finding another use for my mouth. Can you repeat that, please?"

My eyes slowly make their way back up along Drake's magnificent body. I like my lips again.

Drake's hands grip my arms, pulling me closer, his eyes locked on mine with a heat that makes the air between us shimmer. My robe slips further, satin sliding against my skin, leaving me exposed under his gaze.

"Alexia," he growls, voice low and rough, vibrating through me. "You seem a little focused on my dick. …wife. I am up here, babe."

I give him my best innocent smile, but his raised eyebrow tells me he isn't buying it. My tongue flicks out in a teasing gesture, and his expression shifts — half amusement, half hunger.

The tension coils tighter, every breath charged. My body hums with anticipation, my thoughts scattering into fragments of desire and sarcasm. Great. Here I am, supposed to be studying Dark One history, and instead I'm about to become a living example of it.

Drake leans in, his lips brushing mine, his voice a whisper against my mouth. "You drive me insane, Alexia. Do you know that?"

My reply is lost in the rush of sensation as his body presses against mine, the world narrowing to the rhythm of our breaths, the pounding of our hearts. The ceremonial suite, the priest, the tests — all of it fades. There is only us.

I pull away from his mouth and drop to my knees.

I lean forward, maintaining eye contact with Drake while subtly focusing on his erection in my peripheral vision. His facial features change with each swipe of my tongue, paying extra attention to his weeping slit.

Tasting each dewdrop, his male musk of saltiness coats my tongue. Just as Drake closes his eyes, I open my mouth wide and engulf his hard length, enclosing my lips around his flesh, moving my tongue along the underside of his erection, adding some suction.

With a bob, I move my head back and forth as my lips glide along his hot, moist flesh. Remembering not to allow it to travel too far back, or I'll gag.

I have learnt to keep the right amount of suction, hollowing my cheeks and tightening the seal around his heated flesh, and I am determined to make Drake feel good. Using my hands, my fingers from one hand encircle the root of his massive tool, working it, stroking his length while my other hand tickles and then gently grips his ball sack. Occasionally, I place pressure between his ball sack and the base of his cock.

I continue the movement of my head and mouth and the slide of my moist lips along his hot, wet flesh, and hollow my cheeks with an extra hard suck.

My other hand gives his balls a light squeeze and feels them tighten up and slowly lift towards his body. My other hand grips his erection tighter, sliding it back and forth along the heated, wet flesh, working along with my mouth and tongue. Feeling Drake twitch and bob in my mouth, I know he is nearly reaching his limit.

Just a bit more... I nearly have him — I increase the suction.

Lost in determination, strong hands lift me from under my armpits before I can continue working on his hard, silky flesh. It slides from between my moist lips with a wet pop, and I end up flat on my back on top of the bed. My black satin robe untied, exposing my nakedness underneath, my head near the edge of the bed, my long hair falling over the side towards the floor.

Drake positions himself between my thighs. I move my knees up and out towards my chest, causing my legs to separate, exposing myself entirely for his pleasure.

With a hard thrust forward, Drake impales me on his silky granite erection. Filling me, and what air had been in my lungs, whooshes out on a groan of pleasure — sending tingles and erotic sensations throughout my body.

With a swivel of Drake's hips, he starts his erotic dance

and thrusts fast and deep, simultaneously hitting all the right places, filling every inch of space.

Drake's hands keep the pressure on my spread thighs, his fingers biting into my flesh while he hammers my body, holding me still to his fast movements. The sound of our flesh connects and slaps repeatedly — the feel of his ball sack slapping against my arse, enticing the overall erotic sensations to course throughout my body.

Everything around us disappears in our erotic play into utopia. Each thrust brings me closer to the orgasm I can feel building within, knowing this one will be a big, hard one, an orgasm to beat all other orgasms.

My mouth opens, exposing my fangs. I strike. Sinking them into his flesh. His blood fills my mouth, each pull increasing the erotic sensations racing through me. His hips pump faster. His cry reaches my ears before his mouth hovers over my shoulder and he bites down. An erotic feeling engulfs me as my orgasm crashes over me. My mind spirals out of control. Bright lights over around me, or maybe behind my eyelids. Not sure which.

Second, minutes, maybe hours later, pressure against my thighs eases as Drake braces himself on either side of me, his weight hovering but never crushing. My legs tighten around him, holding him close, refusing to let go. The taste of his blood still lingers on my tongue, rich and intoxicating, mingling with the rush of power flooding through me. Something is different. Something magical just happened. With a quick swipe of my tongue, I lick the bite mark.

Our breaths come ragged, hearts pounding in unison, the rhythm of our bodies slowing but the bond between us burning brighter. The bite has sealed more than passion — it has sealed eternity.

Drake's lips brush against my neck, his tongue tracing the marks he left, sealing them with tenderness. His head rests against my shoulder, each exhale stirring my hair. We are still joined, still bound, and neither of us has the strength — or the desire — to move.

A strange sensation hums beneath my skin, a vibration that feels like fire and lightning all at once. My body floats, weightless, caught between exhaustion and euphoria. The world outside this suite fades, leaving only the echo of our union.

As my eyes flutter closed, I know this isn't just sleep. It's the beginning of something deeper. The Joining has changed me. Changed us. And when I wake, nothing will ever be the same again.

Upon waking, I find myself pressed tightly against the warmth of Drake's muscled body. His arms are wrapped securely around me, anchoring me in place, while one of his firm hands slowly caresses my belly in gentle, protective circles. The steady rhythm of his touch is soothing, yet it sparks a strange awareness deep inside me, something I can't quite name.

I stretch slightly, blinking against the dim glow of moonlight spilling across the room, and turn my head to glance over my shoulder. Drake is already awake, his eyes soft and filled with love. When he leans down to kiss me, his lips brush mine with tenderness, sending little tingles racing across my skin. I shiver, overwhelmed by the intimacy of his touch.

"Good evening, my beautiful pregnant wife."

The words fall from his lips with a smile so devastating it makes my hormones spiral out of control. For a moment, I bask in the warmth of his voice — until the meaning of his words slams into me. Pregnant.

My mouth drops open. "What? What do you mean, pregnant, Drake?"

Shock floods me, my brain scrambling to catch up. Pregnant. The word echoes in my head, bouncing around like a bell tolling over and over. My heart pounds, my breath stutters, and I stare at him in disbelief.

Drake's hand continues to stroke my lower belly, calm and certain. "I can sense it, Alexia. It's incredible — similar to when you carried the twins, but different. It's hard to explain, but I know you are pregnant. Here, place your hand with mine and concentrate."

My fingers tremble as I lower my hand over his, pressing against my bare stomach. I close my eyes, focusing, willing myself to feel what he feels. At first, there's nothing but the warmth of his palm. Then — something. A spark. A flicker of life. A pulse that isn't mine.

My eyes fly open, tears already spilling. "Drake... I can sense it. I can feel the life forming. Oh, my Gods. We did it. We're pregnant again."

Joy bursts through me, fierce and overwhelming, but tangled with uncertainty. My emotions are a storm — delight, fear, hope — all colliding at once. Drake's lips brush mine again, his joy radiating through the bond between us, steady and strong.

I cling to him, letting the moment sink in. I am pregnant again. The thought feels surreal, heavy, and luminous all at once.

Memories of the twins flash through my mind — their tiny fingers, their cries, the sleepless nights, the overwhelming love. My heart aches with longing and fear. Can I do this again? Can I protect another child in this world of Dark One rituals and endless expectations?

Drake's hand tightens over mine, grounding me. His eyes shine with certainty, as if he already knows the answer. His faith in me is unshakable, and for a moment, I borrow his strength.

A prayer forms silently in my mind. Hopefully, this pregnancy will follow the typical nine months, safe and risk-free, ending with a healthy, full-term baby. I refuse to let my thoughts wander into darker possibilities. For now, I hold onto the miracle — the spark of new life inside me, the love of the man beside me, and the bond that has sealed us forever.

CHAPTER TWENTY-EIGHT

Watching Doctor Brean walk out through the door of the Joining Ceremony suite is a relief. The large, thick envelope in my hand feels heavier than it should, containing the documentation we have been waiting for—proof that Drake and I are not just mated soulmates but also legally married and officially joined.

I sit back at the table, my fingers trembling slightly as I open the envelope. The contents spill into my other hand: thick parchment, heavy with ink and authority. Our marriage certificate. Our joining certificate. The official documents notify and confirm that Drake and I perform our Joining Ceremony before the ceremonial priest and undersigned witnesses. The old-style swirling script makes it feel timeless, binding us not only in law but in tradition.

Doctor Brean's voice still echoes in my mind. He performs several tests, asks endless questions, and conducts a special medical examination before leaving. "Congratulations, Alexia and Drake. You are expecting again," he says with enthusiasm.

Pregnant. The word still feels surreal. How he detects it this early amazes me. My hand instinctively presses against my belly.

The doctor answers one of my concerns before I can even ask. "Yes, Alexia, you can still breastfeed the twins with this new pregnancy." Relief washes through me. Then, as if reading my mind, he adds, "And yes, you and Drake can continue to have sex, but no rough or extremely strenuous bouts of it."

As if we would. From the corner of my eye, I catch Drake's smile—his quiet nod as he absorbs every word. Typical Drake, calm and steady, while my mind spins in circles.

Doctor Brean explains this pregnancy should follow the average human gestation of forty weeks. Forty weeks. It sounds so far away, yet the thought of holding another child at the end of it fills me with both joy and dread. As long as my baby is healthy, as long as our lives are not in danger, it will be worth it. My last pregnancy is safe, but the memory of hospital stays and assassination attempts lingers like a shadow.

Half listening, I hear the doctor say my blood pressure is perfect—yay me. Drake and I exchange a look of relief. Being a full Dark One, my body remains stable, but the reassurance still matters.

Then comes the question that unsettles me. "Have you noticed any change in your Dark One abilities?"

I answer honestly. "No." But the truth is, Drake and I haven't tried. At times, we have the impression that the ceremonial suite itself blocks us, dampens whatever new powers we might gain.

Even though I can still mind-talk with Mum, I dismiss it as something I already have before the Joining Ceremony. But deep down, I wonder. If we gain new powers, I want strength. I want healing. I want to recover faster if I'm ever hurt again. No more lying helpless in a hospital bed while enemies plot.

Doctor Brean assures us that once we leave the suite, we'll notice differences. Our hearing sharpens, our senses heighten, our reflexes quicken. We'll be stronger, faster, more resilient. That sounds good—for now.

Finally, relief settles over me. We return to the castle, grab my bags, and head home. The twins are safe with my parents, who leave Darshia hours after the wedding ceremony. Knowing they arrive safely back at my childhood home eases the ache in my chest.

I look forward to sleeping in my own bed again, wearing my clothes, being surrounded by familiar belongings and family. But reality intrudes. That annoying school assignment still waits for me, untouched. If I leave it any later, I won't finish before Drake and I return to school.

Oh boy. How am I supposed to juggle twins, breastfeeding, schoolwork, and now another pregnancy— while hiding my Dark One life and all this royalty stuff? The thought makes my head spin. I press the envelope tighter against my chest, as if it might anchor me.

For now, I remind myself: one step at a time.

CHAPTER TWENTY-NINE

I walk casually back into my hospital room with Drake by my side, his hand gripping mine with quiet reassurance. The odour of antiseptic, sharp and unforgiving, radiates from the freshly scrubbed floors, burning my nostrils. Gods, I did not miss that foul smell during our stay in the Ceremony Suite.

Goosebumps rise across my skin. High on the wall, a small heating vent puffs out stale cold air, stirring the unease already crawling through me. I shake my head, trying to clear it, to banish the strange heaviness pressing against my chest.

From the middle of the room, I take in everything. It looks exactly as it did before the ceremonies, as if time here has been frozen. My belongings remain tucked away in the cupboard. The romance novel Mum gave me is still half hidden beneath my pillow. One of the twins' baby blankets lies draped at the end of the bed, soft and familiar. On the side table, a photo of Drake and me smiles back, beside a half-empty glass of water. To anyone who walked in, it would look like I was still a patient, recovering.

Mixed emotions churn inside me. Relief, strangeness, even guilt. I am healed now — finally free of the ordeal of the past week — yet standing here makes me feel like I no longer belong. This room is a shell of pain and recovery, and I am ready to leave it behind. As soon as we pack my things into my bag, Drake and I will head back to the castle, back home, to begin our new married life with the twins.

Married. The word feels foreign, heavy with meaning. My thumb brushes against the warm bands of my wedding rings, and I know it will take time for the reality to sink in. Married. A parent. No longer just a couple, but a family. Our own little family.

If Drake weren't standing here, I might think this was all a dream — that I was still asleep in my bed at my parents' house, safe and ordinary. I shake my head, forcing myself to focus. No more silly, confusing thoughts. There is too much to do.

I am grateful for Nurse Sharonia's meeting with us down the hall earlier. It was more than a courtesy — it was protection. Away from prying eyes, she greeted us with warmth and explained how she had maintained my medical chart, adding notes as if I had never left this room.

The remarkable woman covered for me, weaving stories for anyone who asked. She told them I was sleeping, or in the bathroom, or undergoing a medical examination. Sometimes she said I was walking the halls to strengthen my muscles. She shielded me with lies that sounded like truths, and I owe her more than I can say.

With my talent for breaching mind shields, I resisted the temptation to slip into her thoughts again. I know too well the pain hidden there. Before the wedding, I had accidentally breached her mind and learned of her partner's death. Jake — her love of two years — killed instantly when an overloaded logging truck veered across the road and crushed his car. They had been planning their Joining Ceremony. Instead, she was left alone, with no family, no future.

When I am with Sharonia, I feel a connection, a trust that runs deeper than duty. Perhaps one day I will ask if she would consider leaving Darshia for a while, to become a medical nanny for the twins. She deserves a new purpose, and I would feel safer knowing she was near my children.

As for the other nurses, I didn't bother asking if the Queen had visited me. Instead, I skimmed their minds. It's amazing how much information you can gather in seconds. Grandma Ma never returned to the hospital. She never asked about my health. This morning, she spoke directly with the doctor about another matter entirely.

She must be sticking to her guns, waiting for me to return to the castle.

THANKFULLY, WITH MY HOSPITAL ROOM DOOR CLOSED, Drake's gaze lingers, not with lust but with something deeper — concern shadowing his eyes.

With a brief smile, I turn and sit on my bed. Drake follows and kneels before me, his presence filling the space between my thighs, and gently reaches out, brushing his thumb across my pebbled nipple. The touch sends a shiver through me, but it's not only desire — it's something else.

"Alexia," he murmurs, his voice low, steady. "There's a change. I can feel it."

My breath catches, torn between the warmth of his touch and the unease curling in my chest. "What do you mean, a change?"

His thumb traces lightly, almost reverently, as if searching for answers beneath the surface. "Your body... it's responding differently. Stronger. More alive. It's not just the pregnancy. It's the Joining. Your powers — they're waking."

A tremor runs through me, not from fear but from recognition. The sensations coursing through my body aren't only physical — they're supernatural, a ripple of energy that feels like fire and lightning beneath my skin.

I close my eyes, leaning into his touch, my breast filling his palm, letting the moment ground me. "Drake... I can feel it too. It's like my body is humming, like something inside me is shifting."

He presses his forehead against mine, his voice a whisper. "We'll face it together. Whatever this is, whatever comes next — you're not alone."

His arms wrap around me. Relief fills me. It surrounds me with the lingering heat of his touch. For now, I let myself breathe, let myself believe in the strength of our bond. The hospital, the ceremony, the uncertainty — all fade, leaving only us, bound by love, blood, and the promise of what's to come.

His lips find mine, our love increases as our mouths fuse together in harmony. Our kisses full of heat and passion.

His thumb slowly slides across my pebbling, sensitive nipple, before giving it a slight squeeze. My breath hitches in my throat. "Drake. Do we really have time for... Ah, that feels good." His thumb keeps stroking my sensitive nipple, sending erotic sensations from my breast to my core. I lean into his touch, and my mind, distracted, doesn't notice as our clothing gradually disappears piece by piece.

My back arches, every nerve alive, my body straining to pull Drake closer. Heat floods through me, overwhelming, consuming, until I feel as though I might combust. His touch, his presence, his power — it all drives me into a state of delirium.

My back presses into the mattress, and Drake moves up and over my naked body. In one of his talented moves, he thrusts his hips, filling me. My legs wrap around his waist.

The rhythm between us builds, faster, harder, until my body trembles on the edge of release. My gums tingle, the familiar ache warning me that my fangs are about to descend. The hunger rises with the pleasure, impossible to separate.

Drake tilts his head, baring his neck to me in silent invitation. The sight unravels me. I strike, sinking my teeth into his flesh just as my orgasm crashes through me, shattering me into fragments of light and sensation. His blood floods my mouth, rich and intoxicating, rushing down my throat like bright light mixed with energy on steroids.

The world disappears. My heart stutters, my body floats, and for a moment I feel as though I've left myself entirely.

Through the haze, I barely register Drake's own fangs piercing my skin. His lips seal against me, drinking deeply, and the dual pull of blood and pleasure sends me spiralling into another wave of ecstasy. My body convulses, my mind dissolves, and I lose myself in the bond.

Drake's voice breaks through the storm, raw and desperate, screaming my name as his release overtakes him.

We collapse together, bound by blood, by love, by the unbreakable tie of the Dark One's soulmate bond.

SOMETIME LATER, OUR BODIES SLOWLY RETURN TO US, ENOUGH to notice our hearts beating in perfect rhythm, our breaths racing but steadying together. The connection between us feels deeper than flesh — an unbreakable tether forged in blood, love, and our soulmate bond.

Drake's movements soften, his presence gentle now, extending the waves of pleasure into something calmer, more enduring. The ripples flow through me, leaving my body trembling but whole.

Leaning close, I swipe my tongue over the marks on his neck, sealing the punctures instantly. The bond hums between us, stronger than before, a quiet reminder of what we have become.

A sigh escapes me, heavy with contentment. My body feels weightless, my mind drifting. Satisfaction settles deep in my bones, and I know I could surrender to sleep, safe in his arms, completely at peace.

CHAPTER THIRTY

SLEEPING IN MY HUSBAND'S ARMS, FEELING WARM, LOVED, and safe, is one moment I will always cherish. The knock on my closed hospital room door, however, shatters the peace. Naked, wrapped up in Drake's arms on my hospital bed — awkward doesn't even begin to cover it.

"Oh, shite." Oh, crap on a stick. Did I just say that out loud? The smugness on Drake's gorgeous face confirms it. His arms tighten around me when I try to move. Oh, damn.

The knocking continues, insistent, dragging my focus back to the door. Whoever it is, they're eager. Reaching out with my mind, I scan the presence outside. Only one person.

"Who is it?" My voice sounds calm enough, though my cheeks are burning.

"Alexia, it is I, Doctor Brean. May I come in? Also, yes, I know Drake is in there with you."

Oh, double damn. How does he know? Maybe Drake and I

weren't exactly quiet. Triple damn. My face is on fire. "Come in, Doctor Brean."

I yank the sheet up to my neck, trying to cover us decently.

'Baby, there's no need to be embarrassed. He's seen us in bed before. Hell, he watched us during the Joining Ceremony. So, Alexia, relax,' Drake whispers into my mind.

Relax? Easy for him. He's not the one blushing like a tomato. Still, I feel his annoyance at the interruption simmering beneath his calm.

Doctor Brean enters, closing the door behind him. White coat, serious face, large yellow envelope in hand.

"Good evening, Princess Alexia, Prince Drake." His eyes flick from me to Drake, then to my bag on the floor, then back again. "Are you ready to leave the hospital and return to the castle?"

Oh, just great. Judging me, no doubt. Time to pull my big girl panties up and act like an adult.

"Good evening, Doctor Brean. As soon as I wake up properly and shower, I'll leave for the castle before heading home to my babies." My voice is steady, though my face feels like it's glowing red. "I see you have another envelope. Is that for me?"

He smiles, catching my hint. Good man.

"I am here to give you your last medical examination before release. Plus, I have some... well, hopefully good news." He pauses, dragging it out. "Princess Alexia, while your mother was completing the documents for your marriage and Joining Ceremony, she inquired about residency.

Congratulations — you are now officially a citizen of Darshia."

Say what?

My eyes widen. Officially a citizen.

Doctor Brean continues, "A dual birth certificate, as you would. Since you are next in line for Queen of Darshia, it was wise to correct documentation before you turn eighteen. Your mother registered not only you, but also your female ancestry. As of this afternoon, your mother, your grandmothers, and yourself are now officially Darshian dual citizens."

My mind spins. This could throw a wrench into Grandma Ma's plans. A smile flickers across my face, disappears, returns, disappears again.

"Excuse me, Doctor Brean. What about Drake? Was his birth already registered?"

He shakes his head. "Princess Alexia, Drake is a citizen of Darshia. He was born here. His father abandoned him to your world. If not for his mother arranging guardians, I dread to think what might have happened." His face darkens.

"But how do you know so much about Drake? Was his mother here?"

A flicker crosses his features. "Yes. When you first arrived from the castle, Drake's mother was among the concerned group. Mrs. Smithlyn told me what happened at the castle, what her husband tried to do to you and the twins. We spoke briefly about Drake's past and what she had to do to ensure her baby survived in the human realm."

Wow. So Drake's mother fought for him, made sure he had a life, an education. I'll need to talk to Drake about this — his family, especially his mother's side.

My gaze drifts back to the envelope. Thank the Gods for my mother and her grand plans. *Thank you, Mum.*

Doctor Brean notices. "Princess Alexia, this envelope contains your Darshia birth certificate and dual citizenship documents. Your mother already has hers, along with the rest of the family's. In short — welcome to Darshia."

He places the envelope on the table, then turns to leave. "I'll return in fifteen minutes for your last medical examination. That should give you time to shower and dress. See you soon."

He winks, smiles, and glances at Drake, then exits, closing the door softly behind him.

And just like that, my embarrassment returns full force.

CHAPTER THIRTY-ONE

Within seconds of the door closing behind the doctor, I am quickly out of Drake's arms and my hospital bed. Hearing Drake laughing behind me makes me want to growl at him — the annoying man of a husband he is. Rushing into the bathroom and turning the water on in the shower while waiting for the running water temperature to change to hot, I quickly sit down on the loo, relieving my bladder.

Ah, that feels better. After flushing the toilet and washing my hands at the sink, Drake walks in with clean clothes for us to wear. It looks like Drake is about to join me in the shower. Hmm, I'm unsure if that is a good idea. With no words said out loud, Drake gives me his panty-dropping smile and walks under the pulsing spray of water with his soap and shampoo at the ready.

Ha, talk about being organised, but then he is using my bathroom and showering while I am unconscious, staying with me at the hospital, which means his toiletries are in my bathroom. Turning his back to me, he washes his hair. Water and soap foam glide down his back, over his defined muscles and tight… Hmm, just look at his body — yum.

Look away, Alexia. Look away.

Forcing my attention to the bath, I notice something is missing, something missing from the towel rails — our towels! What about our towels? That is one thing he has forgotten.

Men!

Quickly walking back out to my room, freshly folded towels are sitting on my made bed, waiting for me. Oh yes, I think I might just love Nurse Sharonia. Quickly reaching out with my mind, I find her at once, contacting her mind.

'Nurse Sharonia, Thank you for the towels.'

'You're welcome. Thought they would come in handy.'

Avoiding the sound of her laughter through the mind link, I ask, *'I have a proposition for you. How would you like a change of scenery and come and work for me to watch and look after the twins while Drake and I are back at school in the human realm?'*

'Seriously? Thank you for the generous offer, Princess Alexia. I accept the position.'

Oh wow. I am not expecting her to agree with me so quickly.

'That's fantastic. Welcome to the crazy life of a new princess.
Thank you, Nurse Sharonia.'

'No. Thank you, Princess. When will I be able to start?'

Stunned... Sharonia quickly tells me how she would love
to make a fresh start, a new life away from here, away from
Darshia. I inform her she can begin in a few days, as the twins
are with my parents at their home. Sharonia mentions a few
days will be enough time to organise things here. I let her
know I will pass her contact details before leaving the hospital.

Oh, wow, I just hired my very first live-in nanny!

WITHIN SECONDS OF MY TRIUMPHANT MENTAL ASSIGNMENT OF
hiring a nanny for my children — Princess Alexia, employer
of staff, hear ye, hear ye — I allow Drake to hear my thoughts.
Drake pokes his head out of the bathroom like some smug,
wet Labrador. His hair is dripping, his grin is wider than his
shoulders, and I swear he's about to shake water everywhere
just to mark his territory.

"Did you just hire someone while I was shampooing?" he
asks, voice full of disbelief and amusement.

"Yes," I say, chin high, because apparently multitasking is
my royal superpower. "While you were busy lathering up like
a Pantene commercial, I secured a full-time nanny. You're
welcome."

He laughs again — of course he does — and I roll my eyes

so hard I'm surprised they don't fall out and roll under the bed. Honestly, the man thinks he's hilarious. Spoiler alert: he's not.

I grab the towels Nurse Sharonia left, clutching them like they're the crown jewels. "See these? Proof that women run the world. You forgot towels, Drake. Towels. The most basic of shower accessories. Meanwhile, I hired a nanny. Who's winning here?"

Drake steps out of the shower, water dripping down his chest, and gives me that panty-dropping smile again. Ugh. My sarcasm is strong, but my hormones are stronger.

"Winning?" he says, voice low, smug. "Pretty sure I'm winning."

I throw a towel at his face. "Congratulations. Your prize is drying yourself off before you flood the hospital bathroom."

Inside, though, I'm buzzing. I actually did it — I hired someone. Me. Princess Alexia, employer of staff, organiser of chaos, and apparently, towel rescuer.

Oh wow. I just became a boss. And if Drake thinks he's the boss of me, he's about to learn otherwise.

DRAKE DROPS HIS SOAKED TOWEL AND CATCHES A SECOND towel mid-air like some smug action hero. I know him too well. He always uses two towels. Honestly, if charm were a crime, he'd be serving a life sentence.

"Boss lady now, huh?" he says, realising he's still listening to my thoughts, as he continues rubbing the towel over his hair. "Hiring staff while I'm naked in the shower. That's... efficient."

"Yes," I reply, arms crossed, chin tilted. "I multitask. Unlike you, who can't even remember towels. Honestly, Drake, if I left you alone for five minutes, you'd probably forget pants."

He smirks, stepping closer, water still dripping down his chest. "You'd miss me without pants? I think you'd prefer me without pants..."

"Correction," I shoot back, "I'd miss the silence of you not talking."

Inside, though, I'm buzzing. Nurse Sharonia said yes. Just like that, I've got a nanny. My very first employee. Princess Alexia: ruler of sarcasm, rescuer of towels, and now employer of childcare staff. I should probably get business cards printed.

Drake leans in, lowering his voice. "So when do we meet our new recruit?"

I grin, wicked. "Soon. And don't scare her off with your panty-dropping smile. She's here for the twins, not you."

He laughs again — because of course he does — and I swear the sound echoes off the hospital walls like he's auditioning for Most Annoying Husband Alive.

But me? I'm already plotting. Sharonia's arrival means freedom. School in the human realm, twins cared for, and me finally getting to breathe without juggling diapers and royal duties at the same time.

Oh yes. Princess Alexia is officially in charge. And Drake? He's about to learn that being married to a bossy princess comes with rules.

Showering by myself, without my husband, is a little lonely. I make myself move quicker, rinsing and drying, followed by getting fully dressed, with a light touch of makeup, with time to spare before the doctor arrives. From now on, I might have to make sure Drake and I have separate showers in the mornings on school days if we want to make it on time for class.

Before the doctor returns to my room for my final medical assessment, I open the envelope Doctor Brean left on the little table. With Drake at my side, we look over the documentation. Seeing my new birth certificate for the first time is shocking and a little surreal. I grab my phone, hit the camera app, and take photos of all the documents. Something is niggling at me to make sure I have copies of these papers.

Once I take several photos of all the documents and send myself a copy to my email address, I replace everything in the large envelope and pack it away amongst my belongings in my bag. I walk back into the bathroom, searching all the cupboards, finding nothing left behind. I walk back out to my hospital room, search everything, and check all the drawers and cupboards to see if I miss anything belonging to Drake or me.

The only thing I notice and quickly rectify is the power lead for my phone.

I make sure I write my contact details and Drake's for Nurse Sharonia. I place the paper in my pocket to pass on to her when we leave.

As I close my packed bag, Doctor Brean walks back into

my room. "Good to see you are ready to leave, Princess Alexia. If you can sit on the bed, I will perform a few tests."

Following the doctor's instructions, he performs his routine tests, giving me a clean bill of health. He also informs me he will write nothing down regarding the new pregnancy in my hospital records. Otherwise, word will soon spread of the conception, which will not be safe for myself or the baby.

The doctor also assures me that, at this early stage, I should be safe from Dark Ones, including Grandma Ma, from detecting the pregnancy and keeping our news secret. I should be safe for another few more weeks, at least. Also, by then, I will be back home, in school, and away from Darshia.

Even with my parents, I would like to wait a little while before we announce they will be grandparents again. At least Drake and I are married this time, but come on, being pregnant at nearly eighteen is not a good idea or prospect. I have to finish school first, and that is what I focus on. Oh, and my twin babies, of course. I miss my babies, and I cannot wait until I can see them again.

Doctor Brean's voice interrupts my thoughts. "Princess Alexia. Do you have any other questions for me?"

something is niggling at the back of my mind. How can he tell I am pregnant yet, other Dark Ones would not?

"Um, yes. I do. How is it, that you can detect my pregnancy, yet you said other Dark Ones would not be able to. How is that possible?"

"Ah. You know, you are the first person to ever ask me that question."

"Seriously? Is it a doctor thing?"

He shakes his head. "Darshia doctors and nurses train in

the medical field and learn all there is regarding pregnancy and how to detect it. As for myself, it was part of my new Dark One power, inherited when I became a full Dark One. I can sense a brand new fetus before anyone can. My talent is extremely rare."

"Oh, wow. So, in other words, we should keep this information to ourselves."

"That would be ideal, yes. Thank you."

"Okay," I say and smile.

"Meeting you has been a pleasure, even if I have not said it before. All the best to you, Prince Drake and the twins, and your future together as a family." Doctor Brean looks from me to Drake and back to me again, "…All the happiness and good wishes on your joining and marriage to one another."

Reaching out with his hand, Doctor Brean shakes mine and Drake's hands in a heated, firm, congratulatory grip. "… Good evening, and please, don't take this the wrong way, but I do not want to see you, Princess Alexia. Let me rephrase that — I do not need to see you until it is time for your anti-natal checkup in a month." After everything that has happened to me so far, I giggle at his words. The doctor takes a folded piece of paper from his pocket and passes it to me. "Here is a list of vitamins and pregnancy supplements you should take in the early stages of your pregnancy. They will benefit both of you, but especially your unborn baby."

Oh, wow. I look down at the paper in my hand, making the realisation of the next pregnancy far too real. Glancing back at Doctor Brean, I smile and say, "Thank you, Doctor Brean. Once I am back home, I will purchase these items. I want to ensure this pregnancy is as healthy as possible, giving this new baby the best chance in life."

My hand gently rubs over my still-flat stomach. The benefit of being a Dark One is the ability to heal quickly, allowing my body to adjust and go back to its pre-baby self within a day or so of giving birth.

Drake walks over to our bags and picks them up. Okay, it looks like it is time to go.

CHAPTER THIRTY-TWO

FOR SOME UNKNOWN REASON, I AM NOT EXPECTING TO BE sitting in the front seat of Drake's car when we leave the hospital. It didn't cross my mind how we'll return to the castle, but to see Drake's car completed and sitting in the car park is a big surprise. How did his car get here from home?

What was once a gutted, unrecognisable shell is now transformed. He has built the dashboard and console with modern electronics, replaced every panel, and restored and repainted every inch. The old rust bucket is gone — what we're sitting in now looks like a brand-new 1970 Chevelle SS in Tuxedo Black, but with modern updates.

Since when did Drake obtain a Darshia driving licence. Which is hilarious, considering I know he didn't a car licence before he left me. So how does he magically have one now? No clue. Add it to the ever-growing list of "Dark One mysteries Alexia will never get answers to."

Watching him drive us through the streets of Darshia

toward the castle is equal parts relief and pure surreal insanity. Relief, because thank the Goddess we're not walking like two idiots waiting to be kidnapped. Surreal, because someone is still out there trying to snatch or assassinate me — namely Drake's delightful father and whatever minions he's hired from the bargain-bin of evil.

I sink lower in my seat, praying no one recognises us in Drake's car. Because the last thing I need today is to be murdered at a stop sign.

Reminding me once we arrive home and away from Darshia, I will have to book in to take the driving test for our human driver's licence. I still have over four weeks to go before I can legally drive my car without either of my parents beside me. Pulling my mobile phone out of my pocket, I quickly add a note in my calendar to book my appointment at the motor vehicle licensing office.

Before I forget, I should text Mum to tell her we've finally left the hospital and are heading to the castle. After I send the message, I place my phone on the console to charge wirelessly and lean back, watching the buildings as we drive towards the castle. I still cannot believe the car has wireless charging!

A text notification sounds. I reach for my phone and glance at the screen.

MUM

Letting you know, we are back at our house with the twins. Your father was called in for work. We've been here since this morning.

Oh, ok. At least I now know where the twins are, and tap out my reply.

ME

Ok. Does Grandma Know?

Three dots appear, then my phone dings.

MUM

No. That woman is a worry. Who knows what is going through her mind?

My cell dings again.

MUM

We need more milk. Just about out.

Wow. Good to know my little ones are safe and guzzling the bottled milk.

ME

We shouldn't be long. We'll pick up my stuff from the castle, then head home.

MUM

See you soon. Love you.

ME

See you soon. Love you to. Give my babies a hug from me.

After I press send, I set my phone back on the console, where it continues to charge wirelessly.

The closer we approach the castle, the more unease I feel.

Creepy-crawling sensations run along my spine and down my legs. I am grateful the twins are not with us. Something is very wrong. I do not know what it is, but something is about to happen, and it will not be very nice.

I do not think it will be a confrontation with Grandma Ma, even though that would be bad enough. No. I do not know what it is, but something is very wrong here, with a dark feeling down in my soul. Taking a deep breath, I glance at Drake. Noticing he is concentrating hard while driving, I see his facial features change.

'Drake, do you feel it? Can you sense something is not right here?'

'Yes, Alexia. Something is very wrong. Keep your guard up and eyes open.'

Already sensing the situation, Drake does not have to tell me twice.

One guard I have not seen before allows us to enter the castle grounds and waves us through the big gates towards the front entrance. Driving along the wide driveway, I casually glance around. Where is all the extra security? I look towards the double front doors, trepidation racing through me.

I do not like this.

Out loud I say, "Drake, it will be best to park just over there in the vacant car allotments." We both look at the vacant parking spots at the castle entrance. This position allows the staff to unload the vehicles without blocking the driveway, while keeping them out of the pathway of approaching and departing vehicles by the front doors.

"I think you are right. We need the car close enough to leave. Something is wrong here, very wrong. Where are all the security guards? The ones I notice are none of the men I have ever seen before. Alexia, I think you should change into your steel-capped-toe shoes. I have a feeling you are going to need them."

I think Drake is correct. Something is very wrong, the feeling is getting stronger as I glance over the grounds and back towards the castle. Driving into the vacant car spot, Drake parks his car, pulling the handbrake on as he turns off the ignition.

Reaching behind my seat, I grab for my shoes, seeing a folded-up pair of socks sitting in one of them — handy. I quickly swap my sandals for my socks and heavy-duty kick-arse-fighting shoes. With these shoes on, they are light enough for me to work out in and fight. Also, tough and strong enough to bring anyone down to the ground while protecting my feet and ankles.

Relief fills me when I open the secret compartment on one shoe, finding my switchblade knife still tucked away in its concealed compartment. You never know when a knife or one of its many little accessories might be required. I check the second shoe, open its secret compartment, and find it is still full, with a second folding knife and a few throwing stars.

Grabbing my phone from the console, I check the screen to make sure its battery charge has increased. I switch it to silent and tuck the device away in my pocket on the side of my jacket. I have the feeling my phone will be handy tonight.

Once again, I scan around our immediate area. Something is definitely off. One of the security team should be here to greet us at the car by now. Where is James, that security doorman guy? He usually opens the car door... hmm. Suspicious absence noted.

Turning and looking back at Drake, I know he has been listening to all my thoughts. For once, I do not feel the need to block him. He knows exactly how I feel and what I plan to do. We lean towards one another; our lips meet, infusing with each other. This kiss is more important than any words. I need to feel Drake's body and soul, including his warmth and love, and with his lips, he supplies the feelings of support I require.

Changing the angle of our heads, we both deepen the kiss as it builds and becomes intoxicating to my senses. Our arms move and tighten around our bodies. We hold one another, experiencing his abundant presence, love, power, and body heat, reaching every pore throughout my body and warming me up from the inside out.

Somehow, I rip my lips from Drake's and pull my body away, leaving a gap that feels more like a canyon between us. I never know where I find the supernova strength to end our kiss.

Taking a deep, rugged breath, I brush my lips to his — once, twice, three times — then lean my forehead against his and close my eyes to cherish these final moments together. And say, "I love you — my husband. Always remember that." I brush my fingers along his jaw, savouring his aura. "Let's go inside. Find out what is going on around here. Please be safe."

I need to move before I change my mind and tell Drake to drive away and head for home. With one last quick kiss to his lips, I pull away and open the car door, exiting the vehicle. Before I reach the front of Drake's car, Drake has me in his embrace, hard against his muscled body. His lips kiss mine fiercely. It is not long before Drake rips his moist lips from mine.

"I love you too, my courageous wife, my soulmate. Now, you'd better be extra safe and do nothing stupid."

Ha, as if. Me... Do nothing stupid? That ship sailed the moment we first had sex.

I hope I have enough common sense not to get myself hurt or, heaven forbid, killed. We are no longer home, and I still have much to learn. We are amongst Dark Ones — similar to vampires, with sharp teeth, speed, and inhuman strength. Must remember — Dark Ones can be extremely dangerous and deadly. Especially the one that wants me dead.

With a last fast, hard kiss, we separate enough to lace our fingers together, turn as one, and walk towards the main doors. One thing with Drake is that his embrace and kisses always leave me warm and breathless.

With each step we take, the coolness of the night air turns my warm, moist lips cold. With multiple thoughts racing through my mind, I focus on my pep talk.

Okay, Alexia, it is time to pull our big girl panties up because we will need all our wit, skill, strength, and fighting knowledge to get through whatever awaits us.

Giving Drake's hand an extra squeeze, we make our way silently up the front steps. That is when I notice dark wetness seeping through the slight gap in the barely ajar double doors, the faint odour of blood reaching my nostrils.

Uh-oh. This is so not good.

I freeze, my sarcasm momentarily replaced by survival mode. "Well," I mutter under my breath, "either someone spilled a very large glass of red wine, or we're about to star in a horror movie."

Drake's grip tightens on my hand. His eyes flick to mine, sharp and alert. "Stay close."

"Close?" I whisper back, pulling my knife from my shoe compartment. "I'm practically glued to you. If you sneeze, I'll probably stab you by accident."

We edge forward, the heavy doors creaking as Drake pushes them wider. The smell of blood thickens, metallic and unmistakable, curling into my nose like a bad perfume sample nobody asked for. My stomach twists, threatening to rebel, but my sarcasm steadies me — because if I stop cracking jokes now, I'll probably start screaming.

The dim light spilling through the gap flickers across the stone floor, catching on the dark wetness smeared in uneven streaks. It isn't wine, unless someone decided to host a medieval murder-themed cocktail party. I swallow hard, forcing my eyes to stay open, because closing them won't make the mess disappear.

Drake's hand tightens around mine, his jaw set, his eyes scanning every shadow. He's all warrior focus, while I'm busy wondering if my steel-capped shoes are about to earn their keep. "Stay close," he mutters, voice low and sharp.

"Close?" I whisper back, pulling my knife free from its hidden compartment. "I'm practically welded to your side. If you sneeze, I'll probably stab you by accident."

We step inside, the doors groaning louder as if they're announcing our arrival to whoever — or whatever — left this blood trail. My pulse hammers in my ears, but I force a smirk. "Great. Welcome home. Hope the castle comes with a mop and bucket service."

The air is colder here, heavy with silence, the kind that makes every creak of the floorboards sound like a gunshot. My eyes dart across the hall, catching glimpses of overturned chairs, a shattered vase, and what looks suspiciously like claw marks gouged into the wall.

"Fantastic," I mutter under my breath. "Either we missed one hell of a party, or someone forgot to invite us to the apocalypse."

Drake raises his eyebrow, his body tense, ready. I mirror him, with my bitchy sarcasm locked and loaded. Whatever waits for us in this castle, it's not going to be friendly. And me? I'm ready to kick, hit, punch, and shoot my way through it.

CHAPTER THIRTY-THREE

THE STENCH OF BLOOD COATS MY NOSTRILS, THICK AND metallic, like someone spilled a thousand rusty coins across the floor. My hands ball into tight fists, and bile rises in my throat with each step I take.

Oh, my Gods. What has happened here?

I take in the carnage before me. Scattered clothing, weapons, blood, and who knows what else cover the floor like some twisted yard sale. Who does this? Who could do this? I squeeze through the gap in the double doors, my eyes darting everywhere, making sure no one is about to jump out and yell, "Surprise, you're dead!"

Seeing no moving bodies, Drake and I edge into the foyer of the castle. My pulse hammers. My sarcasm is the only thing keeping me upright.

I quickly reach out to Grandma Ma's mind. *'Grandma Ma. Can you hear me?'*

Several seconds tick by. Nothing. I try again, my mental voice laced with apprehension.

'Grandma Ma. Can you hear me? What is happening? Where are you? Are you safe?'

Waiting. Waiting. Still nothing. What is taking her so long? I should hear from her by now. Reaching out harder, I search for her physical form. Nope. Nothing. I cannot feel her, cannot sense her mind. I cannot tell if she is still in the castle or not.

Now I am past freaking out. Answer me, damn it. Alexettia, answer me.

My foot slips. Drake grips my arm as my shoe skids through a thick, dark puddle, stopping me from face-planting.

It takes my brain several delayed seconds to realise I am sliding in someone's blood. Oh, Gods, no.

"Fantastic," I mutter under my breath. "I always wanted to star in a horror movie. Guess I forgot to audition."

My stomach tightens and swirls as a shudder rocks my body. My heart rate spikes with the carnage surrounding us. My breath races. I sense I'm about to hyperventilate. Shite. Shite. I force myself to take steady breaths and calm my nerves. This is not the time to go into panic mode.

Keeping my eyes moving, constantly scanning all around us, my nerves are on edge as I see blood splattered over the floors and walls, with pools of blood in different sizes near slumped piles of clothing. Why is there clothing everywhere? And where are the bodies to go with all this blood?

Drake's presence fills my mind. Babe, we need to keep moving and be extra vigilant. Whoever did this is most likely still here. I am relieved you spoke with your mother before we arrived, knowing your parents and the twins are safe back at home and well away from all this carnage and death. Come on; I think we better find your grandmother. Have you tried reaching her?

I glance back towards Drake. Yes, I have tried to reach Grandma Ma. But... no, nothing. I cannot feel her, and she is not answering either. I do not know where she is. You don't think she is one of these piles of clothing, do you?

All the piles of clothing — who do they belong to? If you take away the blood and gore, you could almost be forgiven for thinking someone threw a massive party and forgot to clean up.

I sweep the room again, searching for anything resembling Alexettia's clothing. Nothing. Then it hits me. Dust. What is with all this fine dust? It coats everything, clinging to the air, the floor, the weapons, even the blood.

We both stop and inspect some of the clothing as we move through the carnage. Guard uniforms. Castle staff uniforms I do not recognise. We continue searching and checking through the piles for identification and weapons. My hand brushes against something cold, long, and hard. This is not on the list of items I expect to find today as my fingers wrap around the stainless steel spike.

"Oh, wow," I whisper, holding it up. "Do people actually use a spike to kill a Dark One? I thought that was only in the movies. You know — fiction, make-believe, popcorn entertainment. Not real life."

The stake is heavy, solid, and fits comfortably in my hand. Too comfortably.

…Hang on. All the dust everywhere…

Drake, can Dark Ones be killed with a stake, just like in the movies? I ask through our mind link.

Drake turns and looks at me, his eyes moving to the stainless steel stake in my fisted hand.

His presence fills my mind as he answers. *'Yes, Alexia. Just like in the movies, if you hit a fully turned Dark One in the correct spot, right here.'* With his hand, Drake touches his chest, right over his heart. *'A stake straight through the heart usually kills a Dark One. Their bodies disintegrate, leaving what they are wearing behind.'*

Oh, wow — oh, crap on a stick. Does that mean, now we have completed the Joining Ceremony, if we're stabbed in the chest with a stake, this can happen to us as well?

Drake sighs in his head. After a few seconds, he replies, *'Yes, Alexia. Yes, this can now happen to us. The plan is not to let anyone stab us in the heart.'*

'Great plan,' I mutter in my head. *'Don't get stabbed by sharp, pointy objects. Totally foolproof. What could possibly go wrong?'*

My grip tightens on the stake. My mind is running wild, sarcasm blocking the worst of the danger, but underneath it, fear gnaws at me. Grandma Ma is missing. The staff are gone.

The castle is a slaughterhouse. And someone out there is still here.

I look back at Drake and say to him through our mind link, You know, it would have been nice for someone to explain a few more details to me about Dark Ones, especially this little piece of information. For example — Rule 99: Do not get stabbed in the heart, as it will lead to instant death, and your body will disintegrate. Grrr — Dark Ones.

'Alexia, I can feel your upset—'

Is he serious right now? I interrupt him with a raised sharp brow. Upset. Me upset!

'Please don't get me started on how I feel right now, Drake. Come on, let's keep moving.' My free hand waves around towards all the carnage. *'Before someone comes along and finds us here amongst all this mess and tries to accuse us of doing it.'*

I continue moving and sorting through the items on the floor. The Royal Guards and staff deserve to be recognised for their service and remembered, so I keep looking for any identification. At least then, someone can notify the fallen slain's next of kin.

With the thoughts of Grandma Ma, I just hope Alexettia is not amongst the slain — one of the dead — a pile of dust and clothing.

Deciding to keep the sharp stake with its interesting engraved swirling pattern, I slide it safely into my cargo pants, sitting snug in one of the long, narrow side pockets on the outside of my left thigh, within easy reach if I need it. First, I must learn how to stake someone; I just hope I don't get a crash course lesson in staking tonight.

I come across a sharp, long sword resembling a Samurai katana. Something in me insists I pick it up. My hands automatically grip the black and gold handle. My feet separate shoulder-width apart. With a few fast movements — side to side, up, wide circles — I test the blade, watching the silver glint slice the air. The weight feels exquisite, balanced, like it belongs to me.

I wipe the blade against some clothing on the floor, scraping off blood and gore. Deciding the sword is better off with me than left here for someone else to use against me, I look down and notice a hard leather sheath. Sliding the sword into it, I find it a perfect fit. The sheath separates into two straps, designed to be worn across the back. Cool. Pulling my jacket off, I strap it on, secure it around my waist, and slide my arms through the harness.

I pull my jacket back over the sheath, wiggle my arms, test my movement. The strange thing is, the sword feels like it was made for me. I reach back, pull it free in one smooth motion, holding it ready. Cool.

Smiling, I glance up and notice Drake has also found a sword and sheath. He straps it across his back, then pulls it free in one fluid motion. My lips curl into a grin, and I wink at him. Oh my, my handsome warrior man looks good with a sword in his hands.

I nod, slide my own blade back into its sheath, and keep moving through the carnage. The uneasy feeling of no one alive presses hard in my stomach. Where is everyone else? Where are the rest of the castle staff?

Another find: a DXm 40, 9mm handgun. I release the chamber, slide the magazine out. Silver bullets. Of course. Quickly searching the pile, I find two more clips. I pocket them, switch the safety on, and keep the gun in hand. Something black catches my eye.

I pick up a Condor leg rig with several full mag clips. Wow. I strap it to my thigh, slide the 9mm into the holster, secure it with the thumb-break strap. Instant accessibility. I grin. Okay, I think I'm going to like this new attachment.

I'm grateful Dad took Drake and me to the shooting range last school holidays. Guns, reloading, safety drills — all suddenly relevant.

My foot nudges odd-shaped bits of silver. Spent bullets. These little pieces of metal killed most of the people here.

Hmm, I think, maybe a bulletproof vest would help against bullets and stakes. I remember the Safar Body Armor SX02 I tried on at the range — light, flexible, designed for women. Note to self: order them in for Darshia's guards. Something has to be done. I never want to witness this carnage again.

Slowly gathering more identification badges, I find three guards I knew. My eyes mist. These men will never see their families again. One of them is James, my security doorman.

Oh, no. Not James. Tears slip down my cheeks. He was kind to me. A Dark One, yes, but decent.

Taking a deep breath, I steel myself. Time to kick butt. Time to punish whoever did this.

Drake, I think it is time to go to Grandma Ma's office. One

— I need to know if the bad guys are in there. Two — we need to drop these identification badges off.

Drake nods, weapons strapped across his body like me. My eyebrows rise at his new accessories.

What? I can hear you, Alexia. I am your husband, your soulmate. His hand rests on the gun at his thigh. And it is my right to protect you and our unborn child. I will kill if I have to. I love you, Alexia. It would destroy me if anything happens to you.

My defences crumble. My heart melts.

Oh, Drake, I love you too. You silly man, you know I can look after myself. I am, if not better than you, in hand-to-hand combat. I could outshoot you in the targets as well. You make sure you look after yourself. Because if you don't, how will you be there to back me up? Don't play the hero. You started as my neighbour, the guy next door, the one I could rely on. And now you're my friend, lover, husband, soulmate — I love you.

By the time I finish, Drake and I are face-to-face, body to body. Our lips crash together, hard, desperate. This is no gentle kiss; this is the type of kiss you have when your life depends on it. My lungs empty as his arms wrap tight around me. I never want to let go, but we need to move. Survivors. Grandma Ma. The bad guys.

Slowly pulling apart, I look deep into his eyes.

Drake, I love you and our children. Always remember that. Now, let's go. We need to track down the bad guys before they find us.

I love you, Alexia. Be careful. His hand caresses my lower belly.

I nod, turn towards the main hallway. We push our way back through blood, gore, clothing, basically the carnage. I am amazed no one else has come bursting in. Where is the rest of the castle's security? Why is Grandma Ma not answering? And most of all, where are the bad guys?

It is far too quiet.

We move stealthily amongst the shadows, heading towards Grandma Ma's office.

Within minutes, we are near the Queen's office. The little hairs on the back of my neck rise.

Oh, this can't be good.

CHAPTER THIRTY-FOUR

I REACH OUT WITH MY MIND TOWARDS GRANDMA MA'S office. Within seconds, I detect one person. Even though my senses swear there are more people in there — either my Dark One powers are still warming up, or someone has thrown up a protective barrier around the office.

We stop outside the door. My mind senses four individuals inside. Two are on the floor, unconscious, and the other two are busy rummaging through Grandma Ma's desk, drawers, and cupboards like bargain hunters at a garage sale. As hard as I try, I cannot breach their minds.

'Drake, can you detect the four people in Grandma Ma's office?'

My eyes flick to him, waiting for his acknowledgement. With a slight nod, he confirms what I sense.

'I know there are two of them on the floor, unconscious, but I am not sure who they are. The other two are searching Grandma Ma's desk and cupboards for something. Can you pick anything up? Can you work out who they are? Who is on the floor?'

Drake shakes his head. *'Alexia, I can just make out four people in there. It feels like a force field, something interrupts my ability.'*

I nod. I agree. *'It feels like some kind of barrier. Either Grandma Ma set it up, or the bad guys are hiding behind it.'*

Drake's lips curl into a grin. The one when he's up to something. *'Come on, Alexia, let's put our new weapons to good use and practice our workout moves against the bad guys.'*

Oh, goodie. Nothing like a surprise workout session with murderers. I slowly remove the 9mm from the leg rig, slide the safety off, and steady my breath.

We move to either side of the door frame. I sense the handle, checking for traps. Nothing. I nod to Drake. He nods back.

'Now,' we say as one.

Drake bursts forward, slamming the door open, gun raised. He fires instantly, the shot cracking through the air. The first person behind the desk jerks, collapses, and hits the floor.

The second person whirls, his eyes red, gun already lifting. My instincts scream. I raise my handgun, aim, and squeeze the trigger. The kickback jolts my arm, but the silver bullet flies true — straight through the heart. The Dark One disintegrates before my eyes, collapsing into a pile of clothing.

"Oh, wow," I mutter, blinking at the mess. "So that's what happens. Instant laundry service."

My brain scrambles to catch up. I just killed someone. Correction: I just killed something. Numbness creeps in, but sarcasm steadies me.

I shake my head, clearing the fog. No time to think. I scan the room, gun ready, waiting for another attacker to leap out. Nothing.

I holster the gun, crouch beside the unconscious figures. The first is male. Dressed in the royal guard's uniform. I shake my head when I realise who it is. Jones, head of security.

"Oh, great," I mutter. "At least he's alive. Unlike poor James out in the foyer." I roll him into the recovery position, grimacing at the pool of blood under his chest. If only he had better protection on his upper body. "Chest armour. Note to self: mandatory." Since my father introduced me to the ones at the shooting range last year, if the people here had them here, maybe there would be a lot more citizens of Darshia would be alive.

The second body makes my stomach drop. *Alexettia.* Her hair is matted with blood, her leg twisted at an unnatural angle, bone jutting through fabric. Bruises, swelling, puncture wounds. I reach for her neck to check for a pulse.

"Oh, no. No, no, no." My voice cracks. Her heart beat is sluggish.

She's alive — barely.

I reach out with my mind, searching for the doctor. It takes seconds to locate him.

But before I can call him in, movement flickers in the corner of my eye.

"Drake!" I shout, spinning.

Another Dark One bursts from the shadows, blade raised. Where did he come from? Drake pivots, his sword flashing free from its sheath. Steel meets steel with a ringing clash. Sparks fly. As Drake swings again, the Dark One kicks out, sending Drake backwards.

I yank my katana free, adrenaline surging. "Guess it's my turn."

The Dark One lunges at me, teeth bared, strength inhuman. I sidestep, swing the blade in a wide arc, catching his arm. Blood sprays, sizzling against the floor. He snarls, spinning back, faster than human eyes can follow.

"Seriously?" I mutter. "Do you guys rehearse these moves, or is it just natural evil flair?"

He lunges again. I duck, roll, and come up behind him. My blade slices across his back. He stumbles, hissing.

Drake shouts, "Alexia, finish him!"

"Oh, sure, no pressure!" I retort, raising the katana. The Dark One, with glowy red eyes, spins, claws slashing. I block, sparks flying again. My arms ache, but I push forward, driving the blade into his chest.

The scream is guttural, cut short as his body disintegrates, collapsing into dust and clothing.

I pant, sweat dripping down my temple. "Well, that was fun. Ten out of ten for cardio. Zero out of ten for hospitality."

Drake wipes his blade, eyes scanning the room. "Stay sharp. There may be more."

I nod, sliding my sword back into its sheath. How did we not sense the latest pile of clothing and dust?

With my hand resting on the butt of my gun I turn to survey the room. Before I can blink, another stranger with a sword bursts through the door, a side door.

Without hesitation, I raise my gun and fire. The recoil shakes my arm, and a loud bang echoes around me. The menacing stranger's eyes widen in surprise before his body disintegrates, exploding into a cloud of dust. His clothing and sword drop to the ground with a thud.

"Alexia, stop messing around."

My gaze lifts from the clothing to Drake, my eyebrow raises at him.

Seriously! Shake my head and glance back to Alexettia again. She needs help. She needs it now.

Okay, what do I do? Think, Alexia, think. Before I was rudely interrupted, I was about to call for help. Yes, Dr Brean will know what to do. Quickly reaching out with my mind, it only takes seconds to track the doctor down.

'Excuse me, Doctor Brean, Alexia here. Princess Alexia.' I don't give the man a chance to reply, and keep going. *'We have a security and medical emergency at the castle. I am in Grandma Ma's office. Both Grandma Ma and her head of security, Jones, are severely hurt and unconscious. They look bad — as in, I do not know how long they will live. The castle has been under attack. There is a lot of blood...and dust. We need an ambulance here. ASAP.*

Great, now I'm babbling. Fantastic. Princess Alexia, professional rambler in times of crisis.

A moment later, I sense the doctor at my shields.

'Princess Alexia, I have medical and guards on their way, including several doctors and nurses. They should be there in a matter of moments. Do you know if the people who attacked the Queen are still there?'

I shake my head. *'Doctor Brean, I do not know. How am I meant to know — I haven't had time to search the castle! I shot and killed three armed, unknown people here in Grandma Ma's office. Drake has shot and injured another man that is also in the office. Please hurry. I do not know how much longer Grandma Ma will remain alive.'*

Closing my mind link, I carefully place Grandma Ma in recovery, taking extra care of her injuries. My stomach turns and twists at the sight of her leg and arm. Deciding to try again, I attempt to reach into Grandma Ma and Jones's minds. Something blocks me. I cannot penetrate their minds.

Walking over to Drake behind the large office desk, I see him bending down, tying the man's hands behind his back.

A low, gruff voice growls, "Untie me, kid. I will make sure they do not kill your little girlfriend."

Drake snorts. "Do you think I would fall for that old line? As soon as you're free, you'll shoot both of us. Don't take this personally, but we don't believe you. Security can deal with you when they arrive."

"Don't do this, kid. Release me, now."

Drake's tone sharpens. "No. How about you be quiet?"

He turns his head in my direction, his mind brushing mine. *'Alexia, have you contacted security yet or anyone?'*

Uh, what the? Does he think I'm that stupid? I remind myself to stay calm, take a deep breath, and answer.

'Drake. I have medical help on the way; they should be here shortly. Jones and Grandma Ma are both in a bad way and still unconscious. I hope they will make it. Do you know this man or who his accomplices were? I cannot believe I shot someone, and they just poof — disintegrated. Those chest shields we were looking at at the firing range look really good right about now. Also, I was just about to see if I could find any of the security personnel.'

I stop myself from babbling. Time is bleeding away — literally — and I reach out with my mind, searching first the hallway, then the surrounding rooms.

The more I concentrate, the more I notice how I can acknowledge the remains of the fallen in different parts of the castle, as if the castle itself is joining with me, guiding me. A shiver rolls down my spine.

Finally, I find someone alive.

For once, I penetrate their mind. Riley. The other security guard who had been in my hospital room after the failed attempt on my life.

I breach his mind, bombarding him with questions. *'Riley, are you okay? Try not to be alarmed; this is Princess Alexia.'*

Riley freezes, eyes darting around, trying to find me. *'Wow, how are you doing this? Only the Queen can speak with the guards like this.'* Shock and amazement line his voice.

'Get over yourself, Riley. We do not have time to argue. Where are all the other security guards? The Queen and Jones are down. Medical is on its way. I need a thorough search of the castle and grounds for intruders. I also require two or three guards here at the Queen's office to escort the prisoner we have contained. His mates disagreed with the bullet — I shot into their heart. The other didn't like the blade of the sword I had in my hand. They all just fell apart on me,' I say dryly.

Riley stammers. *'You shot someone — you, Princess Alexia, who is just a kid, dusted a Dark One with a bullet to the heart, and a sword.'*

I roll my eyes. *'Riley, it was three. Look, we do not have time for this doubt. Do you have contact with the other guards and security?'*

'Oh, um, yes. One... one moment, Princess Alexia.'

I listen as Riley communicates with his fellow guards, issuing orders. Relief fills me. Security is on its way.

'Oh, by the way, Riley, we need armed clean-up crews in the foyer because it looks like a slaughterhouse. I've collected the identification dog tags from the fallen guards and also found James' dog tags. Could someone please inform his family or follow the proper procedure? Additionally, instruct the staff to handle everyone's remains — clothing included — with care.

'Yes, Princess Alexia. I will arrange for the clean-up crew.'

'Thank you. Oh, and Riley. We need to organise groups to search the entire castle. Whoever attacked Queen Alexettia may still be roaming around. Meet me in the Queen's office in five minutes. Then we can start the security sweep for any remaining enemy fighters.'

'Yes, Princess Alexia. I will be there shortly.'

I exhale, tension buzzing through me. Medical is coming. Security is coming. But the castle is still crawling with shadows, and I know this fight isn't over.

CHAPTER THIRTY-FIVE

I WATCH — SEVEN MEDICAL PERSONNEL AND THREE GUARDS arrive within five minutes of talking with Dr Brean. The medics efficiently place both Grandma Ma and Jones on individual stretchers, IVs already attached to their arms, and escort them to the hospital. Two security guards stay glued to their sides under my orders — protect them at all costs.

I decide it's wisest to inform my parents of Grandma Ma's brutal, almost deadly assault and the attack at the castle.

'Alexia, your father and I will remain extra vigilant. You know we will protect the twins with our lives. Right now, I am more worried about your safety.' How I love my mother. *'Would it be better to leave Darshia and come back home?'* Her mind voice cracks with her plea. *'Please, baby girl. We want you safe.'*

My eyes meet Drake's concerned ones. Before he can speak, Riley and four other men arrive.

'Mum, Riley and his men have arrived. I need to speak with them. Please watch out for any strangers. Keep safe. Love you all.' I end our link before she can reply. My heart can't take it. If I'm to become the next queen of Darshia, I better step up and look after my people.

The last two medics check the prisoner before packing up their equipment. Riley speaks with one of his men, deep in conversation. The dark-haired, solid-built man nods and takes off out the door. Riley steps around the medic as he leaves, stops before me, and shakes his head.

"Princess Alexia. As you are aware, the situation is serious. At least one-quarter of the castle staff and guards are slaughtered. I have three other groups of eight scouring the rest of the castle. As you would have noticed, Haze — I've sent him to oversee the search teams on the lower levels before meeting us back up here."

I nod, turning to face his other men. Okay, at least I know there are guards still alive. That's something.

All right then, time to meet Riley's team. I step forward and offer my hand to the first guard — a tall, solid-built man with short, cropped blond hair and a quiet demeanour. He glances at Riley, nods, and then shakes my hand.

"Hello, I'm Princess Alexia, and you are?"

In a low, solid voice, he replies, "Bl'ack, princess. I am Riley's second." His firm grip releases my hand, and Drake moves closer, introducing himself to Bl'ack.

I turn to the next guard — tall, solid muscle like Bl'ack, with a cheeky look in his eyes and short sable-colored hair. He shakes my hand firmly. "Heya, Princess Alexia, my name is Stiffen."

I nod and release his hand. Well, this one might be the life of the party if his tone is anything to go by.

I face the last member of the four-man group. He's bigger than the others, bald, with the bluest eyes I've ever seen — and carrying enough weapons to stock a small armoury. He steps forward, bows his head in respect.

I watch as he straightens and his powerful blue eyes meet mine. He glances at Drake, then back at me. "Hello, Princess Alexia. My name is Tablot."

"Hello, Tablot. Good to see a man well prepared."

His eyebrow lifts. I glance at his arsenal, then meet his eyes and smile. His lips twitch, and he gives me a slight nod.

"Better to be prepared, Ma'am."

I nod in return. "I completely agree."

'Drake, what do you think of these men?' I ask via our link as I turn to face Riley.

Drake doesn't keep me waiting. *'Babe, I'm relieved to know we have security. Time will tell if they can protect you.'*

My thoughts exactly.

Out loud, I say, "Riley, what is the plan of action?"

His eyes scan my body. "From the weapons strapped to you, you're expecting to tag along?"

My brow raises, and I nod. "You guessed right, Riley. I

know how to shoot and want the bastards caught. Dead or alive."

He looks me straight in the eye for several seconds, then nods. "You can tag along for now. At least you'll have our protection."

My best course of action is to hold my tongue. These men don't know me. They have to earn my trust, just as I will have to earn theirs.

Riley quickly outlines their plan, instructing me to stay close at all times so we can work together as a team. I bet he thinks I will be a burden rather than an asset. We move from room to room, sweeping through each one. Alarmingly, every room we enter has been ransacked, similar to Grandma Ma's office.

Talking with Riley and the three men, they keep their answers short and brief. So I ask, "How did such an attack happen?" I don't wait for an answer; I keep asking, "Do you, the palace security, have access to Special Forces or Special Medical Forces?"

The men look at me as if I've lost my mind. Their smug faces and lack of answers tell me I won't get what I want. If they think I'm a pushover, they'd better think again.

Okay, different tactic. "Riley, if something happens here in Darshia and you don't know how it happened… do you have someone who can perform medical or science tests to fill in the missing details? For example, is there a chemical that affects the men, slows them down? Surely, there are more castle guards. Where are they?"

He pauses, then replies, "Princess Alexia, I will have the lab and hospital scientists run tests in the different rooms, food, water, and also the air conditioning. Just to put your mind at ease and ensure the other Dark Ones will not be affected. Otherwise, no. We have nothing like your human television shows, like CSI. Now, if that is all, we need to keep moving."

Am I annoyed with Riley's avoidance of my two main questions? You betchya I am. First, where are all the security guards? Second, how did the attack even happen?

With that in mind, I search his surface thoughts. It doesn't take me long to discover what he's hiding.

RILEY'S PAST WITH GRANDMA MA LEAVES A SOUR TASTE IN my mouth. Honestly, that is way too much information I do not need, especially when I've sat in that office chair. Blah. Mental bleach, please.

The deeper I dig into his mind, the more twisted the story becomes. Alexettia mistreated him — mentally, physically, emotionally. She degraded him with bizarre sexual acts she forced on her lovers. Riley only stayed at the castle because being a guard meant food on the table and a roof over his head and his son. Wait — Riley has a child? That's news.

I push further, bypassing his mental barrier, and hit a wall of sorrow, anger, guilt, and heartbreak. The truth slams into me: Riley's soulmate was murdered two years ago. Right around the time Grandma Ma demanded he join her in her bed. Tragic doesn't even cover it. Interesting, yes. Disturbing, definitely.

But tonight, Riley and his men had been posted at the

hospital, keeping watch over me. That explains why they weren't here. They underestimated me, though. How did they not notice I slipped away? Rookie mistake.

I enter one of the darkened guest rooms, senses prickling. Danger. My hand shoots out, grabbing Riley's jacket, yanking him back. My other hand lifts, finger squeezing the 9mm trigger. A flash. A bang. The room explodes with light as someone flicks the switch. A thud. Clothing collapses to the floor.

"Oh, crap on a stick," I mutter, heart pounding. Adrenaline surges. That was close.

Reality slaps me — I just shot and dusted another Dark One. And saved Riley's life.

I release Riley's jacket, stumble back into Drake's muscular arms.

"Shit, babe. You are proving deadly with a gun tonight," he murmurs near my ear, half proud, half worried.

Riley inspects the pile of clothing and weapon. Bl'ack mutters from beside me, "Shit, Riley, if the Princess hadn't pulled you back, you'd be dead. She saved your bacon. Man, she's good with a gun. Glad she's on our side."

Riley stares at the bullet hole in the wall, then at me. "Thank you, Princess Alexia." His gaze drops to his feet, then back to my eyes. "I am also sorry for my behaviour earlier. You are new here to Darshia. You don't know about Dark Ones. I should remember that. I have no excuse. Please forgive me."

I nod. "Riley, chances are I'll be around here for a long time. So, I'd suggest you look at me as an equal. I am not my grandmother." With that, I turn and stride out of the room, Drake hot on my heels.

WE ARRIVE ON THE SAME FLOOR AS THE BEDROOM I'VE BEEN staying in. I reach out with my mind, checking in with Doctor Brean for a progress report on Grandma Ma and Jones.

Excuse me, Doctor Brean. Princess Alexia here again. How are Grandma Ma and Jones going? Have they gained consciousness yet?

Even from this distance, I skim his mind. Oh, wow. This is new. And gross. Honestly, I don't want to do this again — being inside a physician's mind is like wading through medical charts dipped in blood. Yuk. It was bad enough seeing the carnage in the castle, but now I'm seeing the severely injured through his eyes. Not fun.

'*Princess Alexia. Hello to you.*' He pauses, struggling to find words. His hesitation makes my stomach twist. Bad news. I can already sense it. '*I have some bad news for you.*' See — told ya.

A SHARP INTAKE OF BREATH FIGHTS ITS WAY INTO MY LUNGS. Hearing those words, ready or not, still shocks my system. Unease swirls in my belly. Oh, no. What bad news? Not Grandma Ma? Then it dawns on me — one of the horrific images I had glimpsed in the doctor's mind. A battered, bloody Grandma Ma.

'Princess Alexia, your grandmother remains unresponsive. For a Dark One of her resilience, this prolonged loss of consciousness is atypical and concerning. At present, we are conducting a full diagnostic workup, including neurological monitoring and systemic imaging. Orthopaedically, we have reduced and immobilised fractures of both her humerus and femur, stabilising them with plaster casts. Thoracic surgery was required to repair a lacerated left lung, and nephrological intervention addressed trauma to her left kidney. Hepatic function is compromised due to extensive parenchymal damage, and we are monitoring her liver enzymes closely. Her chest cavity sustained multiple penetrating injuries; we performed extensive debridement and suturing to control haemorrhage and restore structural integrity. Given the severity of polytrauma and the cumulative blood loss, her prognosis remains undetermined. I must caution you — survival through the night is uncertain.'

Somehow, I understand everything he just said. Thanks to last term's crash course we did to earn more credits at the local hospital emergency department. At least I know I have retained some of that information.

"Oh, Gods, no." Grandma Ma cannot die.

The infuriating woman has far too much left to discuss with me. She promised to teach me the deeper secrets of the castle, about the abilities of the Queen. Too much remains unsaid. Alexettia cannot die — not yet. She wants to know what it feels like to retire after all these years of ruling.

Doctor Brean's voice slices through my spiralling panic. *'As for the guard named Jones. I'm sorry, Princess Alexia. Unfortunately, I hold little hope for him. One bullet we removed was poisoned. Even if he survives the night and regains consciousness, the type of poison we are dealing with is a death sentence for a Dark One.'*

"Oh, my Gods. This cannot be happening," I murmur out loud.

'Doctor Brean, if you have not done so already, I require around-the-clock guards on Grandma Ma and Jones. Only a few of your most trusted staff are to treat them. Do you understand, Doctor?'

'Yes. I understand, Princess Alexia.'

'Thank you, Doctor Brean. I will see you, Grandma Ma, and Jones as soon as we finish in the castle.'

I end the mental conversation, forcing myself to focus on what's happening around me.

CHAPTER THIRTY-SIX

Drake and I step into the hallway, the silence pressing down like a heavy blanket. The castle feels wrong — too quiet, too empty, like the walls themselves are holding their breath.

"Great," I mutter under my breath. "Riley and his merry band of muscle run off, and now it's just us. Perfect time for a trap."

Drake's hand brushes mine, steady and warm. "What do you expect from your Grandmother's security. Stay sharp, Alexia."

"Oh, don't worry. I'm sharp enough to cut glass right now." Just wait until I see Riley next.

We move cautiously, weapons ready, sweeping each corridor. My senses prickle — something is off. The air feels heavier, charged, like static before a storm.

We reach my bedroom door on the third floor. It's ajar.

That's not right... Why is my door not shut? My stomach twists.

Slowly and carefully, we enter my bedroom foyer. Within seconds, I sense someone in my walk-in wardrobe. Drake and I lock eyes, silently confirming we're not alone.

Reaching out through our mind link, I whisper, *'Drake, do you sense who it is?'*

Drake stiffens, his eyes narrowing. His features harden.
He knows.
I try to push into his thoughts, only to slam into a wall.
What the...?
He's blocked me out. How in the world did he manage that?

'Drake, who is it? Do you know who it is?' I demand.

He presses a finger to his lips. *'Alexia, I want you to leave and bring Riley back with the other guards.'*

What... No. Why? Unease coils in my stomach. Whoever is in my room has Drake rattled.

'Drake, who is it?'

His reply is sharp, angry, cutting through my mind. *'Alexia, leave now.'*

Confused and hurt, I back out of the bedroom doorway into the hallway. My chest tightens. Is Drake trying to protect me, or does he think I can't defend myself? Either way, I feel bewildered and stung by his tone. Who in the hell is in my room?

I slip my phone from my pocket, thumb tapping the voice recorder. If Drake is going to play lone hero, I'm at least going to have evidence. Battery life be damned.

As soon as I clear the doorway, I reach out to Riley.

'You better answer me, Riley. You should be here with me!'

His mental shields bounce off my intrusion. *'Yes, Princess Alexia,'* Riley pauses, as if he is choosing his words. *'My men decided, we'll cover more ground by splitting up. You were safe.'*

'Not the point, Riley.'

'So far, by splitting up, we have encountered far too many injured personnel and are in the process of having medical take them to the foyer for assessment. Lives we are saving.'

He is not going to make me feel guilty!

'Riley, you should have remained with me. You know this castle. You are my security.'

'Are you in danger right this minute?'

'Riley, that's the million-dollar question. We have found someone in my room. Drake is insisting on your assistance — right now. Make sure the three guards are with you. Do not let me down — hurry.'

The sound of him cursing and commanding the others to return to me, reaches my thoughts. I don't think Riley realises I can hear all his thoughts and mental commands to his men. *'Yes, Princess Alexia. We will return to you immediately.'*

I sever the link, only to hear swearing, angry words, and the unmistakable sound of furniture breaking. Great. That's my stuff. Drake is fighting whoever's in there.

So much for waiting for Riley and the guards. Why did Drake confront whoever is in there? This is just great — Drake probably thinks he's protecting the baby and me. Will he ever learn?

Pain slams into my head and chest, sharp and biting. My brain catches up — Drake.

He's hurt.

Instinct takes over. I reach out, breaking through his mental barrier.

Oh, my Gods. No. My heart lurches. I can just make out… Oh, no. Drake is fighting …his father. And his father is beating the crap out of him.

Davelt's voice rips through the chaos, dripping venom. "Are you going to give up, boy? I can whip your arse anytime.

You will never beat me. You only know how to fight like a puny little human. What a joke you are to this family, to all the Dark Ones. That little slut you're with will die by my hand, and you will never stop me. You hear me, boy? She is dead, and if you keep fighting me, so will you be."

Rage burns through me. My fists clench. My scorn for the man spikes even as fear claws at me. Oh, fantastic. Family reunion night. Should I grab popcorn or a stake?

A stake sounds good right about now.

Drake roars back, voice raw. "No. Stay away from my wife. You are nothing to me. You stopped being my father years ago. It is you who will ruin our family. You. Not me. You did it all on your own. You are nothing but scum."

From Drake's perspective, I observe Davelt lunging forward with unnaturally quick movements. Drake blocks and counters, delivering a powerful strike to his ribs. The cracking of bone reverberates through the room. For a moment, it seems Drake has gained the advantage.

But Davelt recovers instantly, slamming his elbow into Drake's jaw, sending him staggering. He follows with a brutal knee to Drake's stomach, forcing him to double over. Blood sprays from Drake's mouth, splattering across the carpet.

Drake rallies, spinning with a desperate kick that connects with Davelt's thigh. The older Dark One barely flinches, snarling as he grabs Drake by the collar and hurls him into the wardrobe door. Wood splinters, shards flying.

My heart races. Every blow Drake takes reverberates through me. His pain is mine.

Drake staggers upright, eyes blazing, fists clenched. He charges again, unleashing a flurry of punches — jaw, ribs, temple. Davelt blocks most, absorbs the rest, then retaliates with a savage headbutt that sends Drake reeling.

Blood drips into Drake's eyes, blurring his vision as he looks down. Oh goddess no. Blood drips and spreads on his jumper. He bends, gasping for breath, his strength faltering.

Sensing me in his mind, Drake halts, his focus shifting. His thoughts brush mine, heavy with pain and determination.

'Alexia, remember I love you, baby. My father has stabbed me, there must be poison or something on his weapon. It's weakening me. Hopefully, I have reduced his strength enough for the guards to finish this fight. Please wait for Riley before rushing in here.'

Drake's voice echoes in my mind, ragged and fading. My chest tightens.

Davelt's angry snarl drags me back. "You have to be joking. You married that little bitch? Do you know what you've done?"

I feel Drake stiffen, his anger building like a storm.

Davelt's smug tone cuts deeper. "What have you done to our family? I might as well walk out of this room and kill her right now, and there will be nothing you can do to stop me."

Oh, fantastic. Family drama and death threats. Just what I needed tonight. That pathetic excuse for a man does not know what I am capable of.

Drake explodes forward, fists flying. He lands several hard hits to Davelt's kidneys and a right hook to his jaw. For a moment, I think he might win.

Too late. Davelt blocks, counters, and drives his fist into

Drake's stomach. My husband doubles over, gasping. Then Davelt rains punches down on his head. Each one, a personal blow to me. Pain echoes through me as I sense each blow opening fresh wounds. Blood splatters, dripping into Drake's eyes and mouth.

Without thinking, I race back into the bedroom. Enough is enough.

My focus finds them instantly. Davelt's back is to me, towering between Drake and my bed. Drake staggers upright, bleeding, his jumper staining with dark red patches.

Before I can move, Davelt thrusts forward. A glint of steel catches my eye. A sharp crack echoes through the room. My breath halts as the onslaught of pain fills my chest.

Oh, Gods no. He's staked Drake.

I scream — whether out loud or in my head, I don't know. The sound of bone breaking under the stake makes my stomach lurch.

Drake gasps, struggling for breath. Relief floods me when he doesn't disintegrate. He's alive. But blood blossoms across his chest, staining his jumper.

No. No, Drake. You promised not to get stabbed by sharp, pointy things.

In slow motion, he stumbles. Rage surges through me. I slam my boot into the back of Davelt's knee, forcing him down. Spinning on my heel, I drive my boot into the back of his head. The crack is sickening.

Using my new Dark One speed, I catch Drake before his head hits the floor. Oomph. He's heavy, but I drag him towards the door, as Davelt collapses, hopefully unconscious.

My boot kicks something. The sound of it reminds me of

the sound of metal being struck. As soon as I glance at it, I recognise what it is. The blood-covered stake rolls across the carpet. My stomach twists.

Once outside my room, I carefully place Drake down and rip open his jumper. A jagged hole gapes in his chest, blood bubbling. Panic claws at me. Without thinking, I bite my wrist, letting blood drip into the wound.

I lick the bite closed, then press my tongue to Drake's wound. Air splutters against my face — his lung is punctured. The edges begin to heal, but blood and air keep escaping.

"Oh, shite," I groan. "No. I need help."

I reach out with my mind, slamming into the medical teams downstairs. *'Get your arses up here now. Drake is dying,'* I demand.

I strip off my jacket and long-sleeved top, fold the fabric into a pad, and press it against his chest. Wrapping my sword sheath straps around him, I tighten them to stem the bleeding.

I check his pulse. Weak. His breath rattles. Fear grips me.

I bite my wrist again, press it to his lips, forcing him to drink. My blood slowly seals the wound.

Please let it help.

"Don't you dare die on me, my husband! You must live to care for our little family and me." I kiss his forehead, whispering, "Please, please remember, I will always love you. My soulmate."

Tears streak my cheeks. I wipe them away, forcing myself to stay strong. His heart still beats — slow, but steady.

"Stay strong and do not die, Drake. We need you."

Fast footsteps thunder down the hallway. The medical team bursts in. I pull back, giving them space.

"We will take it from here, Princess Alexia. You did a good job trying to stop the bleeding." Yeah, great. Tried to stop the bleeding. Not exactly confidence-boosting. "The hospital is waiting for us to arrive. Will you be joining us, Princess Alexia?"

They strap Drake to a stretcher, IV already in place. His unconscious body is covered in gauze and tape, blood soaking through. His face is battered, lips swollen, eyes closed. My heart shatters.

Turning back towards the medic guy, I answer his question, "No. I have something to deal with first," I tell the medic. "By the way. Drake's lung is punctured, and someone poisoned him. Make sure he survives. I will be at the hospital as soon as I am finished here."

I kiss my husband's forehead, whispering, "I love you," before they carry him away.

I reach out to Riley and his team.

Nothing but silence.

Right then. I think sarcastically. *Looks like I'm on my own.*

I stand tall, take a deep breath, and turn back toward my room. Time to finish this. Drake's father will not walk away alive.

CHAPTER THIRTY-SEVEN

FIGHT TILL THE END!

A NOISE REACHES MY EARS — MUFFLED COMMOTION COMING from inside my room.

Great. Just what I need. I sigh, already knowing exactly who's responsible.

Drake's father is gaining consciousness. Damn the man. He never stays knocked out for long. For someone who's basically a walking tumour of ego and cruelty, he's annoyingly resilient. I ease back into my room to face the monster who thinks hurting his own child is perfectly acceptable behaviour.

Once I'm past the door, I catch Davelt struggling to sit up. Good to know a well-placed kick can still put him on his arse. He tries to rise, fails, and collapses back to the floor, groaning and mumbling when he notices me.

He spits — a dark blob landing on my carpet. My carpet. "Well, well. It's the little bitch herself." His voice is a wet, ugly rasp. He rubs the back of his head with one hand and his right kidney with the other. Watching him drag himself up to his knees has me thinking I'd better stop him before he gets fully upright. The man does not stay down for long. Like a cockroach with a superiority complex.

"Stop right there, Davelt. You're under arrest." Not my most creative line, but it'll do. I'm multitasking.

Every few seconds, I pause and listen towards the door. The silence in the hallway tells me Riley and his men still haven't arrived. What is taking them so long? I reach out with my mind — nothing. Absolutely nothing. Like shouting into a void. Something is blocking me, and that is not good. I hope the boys are okay. Damn it. I'm going to have to stall until they get here.

The Dark One cockroach catches my attention. "Stop. Stop," Davelt spits. My eyes meet his black orbs surround with a ring of red. "You — telling me to stop." He smirks, blood staining his teeth. "I don't think so, bitch. I'm going to kill you." He sways as he gets to his feet. Good. My kick rattled him more than he realises. He lifts his chin and scowls. "How dare you poison my family's bloodline? How dare you interfere. Because of you, my slut of a wife has left me. Me. Unfuckingbelievable."

He rants like he can't fathom why she'd leave in the first place. Somehow, the man has never looked in a mirror. Or maybe he has and assumed the mirror was lying.

I keep my distance, weighing up my options. My stake might help, but that means getting up close and personal. No thanks. The gun sounds much better right now. Shoot Davelt straight through the heart. Oh, yes. Dusting him has its perks. And honestly, he'd make a very satisfying pile of ash.

I reach out with my mind again — still nothing. No Riley.

Oh boy, this is not good. And Davelt rocking on his feet isn't good either. He's regaining his senses and preparing to attack. Bugger. He should really stay down.

The mantra repeats in my head: *Keep him busy. Delay him as long as possible. Don't die.* That last one feels particularly important.

"Davelt, you're all talk. Anyone ever tell you that?" He scowls, and I lift my chin, refusing to show fear. "You're full of shit. The things you've done to those women and children — how do you even live with yourself?"

His eyes narrow when he realises I know about his past. His face darkens to an angry hue.

Uh-oh. Pushed him too far. Story of my life.

His only warning is a shift in his stiff shoulders before he charges. His boot narrowly misses my head as I roll away and kick him — no idea where I hit, but a hit is a hit. I'll take it.

I roll to my feet, bouncing lightly as I assess my next move. My brain is already calculating angles, distance, and how much pain I'm willing to tolerate tonight. I spin and connect with his head. His body sways sideways. My hand snaps forward, but he blocks most of the impact with his arm.

Before I can react, his hand slams into my arm as I try to protect my head.

Ow. That hurt. He hits hard. Like, *I'm going to feel that tomorrow* hard. If I live that long.

I shake off the pain. My brain is already in fighting mode. I bounce on my toes, inhale, and let my body and mind move as one. My left knee lifts and connects with his kidney; my right fist smashes into his face. I keep kneeing, hitting, punching. Each impact vibrates through my limbs. I push through the pain. I have to move harder and faster if I want to survive tonight.

My left fist slams into his kidney again — once, twice, three times — before I strike the side of his head. His grunts and groans spill out in pained bursts. Before he can react, I snap my right knee up and yank his head and shoulders toward it, smashing his face.

Crack. Crunch. Then more groaning.

Davelt hits the ground hard, rolling across my carpet and scrambling away. Damn. The man has some stamina. And something tells me he's not the only threat lurking tonight.

He spits a thick blob of blood onto my carpet and wipes his mouth with the back of his hand. My poor carpet. It's seen more trauma than half the castle staff. He glares at me with a death stare sharp enough to cut stone.

"You think you know, bitch?" he snarls, spitting again. Blood drips from his broken nose as he wipes it with a shaky hand. "You think you know about me?"

I cut him off before he can launch into another deranged sermon. "Yes, I know all about your pathetic attempt at a super race. Are you stupid or just plain fucking mad, Davelt? I've seen what you've done. All the women you slept with, impregnated, and all the ones you killed — slaughtered. You're nothing more than a monster. Oh, and we know you and your wife aren't true soulmates. You faked everything. Used Mary, her family, and their money for your benefit."

My hand drifts casually toward my leg rig. Casual for me, anyway.

"What do you think you're doing, bitch?" His eyes snap to my hand. "You think you can shoot me with that little pea shooter? I bet you don't even know how to use that gun," he sneers.

My eyebrow lifts. That's all the reaction he gets.

I keep my senses open, listening for the security boys. What is taking them so long? They should have been here ages ago. A sudden movement from Davelt snaps me into action — I roll instinctively.

Gunfire erupts. A hard, hot sting tears through my shoulder.

The scent of sulpha hits my nostrils — gunpowder. Davelt's gunpowder. Followed by blood.

Pain radiates through my shoulder. Oh, Gods. Not again. I've been shot. *Again.* Seriously, what is it with me and bullets?

I tuck myself into a tighter ball, trying to blank out the pain and stay focused. Coming out of the roll feels awkward, like my body forgot how to be coordinated for a second.

The pain is worse than I expected. But my gun is still in my hand, safety off. Small victories. I spin to face Davelt — and he's gone. Damn, he's fast. Not good. My eyes dart around the room.

Where did he go?

Shite, this is not okay. I glance down and see a hole in my T-shirt and a dark, spreading patch of blood. Not my T-shirt. Another one ruined. Honestly, I should start buying them in bulk.

"Oh dear, the poor little bitch got hurt. You going to cry now… bitch?"

His voice slithers out from behind the bed. Of course. He's hiding like a rat. Behind *my* bed. Coward.

"Your kids and mother will die by my hand after I'm done with you," he gloats.

A cold shiver runs down my spine. My heart stutters, then races. That's it. I have to end this man. At all costs. I will do anything to protect my family — even if it means dusting my father-in-law.

I'm standing in the open with no cover. A perfect target. And his smug voice tells me he knows it.

"Well, bitch," he booms, "as soon as I kill you and your little filthy blood brats, I'll enjoy dealing with your mother. At another time, I would have been destined to marry her. Me. Just because my great-grandfather. A Royal Red Blood, was required to marry a Royal Blue Blood — Alexettia's daughter. It was pleasing to hear how their attempt at marriage failed all those years ago."

Is he kidding me? He could have been my father. Or some other horrifying relation. Gross.

He pauses, spits — I hear it hit the floor — and I gag internally. Disgusting man.

"I would never have allowed myself to be shackled to a Blue Royal. Never," he sneers. "When I learned about your arrival, I had to take action. Each attempt on your life failed, but not tonight. I will end you. You will die by my hand. I will never allow my youngest son, that poor excuse, back into the human realm. And I will take over Darshia as the rightful ruler and king."

His words sting, but I shove the hurt aside. I can't afford to let him get into my head. My best option is to roll and shoot before I overthink this.

My senses spike when he moves. Oh shite — if I don't act now, he'll kill me.

I roll, aim, and squeeze the trigger.

Two loud gunshots explode through the room. Another sharp, hot pain tears through my side. Don't tell me the arse-wipe shot me again. That is so unfair.

Pain flares as I hit the floor on my shoulder and side. I roll to a sloppy stop on my knees. Excruciating pain radiates through my body, blurring my vision.

I fight to stay focused, scanning for Davelt — but he's not where he should be. Confusion fogs my brain.

Where did he go this time? He should be standing over me, gloating. I push myself up, stumbling as the room spins. Oh, crap on a stick.

I suck in a painful breath and stagger toward my bed, gun still in my hand. My fingers tingle. A glance shows blood coating them.

That is not good. Not good at all. I nearly collapse as I reach the end of the bed. My head spins, vision blurs. I blink hard, trying to focus. Oh boy. I need medical attention. Now. Or a body bag.

I still can't find Davelt. Can't hear him. Can't sense him. And that freaks me out more than the bleeding. He could jump up and shoot me — or yell *boo* — at any second.

Slowly, carefully, I lean forward and peer over the side of the bed, gun shaking in my hand.

Instead of Davelt aiming at me, I find a pile of clothing and ash beside a smoking gun.

Oh. My. Gods. I shot him.

Holy shite. I dusted my father-in-law.

Relief floods me. It's over. It's finally over.

My family is safe from Davelt. The realisation hits me like a warm wave, and for a moment the crushing weight on my shoulders lifts. I ease my finger off the trigger, click the safety on, and let myself fall backward onto the bed. Injured, hurting, exhausted. The coolness beneath me feels like heaven.

Sleep tempts me. Gods, it tempts me. But I shake my head — I have to stay awake. I have to. Being severely injured is not helping my case.

I force my heavy eyes open. My T-shirt is a disaster — blood everywhere, jagged holes, fabric clinging to my skin. Another one ruined. I swear, I should start a clothing budget just for *"things Alexia bleeds on."*

I need medical attention now. I can feel my life slipping away with every shallow breath. At least Drake is safe in the hospital. He'll recover. He'll look after the twins.

My twins. I would fight anyone who threatens my children and live as long as necessary to keep them safe.

I reach out with my mind, searching for Doctor Brean. My mental voice is barely a whisper.

Doctor Brean... help. Been shot twice. In my bedroom. Need help now.

That's all I can manage before my strength fizzles out.

His reply is faint, but I catch it. '*I'll be right there, Princess Alexia. Hold on.*'

A noise at the door makes me squint. My vision flickers in and out like a dying candle. A man stands in the doorway. I blink, trying to force my eyes to behave.

He looks like Drake.

But Drake is in the hospital. Hurt. Healing. Not here.

I blink again. My vision comes and goes. I squeeze my eyelids shut, then slowly open them and try to focus on the illusion in front of me. The shape and appearance is Drake. But…Something is wrong. This man is not my husband. The hair is wrong. The clothes are wrong. The energy is wrong — colder, sharper, like a blade wrapped in silk.

I must have closed my eyes for a second or two, because suddenly he's leaning over me, touching me.

Ow. That hurts. I groan in my head — it's all I can manage.

I don't have the strength to speak out loud, but I can feel his mind. I can breach his shields if I push hard enough.

'What the hell do you think you're doing? Don't touch me. Who are you, and why do you look like my husband?'

He smiles, but it's cold. Empty. Wrong.

And powerful.

There's something in him — something old, something dark — but threaded with a warmth I can't place. A whisper of magic brushes my senses, familiar in a way that makes my heart stutter. I've only ever felt that around one person… Lucy.

"So, you must be Alexia." His voice is deep, arrogant, and far too calm for a man standing in a room full of blood and dust. "I've heard so much about you. I'm here looking for my father."

His eyes sweep the room, taking in the carnage. They

linger on the pile of clothing beside the bed — all that remains of Davelt.

"You might have seen him," he says softly. "He despises you and what you're doing to my brother."

Brother. My stomach drops. Brother? Oh no. No, no, no.

'What do you mean — brother? Who are you?' Panic curls in my chest.

"Oh, Alexia. Sweet, sweet Alexia." His tone drips with mockery. "Don't you know? I'm Drake's older, better-looking identical twin brother — Devlain. Devlain Deaville Smithlyn, at your service."

Older twin brother.

Identical.

And radiating a power I don't understand.

Oh. Crap on a stick.

And he's looking for his father — who is currently a pile of clothing and dust beside my bed. This is bad. Very bad.

"Alexia, open your eyes. Stay focused. You've lost a lot of blood. Where is Drake? Where is my brother?"

'Drake... my Drake... he's at the... hospital... Davelt tried to kill him...'

"What? No. Please, I can't be too late."

His voice barely registers. My body is cold. Numb. Mind-talking is slipping away. I try to hold on.

'I man...aged to... get my injur...red Drake... away from Da...velt...'

That's all I can manage. Coldness seeps into my bones. Will I ever be warm again?

My vision blurs. Damn it, I must be bleeding more than I thought. The pain in my shoulder and side is fading — which is not comforting. That's blood loss talking. Death is creeping closer. Great. Just another day at the castle. If I survive this, I'm changing bedrooms. This one is cursed. If not... well, I guess I'm going home.

Muffled voices pull me back. I force my eyes open again. Three dark shapes stand beside my bed. One finally registers.

Riley. About damn time.

His voice reaches my ears, even though it sounds far away. "Princess Alexia, can you hear me? Where is Drake? Who does the clothing belong to?"

I'm lifted off the bed. My eyes won't focus. A distant voice reaches me.

"Everything will be okay, Princess Alexia. You're on your way to the hospital."

My last thoughts as I drift into the darkness.

Drake, take care of our twins and tell them I love them. Lucy... wherever you are, please be safe. It's been months since she vanished, and I still can't feel her — not even a whisper. Something about the last month feels wrong in a way I can't explain, like a thread tugging at a part of me I've been trying not to think about. And now there's Devlain... there's something about him I don't get. Something familiar.

'Drake, I hope you can hear me, my husband, my soulmate. I need you and love you. I've met your twin.'

As my world closes in, shadows increase, darkness surrounds me, and I wonder if I'll end up in the same hospital room again…

Then everything goes black.

To be continued

Want to know what happened to Alexia?

Find out in the next book.
Dark Surprises

AFTERWORD

Thank you so much for reading, **The Guy Next Door**.

I am honoured you have selected this book.

I hope you enjoyed being submerged in the world of The Guy Next Door - The first instalment of Sex, Lies And Family Secrets, as much as I enjoyed creating the world of Alexia and Drake. To continue the journey read Dark Surprises - book two.

Without you, my writing would have no meaning. Thank you, make sure you grab the second book and continue to enjoy the characters in the world of Darshia.

If you enjoyed reading this book, please consider leaving a review where you purchased it. This will help other readers make a choice to select this book.

The best way to say *thank you* to your favourite author is by leaving a review. Even if it is only a few or five little words 'I like it' - 'I enjoyed it' - kept me turning the page'

Please visit me at:
http://www.mltompsett.com

ACKNOWLEDGMENTS

To Reece a big *Thank You* with lots of hugs and kiss, without your assistance my book covers would only be half as good. And to you also, Jay.

To the beautiful women with the brilliant minds, the ones I have spoken their names time after time and you have been there, you know who you are. I would still be debating to publish or not. Included in that *thank you* - Robyn, Shelsea, Cheryle, Koula, Sharyn, Nic, Sally, and Alli, thank you for your time, encouraging words and patience, without you, I would still be deciding to create fiction romance on any type of level.

To all my friends and family - Including you - Anthony, Emma and Rachael, as well as my Facebook family, if I had a question, you guys would soon leave your thoughts and comments – **Thank You**.

Thank you, to bookishfixcom.wordpress.com for the fantastic review, much appreciated. (My first review)

To my empty bag of chocolate bullets and the cold, dirty mug. Which provides me with hot, warm and cold tea. (My mug does receive a daily bath.) (Keep an eye out for my new designed mugs) Soon you will be full, hot, and ready to be consumed once more, alongside my trusty hot laptop, with music blaring from the old stereo, pumping the favourite tunes through the speakers and don't forget the small plate (cough cough) sweet biscuits.

Note to self – *must start walking more!*

Thank You
And
Happy
Reading